THE YEAR 2000

All through the middle ages and right up into this present century in the west, there was no future. Tomorrow would be the same as today and any novelties experienced by individuals—death, disease, childbirth—had occurred countless times before to others. In great parts of the world today this attitude and way of life is still in control. But science, and the impact of science, have changed all that for us. Tomorrow is coming and it *will* be different and—the new thing on top of the new thing—we can change the change if we work at it hard enough. Just about the time this knowledge was first penetrating into scientific circles it hit literature in the form of H. G. Wells. He attempted to glimpse the possible forms of the future in fiction form—and SF writers have been following in his footsteps ever since.

OTHER BOOKS BY HARRY HARRISON

THE TECHNICOLOR ® TIME MACHINE

PRIME NUMBER

THE DALETH EFFECT

THE STAINLESS STEEL RAT

THE YEAR 2000

an anthology

edited by Harry Harrison

A BERKLEY MEDALLION BOOK
PUBLISHED BY
BERKLEY PUBLISHING CORPORATION

Published by arrangement with Doubleday & Company, Inc.

SBN 425-02117-3

*BERKLEY MEDALLION BOOKS are published by
Berkley Publishing Corporation
200 Madison Avenue
New York, N.Y. 10016*

BERKLEY MEDALLION BOOKS ® TM 757,375

Printed in the United States of America

BERKLEY MEDALLION EDITION, MAY, 1972

INTRODUCTION

The year 2000. All those zeros in a row seem to exercise an irresistible attraction—2000 A.D., the end of a century—the end of a millennium. What will life be like then? What changes will occur between now and this most interesting date? Is there any way for us to lift the curtain of time just a trifle and take a peek to see what sort of future is lurking up ahead? A number of people are trying to do just that.

This is the second millennium to come to a close within recorded Western history. The first one, 1000 A.D., was steeped in religious significance. The early Christian church had no exact predictions about this date, but there was a widely held belief that Christ would return at that time. Millenarianism and Chiliasm were preached widely and the movements had many followers—that is until the year 1000 slid by without any apocalyptic happenings.

Now the second millennium is approaching and attention is once more aroused. Only this time the attention is scientific not religious, an important indication of the differing natures of the eras. Great minds—and even greater sums—are involved in an assortment of attempts to look into the future and determine just what kind of a world it is going to be when the triple zeros roll up again.

The American Academy of Arts and Sciences has a Commission on the Year 2000 that has already brought out some highly interesting volumes. Herman Kahn and

Anthony J. Weiner have published a book entitled *The Year 2000,* which is subtitled *A Framework for Speculation on the Next Thirty-three Years. The Wall Street Journal* published a series of articles containing predictions for this date, which they have gathered into book form to be published by Dow Jones. In Paris the *Futuribles* project, directed by Bertrand de Jouvenal, is hard at work on this same task, as is the Committee on the Next Thirty Years of the English Social Sciences Research Council.

The future—and the year 2000 in particular—is becoming an interesting place and well it should. Since the industrial revolution science and technology have given mankind the ability to alter his environment drastically. That this ability has been misused goes without saying. In the historical past there was very little that we could do to change the world around us in more than a few localized and specialized ways. Deserts and semi-deserts could be created by the removal of ground cover. Forests were burned and chopped down, while a number of species of animals were wiped out. Yet this is absolutely nothing compared to the destruction now being wrought; the pollution of the atmosphere with atomic debris, the poisoning of the oceans with chemicals, the fouling of lakes and rivers—the Great Lakes turned into an immense cesspool, the asphyxiation of the cities with smog, the deterioration of life through overpopulation, the destruction of lives and property through war. The record is despicable. Therefore it is no wonder that there is now some attempt to plan the future with the vile evidence of the unplanned past all around us.

One of the first studies into the nature of planning the future, "Report on a Long-range Forecasting Study," was done for the Rand Corporation by Theodore J. Gordon and Olaf Helmer. Many more followed. One of the effects of this study was the formation, by Mr. Gordon and others, of the Institute for the Future, a technical organization that is attempting to put predictions into practice.

All of this is shiny new. The reports are just coming out as this is being written—or are unpublished as yet—and the organizations are just being founded. One of the most promising of the plans to direct the course of the future is the Committee for Metatechnology at Illinois Institute of Technology. The chairman is Dr. Leon E. Stover, Associate Professor of the Department of Humanities there. (The establishment of humanities studies in a technical institute is an important step in itself.) Different departments have joined together under the metatechnology umbrella, to focus upon the relation of technology to other aspects of our national culture—and the world condition—that ordinarily are not thought of as relevant. They feel that technology, as the instrument of our material progress, no longer needs promoting. It is so successful that it needs controlling. They hope to build the values of a humane technology assessment into the educational process. In the future, technological virtuosity may be indistinguishable from art. They wish to make sure that a facile technology does not lead to social engineering, believing that social structure will take care of itself, given a humane technology. By the year 2000 they hope to train for that by recruiting into engineering, design, and architecture the sort of students who today are attracted by the liberal arts.

This is a very optimistic program, patricularly since it is the only one of the many projects and studies that seems to be paying much attention to the quality of life in the future. The quality of future life is also one of the things that science fiction concerns itself with, since SF is about the effects of science upon people and institutions. (Not only the future: science fiction is the only fiction that is actually concerned with life *today*. All other fiction is about the past. It is written in the past tense—a very indicative sign—and the characters move through a past orientated world. They may be flying in the most modern jets or moving about the most modern of cities, but when they think of these things—if they think of them at all—they think of them as a logical extension of the past, a sort of natural development that ends at the moment they are then living. Automatic acceptance, almost indifference, is given to all novelties, no matter how startling. In this world 100-pound women drive 4000-pound vehicles without having the slightest knowledge of the mechanism they control; to them the twisting of a key in the ignition is the equivalent of flicking the reins of a horse. You do not need to know the function of a horse's grass-to-power metabolism to make it go.)

Science fiction does *not* predict in the formal sense, which may appear to be a strange thing to say in a book of stories about the future. True predictions must be linear. For example: if the gross national product is so much today and the population so large, and if growth continues in the same way, by the year 2000 the factors will combine to produce such and such an answer. The prediction may be very complex, the combination of a number of factors, and must be computer processed to get any kind of meaningful results. But the operation is still linear. Prediction of things that do not exist today—time machines, immortality, starships—is pure guesswork and not prediction at all. That is the reason why these random factors are left out of formal predictions and why the results of these predictions appear so dull. We look at them and say, well yes, I thought there would be that many people or automobiles in the world—but so what? What will *really* be new? Won't any fascinating and unexpected things happen in the next thirty-odd years?

Of course there will. There will be new discoveries, new inventions, new concepts. But any attempt to predict them, or when they will appear on the world scene, would be merely guesswork.

Science fiction writers are expert guessers. That does not mean that their guesses need be accurate. They just must be interesting and colorful. Linear prediction is also used to provide the flats and props for the story's stage, but these are incidentals. It is the unexpected that makes the story.

If science fiction has an impact to make upon our society, and I think it does, it is in its *attitude* toward science, not in any one-to-one description of things to come. Science fiction is no longer concerned merely with the gadgetry of the future, the Gernsback syndrome where every story could be patented or it wasn't a story. Today it is much more interested in the quality of life. That is the value of this unique form of literature. While fulfilling its prime function of entertainment it considers the realities of existence. It exists in the real present and is concerned about what will happen in the future.

This anthology is a good example of just that. It is a product of thirteen different writers, as different and idiosyncratic as only writers, particularly SF writers, can be. None of them were told what to do—other than to speculate about the future and to set a story in the year 2000. No instructions were issued by me as to topic or content, other than suggestions to certain writers that they consider that year in the light of their own specialized knowledge. A. Bertram Chandler, a ship's master, sets his story at sea, while Daniel F. Galouye, a highly skilled wartime flyer, speculates about airborne transportation. The labels next to the titles of the stories represent, for the most part, a description of the nature of the story after the act.

Although the stories differ from each other in every way and, to my knowledge, none of the authors exchanged information with any of the others during the writing of the stories, they are similar in one important respect. I did not dictate this similarity; it is just the nature of the beast.

All of the stories are about the *quality* of life in the year 2000.

All through the Middle Ages and right up into this present century in the West, there was no future. Tomorrow would be the same as today and any novelties experienced by individuals—death, disease, childbirth—had occurred countless times before to others. In great parts of the world today this attitude and way of life is still in control. But science, and the impact of science, have changed all that for us. Tomorrow is coming and it *will* be different and—the new thing on top of the new thing—we can change the change if we work at it hard enough. Just about the time this knowledge was first penetrating into scientific circles it hit literature in the form of H. G. Wells. He attempted to glimpse the possible forms of the future in fiction form—and SF writers have been following in his footsteps ever since.

A glance at the contributors here will prove how different this form of fiction is from all the others. At a quick look I see an anthropologist, a ship's captain, a philologist, an engineer and physicist, biologist—and more. This is a feedback relationship that only science fiction enjoys. I doubt if any of these stories will ever come true (I hope that most of them won't!), which is completely beside the point. They are involved stories, entertainments that are always related to the real facts of existence. They are important stories in that they reflect a unified state of mind. There will be a future. The future begins today. We will shape the future by today's actions. We can shape the manner of shaping. So—since we are shaping it—let us exercise our intelligence and attend to the creation of a future for the greater benefit of all mankind.

I am happy to report that this anthology will be published simultaneously in different languages, in a number of countries around the world. Science fiction has truly become international and there must be a reason for this. The past and present are already gone the instant you consider them. The real life we lead is in the future, and the peoples of the world are becoming aware of that. It is one world, spaceship Earth, and we are all aboard it. What is decided in the United States affects India. France's filthy bombs poison the Eskimos' fish. These are facts we must learn to live with.

For the publication of this volume I am immensely grateful to Lawrence P. Ashmead of Doubleday & Co. in New York City, and Charles Monteith of Faber & Faber

Ltd. in London. Without their aid, assistance, and understanding this book would never have been possible.

Harry Harrison

London-California, 1966-1969

THE YEAR 2000

AMERICA THE BEAUTIFUL

By Fritz Leiber

I am returning to England. I am shorthanding this, July 5, 2000, aboard the Dallas-London rocket as it arches silently out of the diffused violet daylight of the stratosphere into the eternally star-spangled purpling night of the ionosphere.

I have refused the semester instructorship in poetry at UTD, which would have munificently padded my honorarium for delivering the Lanier Lectures and made me for four months second only to the Poet in Residence.

And I am almost certain that I have lost Emily, although we plan to meet in London in a fortnight if she can wangle the stopover on her way to take up her Peace Corps command in Niger.

I am not leaving America because of the threat of a big war. I believe that this new threat, like all the rest, is only another move, even if a long and menacing queen's move, in the game of world politics, while the little wars go endlessly on in Chad, Czechoslovakia, Sumatra, Siam, Baluchistan, and Bolivia as America and the Communist League firm their power boundaries.

And I am certainly not leaving America because of any harassment as a satellitic neutral and possible spy. There may have been surveillance of my actions and lectures, but if so it was as impalpable as the checks they must have made on me in England before granting me visiting clearance. The U.S. intelligence agencies have become almost incredibly deft in handling such things. And I was entertained in America more than royally—I was made to feel at home by a family with a great talent for just that.

Now, I am leaving because of the shadows. The shadows everywhere in America, but which I saw most clearly in Professor Grissim's serene and lovely home. The shadows which would irresistibly have gathered behind my instructor's lectern, precisely as I was learning to dress with an even trimmer and darker reserve while I was a guest at the Grissims' and even to shower more frequently. The shadows which revealed themselves to me deepest of all around Emily Grissim, and which I could do nothing to dispel.

I think that you, or at least I, can see the shadows in America more readily these days because of the very clean air there. Judging only from what I saw with my own eyes in Texas, the Americans have completely licked their smog problem. Their gently curving freeways purr with fast electric cars, like sleek and disciplined silver cats. Almost half the nation's power comes from atomic reactors, while the remaining coal-burning plants loose back into the air at most a slight shimmer of heat. Even the streams and rivers run blue and unsmirched again, while marine life is returning to the eastern Great Lakes. In brief, America is beautiful, for with the cleanliness, now greater than that of the Dutch, has come a refinement in taste, so that all buildings are gracefully shaped and disposed, while advertisements, though molding minds more surely than ever, are restrained and almost finically inoffensive.

The purity of the atmosphere was strikingly brought to my notice when I debarked at Dallas rocketport and found the Grissims waiting for me outdoors, downwind of the landing area. They made a striking group, all of them tall, as they stood poised yet familiarly together: the professor with his grizzled hair still close-trimmed in military fashion, for he had served almost as long as a line officer and in space services as he had now as a university physicist; his slim, white-haired wife; Emily, like her mother in the classic high-waisted, long-skirted Directoire style currently fashionable; and her brother Jack, in his dress pale grays with sergeant's stripes, on furlough from Siam.

Their subdued dress and easy attitudes reminded me of a patrician Roman's toga dropping in precise though seemingly accidental folds. The outworn cliché about America being Rome to England's Greece came irritatingly to my mind.

Introductions were made by the professor, who had met my father at Oxford and later seen much of him during the occupation of Britain throughout the Three Years' Alert. I was surprised to find their diction almost the same as my own. We strolled to their electric station wagon, the doors of which opened silently at our approach.

I should have been pleased by the simple beauty of the Grissims, as by that of the suburban landscape through which we now sped, especially since my poetry is that of the Romantic Revival, which looks back to Keats and Shelley more even than to Shakespeare. Instead, it rubbed me the wrong way. I became uneasy and within ten minutes found myself beginning to talk bawdy and make nasty little digs at America.

They accepted my rudeness in such an unshocked, urbane fashion, demonstrating that they understood though did not always agree with me, and they went to such trouble to assure me that not all America was like this, there were still many ugly stretches, that I soon felt myself a fool and shut up. It was I who was the crass Roman, I told myself, or even barbarian.

Thereafter Emily and her mother kept the conversation going easily and soon coaxed me back into it, with the effect of smoothing the grumbling and owlish young British poet's ruffled feathers.

The modest one story, shaded by slow-shedding silvery eucalyptus and mutated chaparral, which was all that showed of the Grissim home, opened to receive our fumeless vehicle. I was accompanied to my bedroom-and-study, served refreshments, and left there to polish up my first lecture. The scene in the view window was so faithfully transmitted from the pickup above, the air fresher if possible than that outdoors, that I found it hard to keep in mind I was well underground.

It was at dinner that evening, when my hosts made such a nicely concerted effort to soothe my nervousness over my initial lecture, and largely succeeded, that I first began truly to like and even respect the Grissims.

It was at the same instant, in that pearly dining room, that I first became aware of the shadows around them.

Physical shadows? Hardly, though at times they really seemed that. I recall thinking, my mind still chiefly on my lecture, something like, *These good people are so wedded to the way of war, the perpetual little wars and the threat of the big one, and have been so successful in masking the signs of its strains in themselves, that they have almost forgotten that those strains are there. And they love their home and country, and the security of their taut way of life, so deeply that they have become unaware of the depth of that devotion.*

My lecture went off well that night. The audience was large, respectful, and seemingly even attentive. The number of African and Mexican faces gave the lie to what I'd been told about integration being a sham in America. I should have been pleased, and I temporarily was, at the long, mutedly drumming applause I was given and at the many intelligent, flattering comments I received afterward. And I should have stopped seeing the shadows then, but I didn't.

Next morning Emily toured me around city and countryside on a long silvery scooter, I riding pillion behind her. I remember the easy though faintly formal way in which she drew my arms around her waist and laid her hand for a moment on one of mine, meanwhile smiling cryptically overshoulder. Besides that smile, I remember a charming Spanish-American graveyard in pastel stucco, the towering Kennedy shrine, the bubbling, iridescent tubes of algae farming converging toward the horizon, and rockets taking off in the distance with their bright, smokeless exhausts. Emily was almost as unaffected as a British girl and infinitely more competent, in a grand style. That one day the shadows vanished altogether.

They returned at evening when after dinner we gathered in the living room for our first wholly unhurried and relaxed conversation, my lectures being spaced out in a leisurely—to Americans, not to me—one day in two schedule.

We sat in a comfortable arc before the wide fireplace, where resinous woods burned yellow and orange. Occasionally Jack would put on another log. From time to time, a light shower of soot dropped back from the precipitron in the chimney, the tiny particles as they fell flaring into brief white points of light, like stars.

A little to my surprise, the Grissims drank as heavily as the English, though they carried their liquor very well. Emily was the exception to this family pattern, contenting herself with a little sherry and three long, slim reefers, which she drew from an elegant foil package covered with gold script and Lissajous curves, and which she inhaled sippingly, her lips rapidly shuddering with a very faint, low, trilling sound.

Professor Grissim set the pattern by deprecating the reasons for America's domestic achievements, which I had led off by admitting were far greater than I'd expected. They weren't due to any peculiar American drive, he said, and certainly not to any superior moral fiber, but simply to technology and computerized civilization given their full head and unstinting support. The powerful sweep of those two almost mathematical forces had automatically solved such problems as overpopulation, by effortless and aesthetic contraception, and stagnant or warped brain potential, by unlimited semiautomated education and psychiatry—just as on a smaller scale the drug problem had largely been resolved by the legalization of marijuana and peyote, following the simple principle of restricting only the sale of quickly addictive chemicals and those provably damaging to nervous tissue—"Control the poisons, but let each person learn to control his intoxicants, especially now that we have metabolic rectifiers for the congenitally alcoholic."

I was also told that American extremism, both of the right and left, which had seemed such a big thing in mid-century, had largely withered away or at least been muted by the great surge of the same forces which were making America ever more beautiful and prosperous. Cities were no longer warrens of discontent. Peace marches and Minutemen rallies alike, culminating in the late sixties, had thereafter steadily declined.

While impressed, I did not fall into line, but tried to point out some black holes in this glowing picture. Indeed, feeling at home with the Grissims now and having learned that nothing I could say would shock them into anger and confusion, I was able to be myself fully and to reveal frankly my anti-American ideas, though of course more politely and, I hoped, more tellingly than yesterday—it seemed an age ago—driving from the rocketport.

In particular, I argued that many or most Americans were motivated by a subtle, even sophisticated puritanism, which made them feel that the world was not safe unless they were its moral arbiters, and that this puritanism was ultimately based on the same swollen concern about property and money—industry, in its moral sense—that one found in the Swiss and Scottish Presbyterians and most of the early Protestants.

"You're puritans with a great deal of style and restraint and wide vision," I said. "Yet you're puritans just the same, even though your puritanism is light years away from that of the Massachusetts theocrats and the harsh rule Calvin tried to impose on Geneva. In fact," I added uncautiously, "your puritanism is not so much North European as Roman."

Smiles crinkled briefly at that and I kicked myself for having myself introduced into the conversation that hackneyed comparison.

At this point Emily animatedly yet coolly took up the argument for America, pointing out the nation's growing tolerance and aestheticism, historically distinguishing Puritanism from Calvinism, and also reminding me that the Chinese and Russians were far more puritanical than any other peoples on the globe—and not in a sophisticated or subtle way either.

I fought back, as by citing the different impression I'd got of the Russians during my visits in the Soviet Union and by relaying the reports of close colleagues who had spent time in China. But on the whole Emily had the best of me. And this was only partly due to the fact that the longer I sparred with her verbally, the less concerned I became to win my argument, and the more to break her calm and elicit some sharp emotional reaction from her, to see that pale skin flush, to make those reefer-serene eyes blaze with anger. But I wasn't successful there either.

At one point Jack came to her aid, mildly demonstrating for American broad-mindedness by describing to us some of the pleasure cities of southern Asia he'd visited on R.&R.

"Bangkok's a dismal place now, of course," he began by admitting, "with the Com-g'rillas raiding up to and even into it, and full of fenced-off bombed and booby-trapped areas. Very much like the old descriptions of Saigon in the sixties. As you walk down the potholed streets, you listen for the insect hum of a wandering antipersonnel missile seeking human heat, or the faint flap-flap of an infiltrator coming down on a whirligig parachute. You brace your thoughts against the psychedelic strike of a mind-bomb. Out of the black alley ahead there may charge a fifty-foot steel centipede, the remote-controlled sort we use for jungle fighting, captured by the enemy and jiggered to renegade.

"But most of old Bangkok's attractive features—and the

entrepreneurs and the girls and other entertainers that go with them—have been transferred en masse to Kandy and Trincomalee in Ceylon." And he went on to describe the gaily orgiastic lounges and bars, the fresh pastel colors, the spicy foods and subtly potent drinks, the clean little laughing harlots supporting their families well during the ten years of their working life between fifteen and twenty-five, the gilded temples, the slim dancers with movements stylized as their black eyebrows, the priests robed in orange and yellow.

I tried to fault him in my mind for being patronizing, but without much success.

"Buddhism's an attractive way of life," he finished, "except that it doesn't know how to wage war. But if you're looking only for nirvana, I guess you don't need to know that." For an instant his tough face grew bleak, as if he could do with a spot of nirvana himself, and the shadows gathered around him and the others more thickly.

During the following off-lecture evenings we kept up our fireplace talks and Emily and I returned more than once to our debate over puritanism, while the rest listened to us with faint, benevolent smiles, that at times seemed almost knowing. She regularly defeated me.

Then on the sixth night she delivered her crowning argument, or celebrated her victory, or perhaps merely followed an impulse. I had just settled myself in bed when the indirect lightning of my "doorbell" flooded the room with brief flashes, coming at three-second intervals, of a rather ghastly white light. Blinking, I fumbled on the bedside table for the remote control of the room's appliances, including tri-V and door, and thumbed the button for the latter.

The door moved aside and there, silhouetted against the faint glow of the hall, was the dark figure of Emily, like a living shadow. She kept her finger, however, on the button long enough for two more silent flashes to illuminate her briefly. She was wearing a narrow kimono—Jack's newest gift, she later told me—and her platinum hair, combed straight down like an unrippling waterfall, almost exactly matched the silvery, pale gray silk. Without quite overdoing it, she had made up her face somewhat like a temple dancer's—pale powder, almost white; narrow slanting brows, almost black; green eye shadow with a pinch of silvery glitter; and the not-quite-jarring sensual note of crimson lips.

She did not come into my room, but after a pause during which I sat up jerkily and she became again a shadow, she beckoned to me.

I snatched up my dressing gown and followed her as she moved noiselessly down the hall. My throat was dry and constricted, my heart was pounding a little, with apprehension as well as excitement. I realized that despite my near week with the Grissims, a part of my mind was still thinking of the professor and his wife as a strait-laced colonel and his lady from a century ago, when so many retired army officers lived in villas around San Antonio, as they do now too around the Dallas-Ft. Worth metropolitan area.

Emily's bedroom was not the austere silver cell or self-shrine I had sometimes imagined, especially when she was scoring a point against me, but an almost cluttered museum-workshop of present interests and personal memorabilia. She'd even kept her kindergarten study-machine, her first CO_2 pistol, and a hockey stick, along with mementos from her college days and her Peace Corps tours.

But those I noticed much later. Now pale golden light from a rising full moon, coming through the great view window, brimmed the room. I had just enough of my wits left to recall that the real moon was new, so that this must be a tape of some past night. I never even thought of the Communist and American forts up there, with their bombs earmarked for Earth. Then, standing straight and tall and looking me full in the eyes, like some Amazonian athlete, or Phryne before her judges, Emily let her kimono glide down from her shoulders.

In the act of love she was energetic, but tender. No, the

word is courteous, I think. I very happily shed a week of tensions and uncertainties and self-inflicted humiliations.

"You still think I'm a puritan, don't you?" she softly asked me afterward, smiling at me sideways with the smeared remains of her crimson mouth, her gray eyes enigmatic blurs of shadow.

"Yes, I do," I told her forthrightly. "The puritan playing the hetaera, but still the puritan."

She answered lazily, "I think you like to play the Hun raping the vestal virgin."

That made me talk dirty to her. She listened attentively—almost famishedly, I thought, for a bit—but her final comment was "You do that very well, dear," just before using her lips to stop mine, which would otherwise have sulphurously cursed her insufferable poise.

Next morning I started to write a poem about her but got lost in analysis and speculation. Tried too soon, I thought.

Although they were as gracious and friendly as ever, I got the impression that the other Grissims had quickly become aware of the change in Emily's and my relationship. Perhaps it was that they showed a slight extra fondness toward me. I don't know how they guessed—Emily was as cool as always in front of them, while I kept trying to play myself, as before. Perhaps it was that the argument about puritanism was never resumed.

Two evenings afterward the talk came around to Jack's and Emily's elder brother Jeff, who had fallen during the Great Retreat from Jammu and Kashmir to Baluchistan. It was mentioned that during his last furlough they had been putting up an exchange instructor from Yugoslavia, a highly talented young sculptress. I gathered that she and Jeff had been quite close.

"I'm glad Jeff knew her love," Emily's mother said calmly, a tear behind her voice, though not on her cheeks. "I'm very glad he had that." The professor unobtrusively put his hand on hers.

I fancied that this remark was directed at me and was

her way of giving her blessing to Emily's and my affair. I was touched and at the same time irritated—and also irritated at myself for feeling irritated. Her remark had brought back the shadows, which darkened further when Jack said a touch grimly and for once with a soldier's callousness, though grinning at me to remove any possible offense, "Remember not to board any more lady artists or professors, mother, at least when I'm on leave. Bad luck."

By now I was distinctly bothered by my poetry block. The last lectures were going swimmingly and I ought to have been feeling creative, but I wasn't. Or rather, I was feeling creative but I couldn't create. I had also begun to notice the way I was fitting myself to the Grissim family—muting myself, despite all the easiness among us. I couldn't help wondering if there weren't a connection between the two things. I had received the instructorship offer, but was delaying my final answer.

After we made love together that night—under a sinking crescent moon, the real night this time, repeated from above—I told Emily about my first trouble only. She pressed my hand. "Never stop writing poetry, dear," she said. "America needs poetry. This family—"

That broken sentence was as close as we ever got to talking about marriage. Emily immediately recovered herself with an uncharacteristically ribald "Cheer up. I don't even charge a poem for admission."

Instead of responding to that cue, I worried my subject. "I should be able to write poetry here," I said. "America is beautiful, the great golden apple of the Hesperides, hanging in the west like the setting sun. But there's a worm in the core of that apple, a great scaly black dragon."

When Emily didn't ask a question, I went on, "I remember an advertisement. 'Join all your little debts into one big debt.' Of course, they didn't put it so baldly, they made it sound wonderful. But you Americans are like that. You've removed your angers from things at home—where you seem to have solved your problems very well, I must admit—and directed those angers at the Communist

League. Or instead of angers, I could say fears. Same thing."

Emily still didn't comment, so I continued, "Take the basic neurotic. He sets up a program of perfection for himself—a thousand obligations, a thousand ambitions. As long as he works his program, fulfilling those obligations and ambitions, he does very well. In fact, he's apt to seem like a genius of achievement to those around him, as America does to me. But there's one big problem he always keeps out of his program and buries deep in his unconscious—the question of who he really is and what he really wants—and in the end it always throws him."

Then at last Emily said, speaking softly at first. "There's something I should tell you, dear. Although I talk a lot of it from the top of my mind, deep down I loathe discussing politics and international relations. As my old colonel used to tell me, 'It doesn't matter much which side you fight on, Emily, so long as you have the courage to stand up and be counted. You pledge your life, your fortune, and your sacred honor, and you live up to that pledge!' And now, dear, I want to sleep."

Crouching on the edge of her bed before returning to my room, and listening to her breathing regularize itself, I thought, "Yes, you're looking for nirvana too. Like Jack." But I didn't wake her to say it, or any of the other things that were boiling up in my brain.

Yet the things I left unsaid must have stayed and worked in my mind, for at our next fireside talk—four pleasant Americans, one Englishman with only one more lecture to go—I found myself launched into a rather long account of the academic Russian family I stayed with while delivering the Pushkin Lectures in Leningrad, where the smog and the minorities problems have been licked too. I stressed the Rosanovs' gentility, their friendliness, the tolerance and sophistication which had replaced the old rigid insistence on *kulturny* behavior, and also the faint melancholy underlying and somehow vitiating all they said. In short, I did everything I knew to underline their similarity to the Grissims. I ended by saying "Professor Grissim, the first night we talked, you said America's achievement had been due almost entirely to the sweep of science, technology, and computerized civilization. The people of the Communist League believe that too—in fact, they made their declaration of faith earlier than America."

"It's very strange," he mused, nodding. "So like, yet so unlike. Almost as if the chemical atoms of the East were subtly different from those of the West. The very electrons—"

"Professor, you don't actually think—"

"Of course not. A metaphor only."

But whatever he thought, I don't believe he felt it only as a metaphor.

Emily said sharply to me, "You left out one more similarity, the most important. That they hate the Enemy with all their hearts and will never trust or understand him."

I couldn't find an honest and complete answer to that, though I tried.

The next day I made one more attempt to turn my feelings into poetry, dark poetry, and I failed. I made my refusal of the instructorship final, confirmed my reservation on the Dallas-London rocket for day after tomorrow, and delivered the last of the Lanier Lectures.

The Fourth of July was a quiet day. Emily took me on a repeat of our first scooter jaunt, but although I relished the wind on my face and our conversation was passably jolly and tender, the magic was gone. I could hardly see America's beauty for the shadows my mind projected on it.

Our fireside conversation that night was as brightly banal. Midway we all went outside to watch the fireworks. It was a starry night, very clear of course, and the fireworks seemed vastly remote—transitory extra starfields of pink and green and amber. Their faint cracks and booms sounded infinitely distant, and needless to say, there was not a ribbon or whiff of chemical smoke. I was reminded of my last night in Leningrad with the Rosanovs after the Pushkin Lectures. We'd all strolled down the Kirovskiy Prospekt to the Bolshaya Neva, and across its glimmering waters watched the Vladivostok mail rocket take off from the Field of Mars up its ringed electric catapult taller far than the Eiffel Tower. That had been on a May Day.

Later that night I went for the first time by myself to Emily's door and pressed its light-button. I was afraid she wouldn't stop by for me and I needed her. She was in a taut and high-strung mood, unwilling to talk in much more than monosyllables, yet unable to keep still, pacing like a restless feline. She wanted to play in the view window the tape of a real battle in Bolivia with the original sounds too, muted down. I vetoed that and we settled for an authentic forest fire recorded in Alaska.

Sex and catastrophe fit. With the wild red light pulsing and flaring in the bedroom, casting huge wild shadows, and with the fire's muted roar and hurricane crackle and explosions filling our ears, we made love with a fierce and desperate urgency that seemed almost—I am eternally grateful for the memory—as if it would last forever. Sex and a psychedelic trip also have their meeting point.

Afterward I slept like a sated tiger. Emily waited until dawn to wake me and shoo me back to my bedroom.

Next day all the Grissims saw me off. As we strolled from the silver station wagon to the landing area, Emily and I dropped a little behind. She stopped, hooked her arms around me, and kissed me with a devouring ferocity. The others walked on, too well bred ever to look back. The next moment she was her cool self again, sipping a reefer.

Now the rocketship is arching down. The stars are paling. There is a faint whistling as the air molecules of the stratosphere begin to carom off the titanium skin. We had only one flap, midway of freefall section of the trip, when we briefly accelerated and then decelerated to match, perhaps in order to miss a spy satellite or one of the atomic-headed watchdog rockets eternally circling the globe. The direction comes, "Secure seat harnesses."

I just don't know. Maybe I should have gone to America drunk as Dylan Thomas, but purposefully, bellowing my beliefs like the word or the thunderbolts of God. Maybe then I could have fought the shadows. No. . . .

I hope Emily makes it to London. Perhaps there, against a very different background, with shadows of a different sort . . .

In a few more seconds the great jet will begin to brake, thrusting its hygienic, aseptic exhaust of helium down into the filthy cancerous London smog, and I will be home.

PROMETHEUS REBOUND

By Daniel F. Galouye

Like Triumphant Prometheus, unfettered at last from his storm-thrashed rock, the huge fluxliner heaved up through the final shrouds of resistive atmosphere, majestically treading the fabric of geomagnetic space.

Almost the width of a city block and massing some 350 tons, Transequatorial Fluxway's flagship was a scintillating disk whose 2231-aluminum hull arrogantly flung back the rays of a midmorning sun. Her sheening surface was broken only by circumferential ports—scores of eyes staring out into the depth of space and back at the receding North American coast line.

Ahead—little more than an hour from New York via magnetic field navigation—lay Flight 201's destination: Buenos Aires.

Intrigued with the metaphorical concept of mythology's Giver of Fire shedding his chains, Transequatorial had named its flagship the *Prometheus Unbound,* commemorating Shelley's reversal of Aeschylus' tragedy.

But the metaphor was not entirely consistent. For the *Prometheus Unbound* was indeed shackled—to the very inductive forces which were bestowing her freedom.

Yet she was a proud eagle addressing her wings to the swift updraft, an exultant flying fish hurtling from dismal depths to embrace spray-laden gusts, an emperor butterfly shedding its chrysalis.

Riding inductive currents, Flight 201 finally cleared the adiabatic sink and swung into its second phase of acceleration along a tentatively selected line of force.

"What're you doing, Gil?" Computerpilot Martin impaled his assistant with an admonitory glance. "Grapple her down at L-1.05. Or you'll have the Prometheus sniffing out a lunar transfer orbit!"

"We're *not* on do-it-yourself, Captain." Gilbert spread his arms to absolve himself. " 'George's' fouling up, I suppose."

Martin disengaged the auto pilot, seizing his manual controls. But the ship refused to stabilize on its preassigned geomagnetic shell. Instead, the ascentometer crept upward—L-1.051, L-1.052, L-1.053. . . .

"She's not responding!" he exclaimed, brushing blond hair off his forehead. Unconsciously, he translated earth-radii values into miles of altitude: 204, 208, 212. . . .

Gilbert, too, was extrapolating. He betrayed as much when he mumbled, "Four miles up through the GM shells every ten seconds—twenty-four miles a minute—"

But the captain had already punched his data into an ancillary computer. The answer came out "Sixteen hundred, forty miles."

He winced. "Lower VanAl less than an hour away!"

His cocomputerpilot attempted a weak laugh. "But by then we'll be down-shelling for Buenos Aires, won't we?"

Anxiously, Martin thudded the control column as though the trouble might be there instead of in the drive. "You've just perforated your card for a refresher in magnetonautics," he gibed. "Sure, we'll flux back down in BL space. But only to the gauss value at which we lost control. Then we'll mirror from maglatitude to equivalent maglat—like a volley ball in a hot game."

"What'll we do? Send out a Come-and-Get-Me?"

"Let's try degaussing the drive with excess potential. But, first, you grapple onto our force line-drift vector so we'll at least be fluxing down the slot. I'll check on the passengers."

One after another, Martin switched to all video pickup stations, studying the succession of scenes on his screen. At least, the constant-inertia computer had vectored in the proper flight attitude to balance force-line acceleration with reduced gravitational pull and provide a near-normal G factor. The inclinometer showed that the disk-shaped ship was skittering along in BL space at about a twenty-degree tilt.

Inside, it was an average complement of almost 750 passengers who had only minutes earlier welcomed the green "Steady Inertia" signal. Released from contra-acceleration control, swivel chairs had swung toward view ports which framed the North American coast line to starboard and, to port, the sun-silvered expanse of the Atlantic.

How long would it be, Martin wondered, before anyone properly evaluated horizon curvature and sensed that they were ascending much higher than the programmed 200 miles? Would he then be able to reassure his passengers? What would he say? Somehow the "minor-technical-difficulty" bit didn't seem adequate.

Then he quietly execrated the headlong rush of technology from physicist's blackboard to engineer's drafting table, to manufacturer's plant, thence to general use. Geomagnetic induction drive? Magneto-nautics theory: 1975. Tests: 1981. Military application: '83. Commercial adaptation: '89. First GM passenger flight: 1990.

Now—a scant ten years later—fluxways filled with such shapes as "flying saucer" sightings had, in effect, only prophesied (or perhaps inspired) half a century ago. And still all the bugs weren't out.

Responding to the copilot's goading, the control computer swung the ship gently onto the right heading in gauss-L space while Martin, looking in on Lounge 1, watched two passengers sway—but only slightly, neither spilling his drink. At any rate, the constant-G computer was still compensating almost perfectly by attitudinizing the craft's occupants against inertial change.

"Grappled on drift-bounce vector," the copilot announced. "L value 1.080 and boot-strapping steadily.

That's 320 miles. Ought to have gauss monkeys aboard GM ships."

"Induction engineers, so they *tell* us, would only be drawing twiddling pay," Martin scoffed. "Don't you know *nothing* can go wrong with GM drives? They're simple Rutledge coils mounted on three axes. Sealed units. Foolproof."

Gilbert's dark face responded with an amused smile beneath crimpy, black hair that hugged his scalp. "Ascent control power input on do-it-yourself. *You* want to juice her?"

"No, *you* go switch-happy. Try a 110-plus nudge every two seconds. Careful, though. We don't want to dump any of our cattle on their rumps."

After ten such charges, Gilbert exposed a sour face. "Drive's not buying today."

"Try it at 120-plus for a while."

Gilbert tackled the patently hopeless task of jarring the drive out of its predilection for ascent through the onion skins of geomagnetic shells. Meanwhile, Martin's gaze swept up across the computer-control console to the communications status board.

He tensed. Weak crimson backlighting limned the designation Lounge 2 on the board! In going over his check list before flux grapple at New York's GM port, he had evidently failed to deactivate the pilot-to-Lounge 2 circuit. And someone might even now be looking in on the consternation in the computerpilots' compartment!

He thumbed the Lounge 2-to-pilot switch.

Completing the two-way circuit, the communication screen framed a wizened old man. His permanently furrowed forehead and almost bald scalp, gleaming in the soft light, suggested at least an octogenarian. Stiff finger raised speculatively to the side of a bulbous nose, he was staring intensely at the telescreen in front of him.

"How long've you been sitting there cloaking us? Who are you?" Martin challenged, noting with relief that the audio volume was low and that no one at the bar, visible in the screen's periphery, seemed interested in what was going on in the control compartment.

"Ira Ambrose," the other answered, registering surprise. "And don't try giving me a snow job. I haven't been corking off. I've had the eye on you long enough to know that if you haven't got a runaway prop or oil leak in an inboard engine, you've got some other kind of ants in your pants."

Martin laughed at the caricature. "Everything's AO up here. We're just simulating emergency procedure."

Ira scratched his nose dubiously. "That's what *I* handed my crew once—back in '44. We were droppin' eggs on Dusseldorf. Got our hydraulics shot out. And there I was sitting in that B-24 with my as—" He looked uncomfortably around him. "Let's say with my anus turning up 2400 rpm. I was flying wing on—"

"Sorry, Mr. Ambrose, but I'm going to have to—"

"It's Ira."

"We're busy." Martin reached for the toggle.

"Hold on, Cap'n. You don't over-and-out on *me!* Not 'less you want word to get around that we can't control our rate of climb."

Martin cast a frustrated glance at his copilot, who was still ineffectually juicing the ascent drive, then withdrew his hand from the switch. "What do you want, Mr. Ambrose?"

"I want up on the flight deck. And don't try givin' me the finger. I earned my invitation—from one pilot to another. Twenty-five missions over Europe. Silver Star. Oak Leaf Clusters. Then I helped chase Tojo out of the Philippines and—"

"Flight deck? Don't know much about magnetonautics, do you?"

"Holy cow! Flying's flying. You go up, down; left, right; faster, slower. Plain to see you got a gremlin in your vertical stabilizer control. Stuck, more'n likely. Happened to me once—over Iwo—ack-ack garbage wedged against a cable. Well, if you'd come up by the seat of your pants, like I did, you'd know the answer: Throttle back, hang 'er on her props at full low pitch and hold her just above stall-out. Ain't nothin' she can do then but mush down."

"There *are* no stabilizers on the *Prometheus Unbound,* Mr. Ambrose." Gilbert looked patiently up from his futile attempts to overpower the recalcitrant ascent circuit. "Just Rutledge coils operating on selective induction. No props. Not even jets. No aerodynamic configuration or—"

"Damned *saucers,* that's all they are," Ira grunted.

"Oh, *there* you are, Mr. Ambrose."

Appearing both provoked and relieved, one of the hostesses stepped into the teleframe, soft red hair contrasting her Kelly green uniform. Martin recognized her as the new stewardess, assigned to flight duty just that morning.

"Really, Mr. Ambrose," she scolded, "you should return to your seat. I've been looking all over for you."

Ira scowled. "I'm giving the pilots a hand. Go chase yourself!"

But she deflected his palm before it could deliver a posterior slap. "He won't behave, Captain," she complained, blue eyes boring helplessly out of the telescreen. "He insists on going up to the *flight deck.* I tried to tell him—"

"You'll have to apply whatever measures are prescribed in your handbook, Miss Wesley." The computerpilot tried not to sound abrupt, since he was already entertaining notions of meeting the attractive stewardess at L-1.0 soon. "He's grappled onto the idea that the ship's in trouble. You sluice it from there—and make sure he doesn't panic anybody."

With finality, Martin broke the circuit. But the Lounge 2 call light began flashing immediately.

"Find some micros in every shipload, eh?" Gilbert suggested.

"Even micromicros. What's our L value"

"One-point-one-four-oh. Translates to 560 miles altitude."

Martin swore, punched the datum into an auxiliary keyboard and read the answer. "At least our ascent remains uniform," he said.

"Disgustingly slotted. ETA Lower VanAl—10:05."

"Forty-five minutes off."

"I've never matched orbit with *this* sort of emergency. But"—Gilbert paused to send more peak current surging into the ascent control circuit—"perhaps if we just shut down the drive momentarily—"

"We'd only flop into freefall. Parabolic trajectory. Transequatorial Fluxways' passengers wouldn't appreciate that. When we regrappled, the jolt of sudden induction might twist their guts."

"Then *you* cut the tape." Glistening beads were beginning to stand out upon the copilot's forehead like pearls on dark velvet.

"Well, we've got to cut *something*. Won't be too long before our altitude will become noticeable, even to a neophyte fluxer."

"Time for Come-and-Get-Me?"

"One more try first. If we're going to scrub it down enough to send for help, we might as well scrub it down *real* good. Punch in for a few 150-plus nudges through the vertical Rutledge."

Gilbert's eyebrows rose in surprised disbelief before he began assigning Keyboard C the tasks of computing parameters for the precipitous venture. "Steve, I've been thinking about Ira."

"Who?"

"Flyboy of the forties." The copilot gestured toward the blinking Lounge 2 call light.

"We've got more to think about than him," Martin snapped.

"He could be *all* we've got to think about. The Civil Magnetonautics Bureau has been known to cloak up for computerpilot checks."

"*Ira* A CMB inspector? You're aborting, of course."

"Remember Jenkins? He's not punching a computer-control board any longer. Not since '*Representative* Snyder' got permission to stare over his shoulder and rattled him into letting a negative value creep into his BL space computations."

"Ira—an inspector?" Martin was unable to accommodate the concept. "What would that fugitive from an aeronautical museum know about gauss-earth radii coordinates and driftfield line components?"

"The bureau *has* used theory boys—and some old ones, at that—to evaluate flight crews." Gilbert completed his programming and leaned back to await the computer's signal for manual activation.

"You don't suppose a CMB inspector would actually queer up a Rutledge drive, even if he could?"

"Perhaps not beyond his capacity to restore flight integrity. After all, there *are* 750 paying cattle aboard the *Prometheus Unbound.*"

A green light flared on the console and Gilbert punched the surge control stud.

Anxiously, they studied banks of dials and indicators, watching for hints of change in the ship's response pattern.

Martin swore. "L-1.70—680 miles . . . L-1.171—684 miles. Velocity still uniform up through the gauss shells."

Just then a buzzer blared and the console lit up in a gaudy display of scattered, flickering lights that befitted the latest pinball machine's backboard.

"The inclinometer, Steve!" Gilbert pointed.

Martin riveted his attention on the attitude indicator. The mock saucer-shaped ship was revolving about the dial's surface—changing its inclination constantly, rotating first in one direction, then the other. "We've gone into cyclotronic motion along the bounce line"

He energized the pilot-to-all stations communications circuit, instantly ordering calm on his face. "Passengers will return to their seats and fasten belts. We're maneuvering to strip charged particles off the hull."

The Lounge 2 call light was flashing persistently.

"I'm not one of the cows," Gilbert protested. "So, without the soft-tongue stuff, how about programming me on what's going on?"

"We're not nul-cycing. Subatomic particles in the geomagnetic field travel along lines of force in helical spirals. Somehow we're doing the same thing, even though the Rutledge drive is engineered to scrub out cyclotronic motion."

The analogue craft on the inclinometer dial's face continued to twist, squirm, and rotate. Only such impossible gyrations could blend all errant components of inertia into near-normal, deckward gravity. And this, Martin conceded with respect, was nothing short of a miracle in attitudinization, circumstances being what they were.

"I don't see how the CI computer's standing up under the load!" he exclaimed. "It's handling a three-vector problem—balancing off force-line acceleration with the gravitational variant and, now, with the centrifugal force of cyclotronic motion. It'll fry!"

"Time to send our Come-and-Get-Me?" Gilbert asked worriedly.

"Yes. Anyway, we've got only forty minutes before we reach the VA hots. Hit the call circuit and raise a Guardian."

Leaving his copilot to the task of summoning help, Martin decided to take a look outside. He energized an external video pickup and stared desolately at the screen as earth's misty horizon swung down, paused, tilted sharply, then slid slowly out of view, only to be replaced by the darkness of space. Seconds later, though, the rising western horizon chased the darkness away. As more of the blue-green surface was exposed, he watched the United States coast line slip by, with Haiti looming ahead—but all *so* far below now.

He tuned in on a passenger compartment. Already there were signs of uneasiness. Heads bent together in tense, whispered conversation. Reluctant glimpses through the ports. Two nuns working feverishly over their prayer beads. A stout businessman staring at whitened knuckles as he gripped his arm rests.

Martin envisioned the results of a constant-inertia computer blowout—seats shearing their anchor shafts and hurtling about, together with attached passengers, like gravel in a concrete mixer.

"Raise a Guardian yet?" he asked.

The copilot spread his arms impotently. "I'm putting the call out to three Surface Guard stations—one orbiting at 800 miles. But there's a lot of interference." The screen on his right displayed only jittery snowflakes, accompanied by squawks and howls.

Relentless flickering of the Lounge 2 light betrayed Ira Ambrose's refusal to return to his seat and reminded Martin of the old man's threat to spread word that the ship was in trouble.

Energizing the pilot-Lounge 2 circuit, he admonished, "Mr. Ambrose, you were requested to go back to your—"

The screen cleared sufficiently to produce a weak picture of Ira, squeezed into the stewardess' seat along with Miss Wesley. Half in the old man's lap, the hostess squirmed protestingly.

"Elaine!" Martin called out. "Are you all right?"

"Hell's bells, son!" Ira pouted. "Been thirty years since any broad *wasn't* 'all right' with me, even a chick like this li'l pinup."

Elaine twisted around to face the screen. "The only way I could get him belted down was by sharing my seat with him."

Martin watched the chair swing slowly to the left, then to the right, listing, tilting. The CI computer was supplementing ship attitudinization with seat attitudinization as a desperate means of synthesizing near-normal gravity. In the background, the lounge had apparently been cleared and all gear stored.

"Now—about this spin we're in." Ira plucked at an eyebrow. "Easy to spot what happened. No buts about it. You let your air speed fall off too much when you were mushin' down. You stalled and dropped off—"

"Mr. Ambrose," Gilbert said doggedly, still casting for his Come-and-Get-Me response, "we've told you there're no aerodynamic principles in GM flight. This cyclotronic motion—"

"He's right—about our being in trouble—isn't he?" Elaine asked, frowning.

"Of course not," Martin lied. "By slotting in cyclotronic motion for a while we're purging the Rutledge drive."

"Bull s—" Ira coughed and glanced deferentially at the girl. "What say we shake a leg and get out of this spin? First: Power off, stick full forward and kick hell out of your left rudder; hold it down, *hard!* Next: Power on—*full!* Then ease back on the stick. Ready to give it the ol' college try before she winds up too tight?"

Elaine unlocked the safety belt and bolted from the seat.

"Ira!" Martin shouted.

"For cryin' out loud." The old man displayed his hands in sheepish innocence. "You don't think I goosed the gal?"

The stewardess, swaying against all the forces acting on the *Prometheus Unbound,* tight-roped toward the nearest passenger compartment. "I told Mrs. Callahan to use the baby belt for her child," she explained. "But she's still got the kid on her lap."

"I know what's going through your noodle—that I'm an 'ol' codger.' Right?" Ira ventured as the girl walked out of the frame. "Thirty-five years ago I was sacked in at the VA hospital. There was this *real* 'ol' codger' there—a mule skinner from Pershing's campaign in Mexico in '16. Eighty years if he was a day. He had a visitor—his grandson—a jet pilot in the Air Force.

"Let me tell you somethin', Mr. Computerpilot: That mule skinner—garrulous ol' bird—claimed his grandson's jet wasn't any more of a machine than the mule. Claimed the most important thing either a pilot or mule skinner had to watch was his point of no return. Only difference was: One had to keep an eye on the water barrel, the other on the fuel tank.

"Mr. Mule Skinner had found out all about the point of no return when the barrel went dry, his mules keeled over, and he had to walk back to Parral—in '16. Barely made it. Mr. Jet didn't get his grandpa's message. *He* forgot all about the fuel tank once; had to hit the silk and lay 'em down from behind Cong lines in '67. Didn't make it.

"Point is that technologies change, but the new ones can always learn something from the old ones. You think about that awhile and—"

"Here we are!" Gilbert broke in. "Come-and-Get-Me response—from Guardian Station 14-A. In polar orbit."

Flipping the switch, Martin dismissed the old man and turned eagerly to Gilbert's screen. Worsening interference was draining the picture of all resolution. But a scratchy voice, having identified as Station 14-A's monitor, was struggling through:

". . . understand your situation. We'll peg you high on priority pickup. But I'm afraid we'll be dragging it some before we can spare a rescue craft."

"*Spare* a rescue craft!" Martin shouted. "Don't you realize we've got a herd of 750 that'll soon be locking horns with the VA hots!"

"And don't *you* realize, Captain, that the Guardians have been fraying their wings for hours now—snatching thousands off meterological, observational, experimental and private platforms? Sure, you've got your trouble circuit on positive feedback. But you should have yelled for an angel as soon as your malfunction developed—especially with a double-red peak due on the solargraph. We'll keep in touch and do the best we can."

Martin started. A double-red peak! When? How—?

Then he slumped. Of course. He *had* been aware of the *cis*-Venusian station's warning—*had* known that the severe proton storm from the sun's photosphere was due to swamp earth's magnetic field before Flight 201 landed.

But by then the *Prometheus Unbound* (or, he asked himself, shouldn't it be *Prometheus Rebound?*) was to be vectoring in on Buenos Aires, well below its *intended* maximum altitude of L-1.05. Even at 200 miles, however, there would have been no danger for the lightly shielded ship—not with the Van Allen belts protectively sopping up all the suddenly intensified radiation. That was why he hadn't bothered to commit the double-red datum to the main computer's alarmfactoring system.

But now they were *approaching* the lower VanAl. And

just when they reached peak mirroring altitude in half an hour, that area of BL space would be seething with bristling solar-injected protons! Radiation level a thousand times normal. Almost instant, torturous roentgen sickness. Death—for everybody aboard the *Prometheus*—within hours, even if exposure were for only a few seconds.

Gilbert set his Come-and-Get-Me contact on standby. "About our being peeled off by the Surface Guard—of course, it doesn't matter."

Openmouthed, the captain only stared at him.

"With the ship cycing like it is, the Guardians wouldn't be able to pick up our herd anyway."

It was true, Martin conceded. No rescue craft could draw close enough even to *try* a ventral hatch grapple—not with a twisting, twirling, squirming, bucking ship.

The Lounge 2 light was flashing furiously now. But the captain just ignored Ira. "What's our L value?"

"One-point-two-six-oh."

Martin glanced at the radaltimeter. But its readings, fluctuating crazily, were useless.

Gilbert bent over an auxiliary console. "That computes to 1040 miles. Correction—1044." He paused a few seconds. "Now 1,048."

"Still rising. Wring out a drift-force line velocity component."

Gilbert deftly fingered the keyboard. "Almost 4500 mph. Should be nearing the magequator. What about reversal and backdown?"

"If we can't harness our beast, we won't have to worry about decelerating along the line."

The copilot clasped his hands in front of his chin. "If Mr. Props *is* a CMB inspector, do you suppose he'll drop his mask?"

"If *he* triggered these emergency situations, he certainly should have dropped it long before now."

"Unless he has pop-up solutions to all our troubles."

Martin raised a dubious eyebrow. "That old bird

couldn't have instant answers to anything."

"Remember—the jet pilot and the mule skinner? Ira didn't seem very much like an 'ol' codger' when he started spinning his philosophy about technological change, the new learning from the old. Could he have been helpfully coaxing us to look under the surface of his 'ridiculous' suggestions on how to get out of our trouble? Maybe he's letting us kick his veiled hints around a bit before he pulls from his incognito trajectory, spits out the solutions, and banishes us to the limbo of ex-computerpilots."

Martin only snorted. Then he glanced suspiciously at the Lounge 2 call light, now blinking at emergency frequency. (Damn the old man!) But, in addition, six other lights were flashing for attention.

He selected a passenger compartment at random and energized its two-way circuit. Again, only interference patterns filled the screen.

That *his* image was getting through clearly, however, was indicated when a static-harassed feminine voice at the other end of the connection whispered, "We're flux-scrambling pretty bad, aren't we, Captain? What's wrong?"

The screen cleared and there was the troubled face of the section stewardess, belted in her chair at the head of the compartment.

"Nothing to be alarmed about, Miss Holmes," he said.

"Well I can't pacify my cattle any longer," she grumbled. "They won't graze on that alfalfa about 'stripping charged particles off the hull.' "

He stared at the passengers. It was even worse than he had feared. In unison, the seats were gyrating, bucking, tilting. Mounting fear tugged at almost everyone's face. Several were bent over plastic bags. From the rear of the compartment a woman screamed. The shrill sound joined a growing chorus of more subtle groans. Through several of the view ports Martin could see earth and sky reeling, dipping, bobbing as the ship wound into progressively tighter cyclotronic motion.

Abruptly, he shifted his gaze from the screen to the constant-inertia computer. Did he detect acrid fumes rising from its louvered console? If the CIC blew now, what would happen? He knew the answer, of course. Stripped of proper attitudinization, the ship would be crushed and scattered by all the forces acting randomly upon it.

Martin brushed aside his grim speculation and switched the communication circuit to an all-stations hookup.

"This is the captain," he addressed his passengers with authority. "We're experiencing minor difficulty, but order will be restored shortly. Transequatorial Fluxways arranged a surprise on this hop. We selected a line of force that would take you higher than any commercial flight has ever gone—for a view of earth enjoyed only by professional spacemen. Unfortunately, you are also experiencing cyclotronic motion. Something to tell your grandchildren about. But our automatics are being programmed to cancel that out." He switched off.

"Now." Gilbert japed, "all you have to do is punch it out proper."

"Wiseling! If you've got the solution, *you* punch it out."

"Look, Steve! Our ascentometer!"

Martin gaped at the dial: "L-1.290." He waited ten seconds: "L-1.290." After another ten seconds: "L-1.290."

"Ascent factor's been phased out!" he exclaimed.

Using the L value as a whip, he flogged an ancillary computer and interpreted the answers: "Eleven hundred and sixty miles altitude. If we stay stabilized on this shell we'll peak in five minutes."

"Then we'll be down-shelling," Gilbert said hopefully.

"But we won't flux far if we don't start nul-cycing."

Martin swore at the irrepressible Lounge 2 light and angrily tweaked the toggle switch. "What do you want now, you damned—"

"Like I was saying," Ira resumed, clinging to a seat that was precessing on its swivel like a gyro, "you've got to rustle the bushes and get us out of this spin. She's winding up pretty bad."

There was motion at the edge of the screen and Elaine

stumbled into the frame. The deck zoomed out from under her and she fell sitting, legs splayed, uniform skirt disheveled about her thighs. She skittered, twirling, across the deck, reversed direction and came sliding back past Ira's tilting chair.

"Give me some skin!" the old man shouted. He caught her outstretched hand and helped her back into the seat beside him.

Gilbert wiped perspiration from his brow. "We're really slotting down the misery range now, Steve. Spray the compartments?"

"Yes. Trigger off the sweet-dreams system. A fifteen-minute shot. If we're not over the hump by then, it won't matter."

"Too bad the lounges aren't on the spray circuit."

Martin readily admitted that it *was* unfortunate. Face buried in her hands, Elaine was crying now, while Ira tried to comfort her against the sickening, jolting motions of the seat.

"All right, Ambrose—or whoever you are!" Martin shouted at the screen. "We're just about fused out! Spout your theory and tell us how to unscramble!"

"Eh?" said Ira.

"Are you or aren't you a Magnetonautics Bureau inspector?"

"Eh?" Ira repeated. Then his puzzled frown was buried under an expression of senile amusement. "See what you're getting at. You think—" He paused, croaking out a laugh. "No, I'm no quisling. Flew for the airlines after the war. And there was this goldbricking CAB inspector who came pussyfootin' around and —"

Elaine's sobs drowned out his words and she exposed a tear-streaked face. "It's not him," she said remorsefully. "It's me."

"*What's* you?" Martin asked, confounded.

Her seat dipped almost to the horizontal, rotated, then swung back toward vertical. "*I'm* the CBM inspector," she sobbed. "I shorted out the erect Rutledge coil lead with a bobby pin—to see how you'd react."

"You *queered the drive?*" Gilbert asked, astonished.

"Chick's just a damn gremlin!" Ira observed. "I remember back in '45, flyin' out of Luzon. We had this gremlin in our—"

"Well," Martin roared, "you just go get that damn bobby—"

"I already have." She held it up in front of her.

"That's why our ascentometer quieted down," Gilbert offered.

"But," she went on desperately, "I had nothing to do with your nul-cycing trouble. I swear it!"

"I'll take care of you later—asurface," Martin threatened. "Meanwhile—you're a theory girl; suppose *you* tell us how to shake off this cycing before it wrecks the *Prometheus.*"

"I—I can't. I don't know how."

Martin swept the screen clear and settled disconsolately back into the glum silence of the computerpilot compartment.

"I think I see what happened," Gilbert ventured.

"I do too—now. Basically, this ship's drive is comprised of three Rutledge coils, with our cyclotronic damper resonating and operating in parallel with the vertical coil. Sympathetic coupling. Vertical coil lead gets shorted and the regulator suddenly has its hands full meting out proper current to the surviving nul-cyc circuit. The overworked regulator makes a slip, delivers excess potential, and a relay gets stuck. Results: We quit phasing out cyclotronic motion."

Gilbert nodded in agreement. "What can we do about it?"

"Operating with sealed units, I can't think of a more futile question."

Martin looked in on a starboard passenger section. The seats were dancing on their swivels like filings in a rapidly shifting magnetic field. Fortunately everyone was sedated, heads held rigid by cushion-mesh nets that had snaked around their foreheads. Nobody would even know when the chairs began snapping their shafts and hurtling about.

Through a port in the compartment, erratic motion of earth and sky attested to the ferocity of the "spin," as Ira had called it.

Martin straightened alertly. Mr. Props had tried to equate cyclotronic moment to aerodynamic spin. Was it possible that—?

"Gil, what was it the old man said? About a stalled-out, spinning aircraft?"

"Something about throwing the stick forward and—"

Martin dug deep into his early courses on the development of flight. "In other words, you're stalled out, nose down, spinning because you've got lift on one wing but not on the other."

"Sorry, but you're not slotting down my channel now."

"Normal reaction would be to fight the spin, try to get your nose up. But you *don't* do that. Instead you go *along* with it!"

He hesitated thoughtfully. "By throwing your nose *down,* you get enough velocity to restore lift to the stalled wing. *Then* you correct your spin, apply power, and pull out."

"But—"

"Mr. Props may have stumbled onto a solution! If we go along with this cycing—one quick surge at the top of the spin to *accelerate* us in helical motion—maybe then we'll strip the nul-cyc circuit of all inductive force and free that relay!"

"Maybe," Gilbert mused aloud, "it's as Ira says: New technologies can always learn something from the old ones—even if only by accidental analogy."

Martin wrested time, attitude, force line and drift values from his computer. Then he programmed it for instant activation.

It came in a moment. There was a split-second, twisting jolt as he studied the passenger compartment on his screen. A final, brief, whipping motion of the seats. One of them snapped its shaft, but only tumbled gently to the deck, landing on its back, not moving. For, in the same instant, the fluxliner was properly attitudinized in BL space.

"Shut down all drive units!" the captain ordered.

"But," Gilbert protested, "we'll flop into freefall!"

"We can afford to now. We're slotting almost 5000 mph along the line. And if—" He paused to operate an auxiliary computer. "And if we go into freefall we'll take about twelve minutes to drop to 200 miles. But it'll be along a gentle parabola, considering the magnitude of our force-line velocity. We'll be able to ease gradually back onto our proper GM shell with only a mild jostling."

Half an hour later, the captain secured his computer-control gear, stretched, lit a cigarette, stepped out of the compartment and headed for the pilots' ready room.

"Don't go off," Gilbert called wearily after him. "We're booked to pick up the Bombay to New Orleans flight on telemetry switchover."

"Not me." Martin paused at the synchronous satellite's main view port. "We've had three flights today, without stepping out of that damn little box. Let them get another crew. Anyway, I've three weeks accumulated leave coming and I'm claiming them as of now. I'll be jumping asurface on the next shuttle."

Twenty-two thousand, five hundred miles beneath Transequatorial Fluxways' flight-control nexus for the Western Hemisphere, earth was a huge, brilliantly illuminated ball of pastel shades. The southeast coast of South America was almost cloudless. Martin could even see the Rio de la Plata and distinguish Buenos Aires' location.

He envisioned the *Prometheus Unbound* (*Rebound, Reunbound?*) passengers streaming to customs at the GM port there. Bringing up the rear, he felt certain, would be a much chastened Elaine Wesley.

"Anyway," he added, "I've got a little nonmagnetonautics theory to thrash out with our theory girl down there."

[illegible]

[illegible] period, remembering the [illegible]

[illegible]

[illegible]

[illegible]

[illegible] new short-sleeved white shirt and [illegible] for eternity, the soft gray boots that [illegible] the only concession made to outdoor work. He

FAR FROM THIS EARTH

By Chad Oliver

Stephen Nzau wa Kioko dressed quietly so as not to awaken his wife and son. It was still early—the African sun shed pale light but no heat against the windows—but he felt a nagging irritation even as he tried to move without sound. In the old days, his wife would have been up first. His breakfast would have been waiting for him: the thick hot sweet tea mixed with fresh milk from his cows, the steaming porridge made of the ground maize from his shambas. His son would have already started the beautiful thin cattle and the sheep and the goats out of the kraal on their long walk toward water. Stephen grunted softly with annoyance. Elizabeth seldom got up before noon these days and her complaints would have been a blasphemy to her mother—old Wamwiu, so wrinkled and worn, her gums collapsed over the wreck of her teeth, dead now these twenty years. And Paul—one son, imagine only one son, one child. Paul with his idiot's beard, his single feather stuck in a headband like a red Indian. Paul!

Stephen set the dials for his breakfast. Fish cakes and eggs, toast and coffee. It didn't take long, a precise minute and a half. It wasn't worth the wait. The food was neither good nor bad. It simply kept a man going, like petrol in an engine.

He dressed with care: short-sleeved white shirt and tie, brown trousers creased for eternity, the soft gray boots that were the only concession made to outdoor work. He stepped outside and the door closed silently behind him.

Stephen's house stood on a high ridge, flanked by a thousand other houses that were exactly like it except for minor variations in color. He hated the houses and his hate was a constant source of surprise to him. As a boy, he had dreamed of houses like these. He had told himself that one day he would live in such a house, but he had not really believed it—not even after the promised *uhuru* had actually come and so many things had suddenly seemed possible. He remembered the old house, the sun-dried brick that crumbled when the rains came, the thatch on the roof, the good rich smell of smoke from the cooking fire. He had been told that the old house was not a good one and he had believed it—then.

He stood for a moment, drinking in the morning. To the north, not far away, he could see the outskirts of Nairobi. Already, a smudge was staining the air above the industrial complexes that ringed the city. He looked westward, across the plain that had once been Masailand. The great sky, that vast incredible Kenya sky, stretched away as it always had. The grass still grew—taller now, with better land management—and the flat-topped little acacia trees were still starkly black in the new sun. Unhappily, perhaps, a man could see far across that ancient savannah, and he could see clearly. Stephen could not ignore the glint of the electric fence that sealed off the game park and he could see the swollen metallic bubbles and gleaming towers of Safariland in the distance. Safariland was not open yet; the copters and the monorail would not begin to disgorge the tourists from Nairobi for another two hours. Filled or empty, though, it made no difference across the miles. Safariland was an alien thing, a growth that cut the earth but had no roots. Stephen knew it for what it was: garish, tasteless, a polished machine that sucked in money the way a hippo swallowed vegetation. And yet, he was strangely drawn to it. In a way, it was a part of his youth. He had wanted this, or something like this. It had not been forced upon him. He had welcomed it, grasped for it, fought for it. He had it now, and of course it was too late. The boy would have been enchanted, but the man was too old. The man had learned the hard way that the best dreams are not always those that come true. Still, a man can dream again, he must. . . .

Stephen tore his eyes away. He had more urgent problems. For one, the problem of the disappearing rhino horns. For another, the problem of the cattle that ate the forbidden grass—

He climbed into his car. It was only three years old, a Chevrolet. It was painted with black and white stripes that were supposed to look like zebra markings. There was neat, discreet lettering across each of the front doors: WARDEN, KENYA GAME COMMISSION. There was a good rifle, a .375 Magnum, clamped under the dashboard. On the back seat, resting casually as though it had just been tossed in as an afterthought, was a wooden staff about six feet long with a fork in one end. It was always there now when Stephen worked.

He drove the car down from the hills and turned west, away from the city. The climbing sun was behind him. Ahead of him was the grassland and the wind.

He showed his identification at the gate, trying not to look at the huge signs. He had to look at them, of course; that was the kind of sign they were. One read: SEE WILD AFRICAN ANIMALS IN THEIR NATURAL HABITAT! That wasn't too bad, although many of the animals in the park were not really wild any longer and one could quibble about how natural the carefully managed habitat was. Another sign: SEE SAVAGE MASAI WARRIORS SPEAR A LION! The Masai weren't very savage these days, those that were left, and the spearing was a bloodless charade. Another: SEE SPEKE DISCOVER THE SOURCE OF THE NILE! That was staged in Safariland; the park was a long way from Lake Victoria. Another: SEE MAU MAU FREEDOM FIGHTERS! Well, they were at least in the right country, although the Mau Mau in Safariland were a far cry from the ragged, desperate men Stephen had known—when?

Long ago, long ago. He had been a boy of seven when the Emergency had been declared. Another: SEE THE BASE ON THE MOON! It was a long way from the Mau Mau to the conquest of space, in more ways than one. But the broad theme of Safariland was exactly what the name suggested. A safari was just a journey, an expedition preferably into lands unknown. As a matter of fact, the space exploration exhibits at Safariland were among the best in the world. They were almost as good as those at Disneyland, which Stephen had visited. The Kenya government had been anxious to emphasize the future as well as the past in Safariland, and money had been spent.

Stephen drove into the park and there were no more signs. That was a blessing. At this time of the day, before the vehicles fanned out over the roads, a man could almost believe. . . .

He remembered this country as it had once been, not so very long ago. Stephen was a Kamba, and he had been born in 1945 in the hills near Machakos. (No tourist had ever heard of the Kamba; his people had not been colorful like the Masai or leaders in Mau Mau like the Kikuyu. A couple of anthropologists had written books about the Kamba, but no one had read them.) Stephen was now a man of fifty-five, but he had known this land well as a younger man. It had once been Masailand, which bordered on his own tribal territory of Ukambani. He had been here when there was no game park. He remembered the brown grasses, the clouds of red dust, the scummy green water in the shrinking pools. He remembered the Masai as they had been: the tall thin warriors with their cloaks the color of the red ocher they smeared on their faces, the long iron-bladed spears, the great herds of skinny zebu cattle, the brush fences around the brown breadloaf houses plastered with mud and manure, the flies everywhere. He remembered the fear that came with the Masai raids on the Kamba kraals, remembered his own father running for his bow and poisoned arrows. . . .

There were no Masai visible now, although some would be on duty later, in costume, at Safariland. He *could* see some animals, even from the main road. (Stephen could remember when there had not been a single paved road of any consequence in all of Kenya outside the cities.) There were five giraffes in the bush to his left, their stalklike heads poked up above the screening acacias and watching him with typical giraffe curiosity. If he stopped the car and waited, they would walk right up and try to stick their heads in through the windows, their great long tongues uncoiling like snakes. There was an ostrich trotting with imperturbable dignity along the side of the road, looking for all the world like a long-distance runner in training for the Olympics. There were Tommys—Thomson's gazelles—everywhere, some of them stotting in their characteristic stiff-legged gait. It was odd, Stephen thought. As a boy, he had shared the attitudes of most Africans about wild animals. They were meat, pure and simple. He had saved his affection for his cows. Now, he had learned to admire them, even to envy them at times. He was not sentimental about them, like some of the British he had known, but he welcomed their presence on the land. His people needed them, yes; they brought in the tourist money. But it was more than that. They were not cows, but they were something. Of all the changes he had known in his life, this was one of the greatest. It was one of the few gifts of the white man that did not corrupt.

It took him nearly an hour to reach the field station. The sun was higher in the great sky, flooding the plains with golden light and welcome warmth. It was not hot and would not get hot even in the afternoon. Kenya was on the equator, but most of it was high plateau country and the air was cool and dry. For real heat you had to go to the coastal lowlands, to Mombasa on the shores of the Indian Ocean. But Stephen had no desire to go to *that* tourist trap with its swarming beaches. They called it the New Riviera, but to Stephen Mombasa would always be tainted. Mombasa had been the mainland starting point for the slavers from Zanzibar, and some of those Arab slave caravans had reached hungrily into Ukambani. . . .

Ah no, he did not deceive himself. The good old days

had been no Eden. He had lost three sisters and a brother, all dead before they reached their fifth year. He remembered his father, so drunk on sugar-cane beer in the afternoons that he could not speak. He remembered his mother, toiling endlessly in the fields, so bent over at the waist that she could hardly stand erect. He remembered the killing oaths, and the witches. He would not go back if he could. That dream was for the foolish young, who had never been there and so could not remember. And for the very old, perhaps, the elders lost in a new world and groping for the only alternative they knew.

He tried not to think about it as he checked the reports. He knew what he would find, out there on the sunlit savannah. He knew that they could not escape him.

His heart was heavy when he went out to the waiting copter. He did not relish this part of his job. It had to be done, yes, but it could not be done with joy. The past had been murdered enough.

The chopper climbed into the vault of the sky and swung toward the southwest. There was no Safariland here and only dirt trails cut through the thorny bush. Elephants, not gray as they were in zoos but rust-colored from the dust. Fatbellied zebras, breaking into an oddly clumsy gallop as the shadow of the copter passed over them. Kongoni, those most ungainly of antelopes, unconcerned as always. One lazy lion, a male, flopped down asleep in the tall grass. Stephen knew him. They called him Lord Lugard, and Stephen was worried about his teeth.

"The damn fools," the pilot said. "Won't they ever learn?" He spoke in English. It still surprised the tourists, but English had been the major language in Kenya for years. The tribal languages were fading out, and Swahili was not what the doctor ordered for a nation trying hard to be modern.

"Wait a bit," Stephen said. "You'll get older and disappoint the old lady some night. Then you'll be out hunting rhino horn with the rest of them."

The pilot looked at him blankly. "I meant the cowboys."

Stephen did not reply. Cassius, the pilot, was a Luo and too clever by half. Stephen found him pretty hard to take. He was deliberately obtuse with Cassius, mostly to shut him up. It seldom worked.

"I mean, they haven't a chance when we can spot them from the air," Cassius said. "If they had half a brain between them they could figure that out."

"Africans ain't got no brains, don't you know that? We are like children."

Cassius lapsed into silence. He wasn't angry, just puzzled. Stephen was aware that he was something of an enigma to his colleagues, and he rather fancied the role.

The copter droned on, flying a search pattern. Stephen didn't bother to use his glasses. He could see well enough. He wouldn't miss a herd of cattle, not from the air or from the ground. He knew about where they had to be. Close enough to the fence to get them out at night, using a portable wooden walkway to get the animals over the electric fence. Close to the Tanzania border, away from the tourists and the game patrols.

Cassius was right. They were fools. But they were other things as well. He thought of his father, and of his grandfather. He thought of all the men of his clan, stretching backward into the mists of time, the men and their cattle, always the cattle. . . .

He saw the two peaks of Kilimanjaro thrusting up through the clouds, sharing the sky to his left. The snow and ice gleamed on the summits. According to legend, the Kamba had once lived on the slopes of Kilimanjaro. And now he was coming back—

"In a great silver bird," he muttered in self-mockery.

"How's that?"

"Nothing, man. An old joke."

The copter flew on. The sun climbed high in a sky that was a brilliant blue.

Quite suddenly, Stephen spotted them. They were nakedly exposed on the plains below. They could not hide any more than ants could hide on a greasy white plate.

"Take her down, Cassius."

Cassius stared at him. "We going in alone? Don't you think—"

"Take her down, Cassius."

The copter started down.

Stephen climbed out of the copter, his boots crushing the soft, fragrant grass. He carried no weapon. Cassius stayed behind, shouting into the radio. Stephen walked forward, hating what he had to do.

Almost, he thought, it was a timeless scene, a frieze from a ruined temple. There were the hump-backed cattle, beyond any man-made law, munching on the grass. And there were the herdsmen with their staffs, frozen like statues, only the eyes alive. Hostile eyes, fearful eyes, resigned eyes. Eyes that looked again on the destroyers of herds. . . .

But it was like all scenes now. There were distortions, bits and chunks of wrongness. A man had to edit to see what he wanted to see—or look beyond. There was the copter, for one thing, and that in a way was the least of it. The herdsmen—there were three of them—were very old, too old to be taking cattle to grass. That had been a job for boys, back when boys still did such things. The men were dressed in ragged, baggy suits—ripped by the thorns, stained by years of filth. One man even wore a tie although he had no shirt. And there were only sixteen cows in the herd. Three men for sixteen cows!

Stephen recognized one of the men as a Kamba. He could tell by the way his teeth had been filed, a custom that hadn't been practiced in fifty years.

Stephen spoke to him gently, the old language strange in his mouth. *"Nouvoo, mutumia?"* Is it peace, elder? A standard Kamba greeting once, but it had a literal meaning now.

The old man looked surprised, subtly pleased by the use of his language and his title. Hope flickered briefly in the cloudy eyes. He hesitated a moment, then nodded. *"Ii nesa."* The ancient response. Yes, it is well, it is peace.

Stephen knew his job. Elders did not fight. "Old man,"

he said softly, "you cannot herd your cows here."

"Where can I herd them?" The elder's hands were trembling, more with age than fear.

"You cannot herd them anywhere. There is no land for cattle."

"There is land here. Much land."

"Not for cows. For wild animals."

The elder shook his head. This was madness. Stephen knew the memories in the old man's mind. When the British had come, it had been the same. The people had been moved to protect the animals. Then the white men had come to shoot the animals. It made no sense. "I must have cows," the old man said simply. "I have always had cows."

"That is all over. I am sorry." Stephen did not try to explain. There were no words to reach this man. Population growth rates, land shortages, the necessity to increase agricultural yields—these things had no meaning for him. Irrigated farmland could support twenty times as many people as the same land spent on herding. Kenya could not support the luxury of cows.

The elder was beyond tears. He did not attempt to argue. He had suffered many blows in his long lifetime. He stood there, leaning on his staff, waiting for the next blow to fall.

Stephen waited with him, in silence. It took several hours; the sun started down the arc to the western horizon and the air was still. The flies were very bad. In time, the police trucks rolled up in showers of dust. The cattle were loaded. The three old men were arrested and put in with the cows. The trucks drove off.

That was that. Stephen looked for a moment at the distant Kilimanjaro. He could see only its dark base, rising so improbably out of the level plain. The peaks were hidden by clouds. He walked back to the copter and climbed in.

"Okay, Cassius. Another heroic mission accomplished. Chins up and all that."

"You're lucky you didn't get an arrow through you."

"You just don't understand savages, old boy. Just have

to look them right in the eye and speak in a loud, clear voice."

"Ah, go to hell."

"Filthy superstition. I'm disappointed in you. Shall we have a go at the bloody rhino poachers?"

"What's with this crazy colonial talk? You could find yourself in a mess of trouble, Steve."

Stephen thought: We took their houses, their cars, their clothes, their schools, their courts, their money, their cities, their clubs, their guns, their books, and their whisky. Why not their patterns of speech? He said, "Some of my best friends are natives. I used to be one myself."

Cassius clamped his teeth together and turned to the controls. The chopper lifted with a great clatter into the blue sky. Down below, the good grass undulated in the wind from the whirling blades. Then all motion stopped and there was nothing.

They wasted a couple of long afternoon hours searching for signs of the rhino hunters. They found one dead rhino, its grotesque carcass bloating in the sun. The animal had been dead for days. The horns, both front and rear, had been neatly detached from the skull. The horns were missing, of course.

Stephen felt an anger that he had never been able to feel against the old men with their cattle. This rhino horn business had been going on for centuries. The passage of time does not necessarily make people less gullible. There were still millions of persons—in the Arab countries, in China—who believed that rhino horn was a cure for impotence. The horn, which was not a true horn at all, was ground up and served in a potion. It was incredible, but perhaps no more incredible than—say—astrology or statistics. Stephen didn't know how it worked out in the bedroom, but he did know the result in Africa. The rhino was virtually extinct.

It was no great trick to find the rhino carcasses, but catching the killers was something else again. It was not like trying to spot some old men with a herd of cattle. The poachers were well organized, and they could work at night. A rhino horn could be carried out of the country in a briefcase.

There was no point in aimless cruising, and the fuel was getting low. Cassius flew the copter back to the field station and landed. It was nearly five o'clock—quitting time.

It had been a depressing day and Stephen was in no mood to hurry home. He checked out, climbed into his Chevrolet, and drove the other way, toward Safariland. The highway was crowded with cars going back to Nairobi. Stephen studied the drivers as they flashed by. Black, brown, yellow, white—they all looked the same, faces tense, films exposed, wives bedraggled, kids sullen. There were times when Stephen felt very much alone.

Safariland was technically closed when he got there, with the maintenance crews engaged in picking up the day's debris. Stephen had no trouble in getting in; Safariland was situated in the game park, and Stephen was a senior warden. He preferred the place without the tourists and without the gimmicks. He had eyes. He could use them.

He ignored the buildings devoted to Africa's past. He didn't much care whether Stanley ever met Livingstone, and the source of the Nile was not a burning issue to him. He went straight to Spaceland and entered the great bubble of Moonbase.

He sat down in silence and looked at another world. He was the only one there. It was a good feeling.

The stars on the dome were very close, very bright. The animated lunar vehicles were still now with most of the power switched off for the night. The rockets were in their cradles with no fire in their tails. The helmeted human figures—so small, so lost in grandeur—did not move. The craters pocked the surface. Far away—it seemed—a lunar range thrust its ragged peaks into an unearthly sky.

The Mountains of the Moon. Once, they had called the Ruwenzoris that, those snow-capped mountains that separated East Africa from the Congo. Once, if it came to that, they had believed that the Ruwenzoris were the source of the Nile. . . .

Stephen felt a kind of peace growing within him. More than that, a kind of hope. (He remembered the false hope in the old herdsman's eyes. But a man had to have hope.) Here, of all places, there seemed to be an opportunity, a second chance—

It wasn't just the moon. The moon was nothing, a big hunk of barren rock. But the base on the moon stood for something, for everything. It was a sign for those who could read. It said: *It can be done.*

Stephen was not, by some standards, an educated man. He had finished high school, no more. But Stephen had read books and he had a brain. It was not a combination that led to happiness, but it had its uses. Stephen had been eighteen years old when Kenya became an independent nation. He had been in the Youth Wing. He had thought himself quite enlightened; he had dispensed with the past. Everything was going to be modern, up to date. He was going to have a car, a big house, a television set, a representative in the United Nations. . . .

Well, he had those things. When it was too late, he discovered what he had lost. Not just the old ways, although he saw the good in them now. It was not innocence that he had lost. No, the loss had been in the power of choice. By his eagerness to be "civilized" he had thrown away all of the alternatives. His people had given up what they had. In its place they had taken a bastard culture, and they had *wanted* to take it. Instead of the Kamba, the Masai, the Pokot, the Taita, the Samburu, they were all the same, ants in a western anthill. Not just the Africans. The whole world was stuck with the same culture—cities, industry, money, loneliness in the manswarm.

Stephen could not accept it. He did not believe that this was all that man could be. Other lifeways could have flowered from the old roots; even manure makes good fertilizer. There could have been warmth, kinship, purpose, fulfillment. For him, for all those on the earth today, it was too late. But clans do not die, they go on down through the generations. And one day, somewhere—

Space was vast. There were many worlds, not all of them barren like the moon. Mars was not the end. There would be other suns, other rivers, other grasslands. Surely, on just one world, at some time unimagined, man would find a life worth living. Perhaps even with thatch-roofed houses and cows and food plants that took root in good soil—who knew?

There was just one way to *get* to the stars. Stephen understood that. But then?

He took a last look around the silent Moonbase. He felt better. A million to one shot, a billion to one shot, was better than nothing. He went back to his Chevrolet and started the long drive home.

The lights were on when Stephen reached his house in the hills. Stephen felt a little guilty at being late but as always after a visit to Moonbase he was filled with his vision, he wanted to talk, to communicate—

He stepped inside. Elizabeth looked up coldly. "Where have *you* been?"

Paul was stretched out on the floor, staring at a Western on television. He had his feather on. Like so many of the young people, Paul didn't believe in anything. The Indian feather was the badge of his generation. It was worn precisely because it made no sense. Paul didn't bother to greet his father.

Stephen felt a hot, sudden, irrational anger. His family seemed a waste and a betrayal. They had accepted it all, wallowed in it. They were blind, just as he had once been blind.

Stephen turned on his heel and walked back to his car. He took the wooden staff from the back seat. It was an elder's stick with the traditional fork at the top end; he was entitled to it at his age, even though the old age-grade system no longer had much significance. He went back into his house and crossed over to the TV set. He swung the staff once. Glass tinkled, a few sparks shot out, and the TV sputtered into silence.

Paul leaped to his feet, finally jolted into awareness.

"Are you crazy? What did you do that for?"

Stephen gripped his staff. "You watch that damned thing too much, Paul. You should be studying. You should be reading."

"For Christ's sake!" Paul turned to his mother. "What's with him?"

Elizabeth fluttered her well-manicured hands. "Really, Stephen. I hardly know what to say."

"Don't say anything then. Paul is throwing his life away, can't you see that? It's *not* all over. There are things to do."

"Paul does very well in school. He's got a C average."

Stephen said a word—traditional indeed, it went all the way back to Anglo-Saxon. "Paul is going to learn the important things. He's going to be an engineer, a scientist. He's going to do it if I have to beat him with this stick. I'll call in the lineage elders. . . ."

"Lineage elders!" Paul threw up his hands. "What'll they do—buy a goat to sacrifice? You know what you are, Pops? You're an Uncle Tom. A chief. A neocolonialist!"

Stephen advanced on him with his staff. Paul ran away and locked himself in his room.

Elizabeth looked at her husband, then lowered her eyes. She knew his moods. Stephen was a little mad sometimes. It was embarrassing, really. Why, he might even strike *her*.

"Fix me something to eat, Elizabeth. I'm going out."

Stephen went into their bedroom and changed his clothes. He knew he would be out all night. His anger was gone. The despair was back. He had handled Paul badly, as usual. He could not reach the boy, could not make contact with him. And yet he *had* to get through to him. He had to try. If fathers gave up on their sons, there was no hope, no chance. He remembered his own father. God knows, he had had reason to drink.

He ate his dinner. Elizabeth said nothing to him. He touched her when he was through. "I'll get the TV fixed tomorrow," he said. It was an apology of a sort.

"Will you be back tonight?"

"No. I'm going out to check the herd."

"You have no cows."

"I have a few—for a while."

She watched him go. Her face was hurt, puzzled. Stephen thought that the expression was better than the normal blankness.

He drove back into the park under the stars. The deep African night closed in around him, sheltering him. The blaze of the Nairobi lights was an intrusion, but he did not try to edit them out. You had to have the Nairobis to reach those stars.

He knew that the lions would be hunting this night. If he stopped the car he could hear their coughing roars, perhaps see their gleaming eyes. He did not stop, but it was not fear that prevented him. It was not lions that he feared. People were the problem, always, forever.

He drove to the silent field station and parked the Chevrolet. He walked to the holding pens. The cattle were there, the sixteen cows he had confiscated that day. They would be slaughtered after they had been inspected tomorrow. The meat would go to the hotels in Nairobi.

He opened the gate and went inside the pen. He closed the gate carefully behind him. He sat down on the earth. He had no plan. There was nothing he could do.

It was far different from the kraals he had known as a boy. The fence was steel, not thornbrush. There were no calves. There were no thatch-covered houses in the moonlight, no drums in the distance, no old man singing drunkenly along the trails.

But the smells were there, the warm rich milky smells of the cows. The cows were there, the feel of trodden earth and dung and hairy hides. There was a kind of continuity. A Kamba and his cows. . . .

Stephen smiled, alone there in the great night. Perhaps he was a little mad. Perhaps a man had to be a little mad in these times. He knew that he would never surrender. He would do his job as best he could, preserving something. He would keep after Paul, all the Pauls. Study, learn, work. Find the way. And then go, take the long way home—

It might never happen. For him, it would certainly never

happen. But there were other men, other times. Clans do not die. When he too was a forgotten ancestor, the clan would live.

Stephen stayed there with the good smells all that night. He watched the red sun rise over the hills. He said good-by to the cows and got in his car.

He drove down the paved road to Safariland. He parked by the gates in his zebra-painted Chevrolet. He watched the tourists come in for a new day. They were all the same—black, brown, yellow, white. Dead people, groping for life.

For you too, Stephen thought. *For you. For you.*

AFTER THE ACCIDENT

By Naomi Mitchison

Naturally I knew the chances. It had all been plotted with a standard margin of error and for those who, like myself, knew which ancestors had been in fallout areas, the probabilities were reasonably clear. Of course many of the mutations were lethal, though not always at an early stage and when they were late-stage, one might be involved in considerable unpleasantness. So it was better to avoid the whole thing. As a young girl I had been somewhat obsessed with this: inevitably it took me into history and biology. Once one was aware of the connections, the tension eased off.

But I was affected by the Better Humanity writings and telepropaganda. I saw this return to genetic normalcy and advance to super-normalcy as something desirable, deeply clean, to be reached for. And I was well aware of the flaws in my own make-up. Most of my friends had the same problem; most of us had been constrained, reluctantly on the whole, to turn down date-mates whose heredity would have increased the problems. If a man appeared to be lying, as some of them did, lies being so much a male weapon, it was easy enough to check up on the probabilities. The seconds were open, at least in our sector. Occasionally one of us would take a chance, but there was always an element of guilt. Those who were genuine Better Humanity converts had of course to agree to instant destruction if the result was not perfect. And how seldom it could be!

Naturally we dated and all that, but did not mate, and, as time went on, found a certain lack. In this comparatively empty world which the Great Accident has given us, we wished to give and not merely in the matter of data, observation, and synthesis. We wanted to people some of the new spaces, as they became tenable once more, to sample some of the new growths, the genera of plants for which names had perhaps still to be found, to see how rapidly adaptation and selection could take place. Above all we wanted to meet some of the cut-off communities who were also in the Better Humanity network, not merely over telecommunication but face to face. Yes, how we wanted to give. To be fertile. But—Better Humanity? There were moments when we shivered away, back to other dreams.

My own sector had barely been space-interested. Before the Accident space travel had made sense; the beginnings were there; now it had become academic. And yet, once the techniques were there, even on brain level, it was not possible to disregard them. At least not for some.

That was how Hari arrived, gliding into my life like a virus into a cell. But—a virus of happiness, delightful, but as important as other viruses to control. He had managed an inter-community capsule, of a kind none of us had envisaged. Both it and he were new. I took him off and he did not seem unwilling. Nor would I have expected him to be.

He had been working on one of the main space-travel projects; his own capsule was a by-product of this. The work was slow of course. So much had to be improvised: not the ideas but the methods of carrying them out, especially now that large-scale power methods were no longer possible. Many of the necessary raw materials had quite simply been destroyed during the Accident. Others were in no condition to be touched. And the space projects needed considerable groundwork. It was only gradually that I realized that under Hari's apparent lightheartedness there was a feeling of hatred against the makers of the Accident which was even greater than our own.

We all have hang-overs from earlier cultures. There came a time when Hari showed me a small ivory carving of one of his goddesses—Kali, I suppose—with a recognizable head of a late twentieth-century statesman in each of her eight hands. Three were Asians, four were European or American, one was African. I wondered whether there would have been exactly the same choice had it been made elsewhere. But I was more interested in the ivory, whose grain I recognized. "Have you seen one of *them?*" I asked. "Dead," he said and added. "One of the central vertebra usually snapped. The main leg bones were adapted to the weight, but if they got into wet ground which they usually did, looking for fruit trees or high crops to eat, the strain on the middle of the spine, which took most of the weight when getting out of the mud, usually did the trick." He looked away from me and went on, "The one I saw had fallen on two or three houses; it took us a day to get it off. I was still a student in those days. There were some children squashed into mud. Yes."

"Are they all gone?"

He nodded. But I would have liked to see an elephant fifteen meters high.

Most of the worst giant mutants had been destroyed or more usually had died out because of their own inability to come to terms with their environment. But there were occasional lurkers in the less populated zones. Such really nasty ones as were left were almost wholly aquatic, since water is more accommodating than land to large displacements and easier to hide in. We used to read sometimes about swimming in seas or rivers in the old days, surf riding and above all underwater exploration. How wonderful it must have been! I ask myself whether pre-fallout people ever realized how fortunate they were. Such activities are hopelessly dangerous now.

There was still work to be done on many other mutants, especially of course the bacteria, which had developed with predictable rapidity. Some had to be eliminated, but there was always the danger of a fresh invasion. And there were the happy-making viruses which, however, had to be strictly controlled, as we learned through some very alarming periods of trial and error. But at least we biologists were never bored.

Some of the work we were doing was quite new to Hari, and of course there are few things more enjoyable than explaining one's work to an intelligent listener. Quite apart from little things like the sudden, excited movement of a hand catching at one's own, the bright widening of deep brown eyes, there is the mental effect on oneself: new aspects are suddenly uncovered; something which has puzzled one for weeks shows itself in a curious flash, which, if one could catch it—and this was largely a function of the listener—short cut hours of plodding and worry and fake analogies. But such exchanges of intellectual sympathy must be mutual. I listened to Hari talking about space travel, and listened just as carefully when my fingers were also tracing his eyebrows or pushing back his black, wavy hair.

It started from his explanation of the simple, but to us new, technique of his inter-community travel capsule, which traversed the danger areas where fallout reactions were still predictable. After his account of the type of travel mechanics and propulsion, he began to talk about the plans for landing on heavy and light gravity planets, of which the former seemed most likely to have possible atmospheres and some kind of life. Much of this was based on work done before the Accident, but now perhaps we could get a calmer and longer term perspective. There had even been some survivals of the plants which had been specially designed for human food during space travel and on arrival. And here came the next step: the colonists.

It would be at the earliest fifteen years, at latest twenty-five, before any possible start; we could not get together the enormous and costly pre-accident space-travel gadgetries. In fact our methods were based on a different philosophy of techniques. But training for colonization would take a long period, in fact it could not be started too young. I did not see where this was leading until Hari explained that he had looked up my records. He seemed to be rather ashamed of this, though I could see nothing wrong with it. Such records are and must be, public. Apparently this was not entirely so in his culture, at least for women. He had equated with his own. There was a very high probability that the gene pattern would be such as to produce the perfect high-gravity colonist, almost legless and with certain other modifications from the normal human evolved for an earth environment: the ideal of Better Humanity.

Would I?

I went through a difficult time. At first I was deeply shocked, I could not bear to see Hari again. Then I did see him one day, standing very still, looking desperately sad and carrying a long piece of silk. I had of course heard of silk, but had never seen it, or rather only in one of the collections where it had partly crumbled and did not appear at all desirable. We had, after all, plenty of textiles. But it was interesting and attractive, and so was his sadness. He did not speak a word of what had upset me, but when at last I spoke to him, he told me that this was the kind of dress which his sister sometimes wore. As a matter of fact it was quite true that he had a sister; I saw a picture of her, a tough girl in lab jeans carrying a spanner. But quite possibly she did wear this kind of dress sometimes.

I did not put it on at once. He held it up and played with the silk, which certainly produced beautiful reflections. I touched it with one finger. He threw an end over my shoulder, and his fingers brushed my neck, accidentally on purpose. No doubt if I had genuinely not wanted him I would have reacted badly.

But I did not. I let him dress me in this silk: this fancy dress so different from standard lab wear or play wear. I became confused, the length of silk wrapped me and tripped me. He began to talk about his sector of humanity. Much of India had escaped, or had not escaped but was now habitable, and being cleared of mutants. I began to think I wanted to become somehow involved in it. And then he was showing me gods and goddesses in deep color stereo: pictures one could wander into. Not that Hari believed in them as such, any more than I believed in my own religious hang-overs, some of which are pretty enough. Yet, as I fixed my attention his gods began to affect me. And I wanted them to.

By the way I have not yet made my work clear. I am, of course, a biologist, but I was also developing a technique of intellectually aware appreciation of historical objects and artifacts, which could lead to a reaching out into past lives and consciousness, which could in turn clarify historical problems, especially those where one was quite out of touch with contemporary motives. It was particularly useful in dealing with pre-fallout situations where our ancestors had allowed themselves to be pulled into the most extraordinary and evil activities through religious or political convictions.

Some people said all this was pointless: better to ignore the incomprehensible past when we had so many of our own immediate and directly fascinating problems. I remember an argument I had about this with Motaba, a friend of mine. I had been concentrating on something directly concerned with some of her ancestors: the impact of the Christian missions in southern Africa. I had come across some old letters—so curious, which archives did and which didn't escape the Accident!—and I was concentrating on them, especially the slight change in handwriting when certain highly charged words occurred. I was now looking for typed material of a slightly later date to see if this change would still occur.

"I wish you wouldn't!" said Motaba, one fine-boned hand on mine, but oddly a different shade from Hari's, who was, however, not a cross.

"You're getting angry," I said, "why?"

She said: "It was all such a waste! Five generations back—only that—my grandmother's people had to become Africans again. It was good that they did— No!" She caught my eye. "Not good, Chloe. But it had to be done. Because of what you are reading about. But it made my people do horrible things. Horrible!" Her face went into a twist. She was thinking of a story about a mission which had not withdrawn in time and of her great-great-grandfather, who had started as a mission-Christian but ended—well, it was all over. Or was it? The story hurt her still.

I said: "What I'm trying to do, Motaba, is to reconstruct the reason for the missions first going in and then staying on."

"To open a door to trade," said Motaba bitterly.

"Yes, yes, dear Motaba, we know all that and it's a bore. I'm getting down behind it. You'd be interested if you could bear to think about it."

"But it doesn't matter any longer. Everything's changed. We're different. My people were converted by the mission. My people tortured and murdered the mission. That's past. Nobody could behave like that any longer: like my people or like the mission. We've moved on."

"Sure?" I said.

"Yes! We've moved on to molecular bounce. Oh, Chloe, it's so marvelous, isolating the states; when it all clicks together. It's not in the same world as murder and conversion—is it? So why bother? Aren't you thrilled about bounce, much, much more than those old letters?" She was excited, she pulled my hair gently. Yes, bounce was all right, but conversion was still real.

I said: "We have to know everything about belief and conversion reactions because they still go on. You're keen on Better Humanity, aren't you, Motaba?"

"Yes, Chloe," she said, clearly trying to be truthful but to keep all emphasis out of her voice.

"And I am considering becoming pregnant with a mutant," I said.

"No," she said, "No! Even if you are so much in love—"

"But I'm not," I said. "Only I'm thinking of leading an experiment." She covered her face with her hands, muttering something to herself. I rubbed it in: "A mutant, quite a long way off standard. Now, Motaba, remember your great-great-grandfather."

And I felt that she had, that the shock which was graying her lips came from deep in. And it was something which I shared; we had all accepted part of the ideology. It was fascinating, for I could feel the same thing, but attenuated. The converted soul coming up against a nasty fact. Yet we were in a civilized environment. But how civilized was it? Where was the breaking point? My research on the letters might give me some of the data for that.

And, using the same techniques, I began hard concentration on Hari's gods and goddesses. There was the eight-armed Kali again brandishing the weapons of technology. There were beast-headed avatars, many-faced Siva. The four-armed dancing god Nataraja was more beautiful than a normal, indeed a perfect, human. There was the inelegantly bodied but attractive elephant Ganesa, the half-human monkey, the lion with the head of an angry, overeager man. There were protruding eyes and tongues, semi-serpents. There was also a very strange trio of gods from Puri in Orissa, and they, above all, were like some mutants, stump-legged and stump-armed. At first I was alarmed and half angry, clutching out of their reach toward Better Humanity. Then I began to accept them, as I had accepted Hari's silk.

I knew it was all on purpose. I knew that Hari and his whole space-travel setup had planned this, talking it over carefully; they had made the pictures of the gods, and I was not the only object. I knew that Hari's mind was not on me, but far ahead on his high gravity planet. Not that he would be there, only his children. But that was as it should be, between scientists. Yet I could not have accepted it without a certain degree of thought-changing, of alienating myself from earlier resolves. I ask myself, could I have accepted if Hari had moved with less beauty, if his sadness and quivering joy had not affected me so deeply, if his hands adjusting the silk, had avoided the delicious nerve touch? Is a true answer possible?

During my pregnancy I asked him many questions. He wanted more colonists and I helped him to find mates among my friends with suitable genetic make-up. Another genotype was of course necessary for those who would act as mechanics during the space voyage, probably doing repairs, internal or external, while in a state of weightlessness. But Hari was not a suitable parent for these; he had to concentrate on colonists. Apparently it had not worked out with any of the mates in his own sector: all had produced lethals. However, this was partly due to sloppy methods of recording and partly to the fact that they had apparently no drug like our neo-thalidomide, which would allow potential lethals to develop. The only thing they used was a local plant extract with a somewhat uncertain action; it had not yet been at all thoroughly analyzed. In fact, it may be better than neo-thalidomide. One does not know yet.

At an early stage I had an amniotic fluid analysis; a lot could be discovered from the chromosome arrangement —or misarrangement. It appeared that the predicted result of the meeting of zygotes was happening. Looking at the chromosome pattern, it seemed to me probably male, but certain elements were jumbled about and unclear. I could not be sure. And if the colonists were to breed successfully, sexes must be separate.

I began to take neo-thalidomide. And yet, every now and again I was shaken. Perhaps all women, in some curious way, suppose that their first pregnancy will produce a divine creature, something of consummate beauty and worth. The experience of many centuries has not altered that. This time I knew that, whatever I gave birth to, it would not, by human standards, be divinely beautiful. Yet it must be given love if it was to survive and have the confidence necessary for its task. Could I manage that?

I was concentrating meanwhile on Hari's gods and on the state of mind of those who had made them, who did not insist that divinity could only manifest itself in the perfectly human. And I was not neglecting my work on the African missions. I was watching Motaba and her reactions to my pregnancy, my deviation from the genetic norm to which she had given the enthusiasm of conversion. But now I thought that I had better be more certain and asked for an X-ray. While I waited I explained that this was an experiment, designed to solve some of the problems of space travel.

Those who had seen the earlier chromosome analysis had assumed that I would discontinue the pregnancy, if it did not discontinue itself, as it would probably have done without the drug. The research physician in charge at the center was herself a very keen Better Humanity convert. The walls of the clinic were covered with stereos and even imaginary pictures of the recognized ideals, in the several branches of mankind and their crosses. I noticed that India figured less than Africa as a basis of mixture and was obscurely annoyed.

There was some surprise that the pregnancy had continued. The X-ray picture of the fetus showed a colonist. What I had intended. But I was suddenly afraid. "Don't you think, my dear," said the physician in charge, looking very gravely at the shadow picture of the still curled fetus, "that this experiment has gone far enough?" And for a moment I almost said yes. "Stop taking the neo-thalidomide and the thing will probably abort on its own. We'll look after you. Give me the tablets, Chloe."

I can remember how near I was to putting them into her hand. But I managed not to. The interest of the experiment succeeded in containing my fear; I reacted as a biologist. I said, "I don't think you quite realize the nature of the space-travel difficulties." And as I said this I suddenly knew that the fetus with which I had doomed myself, if that was to be part of my reaction, was not forever: its destiny was not of this world.

There were weeks and months more to go. Motaba was still not reconciled. "It is the example," she used to say. "You may have good reasons, Chloe, but others might be encouraged to—to mate thoughtlessly." And then added, "As I almost did once."

She told me about that, how she had longed for a child, tried to persuade herself that it might be normal; but her gene pattern was too bad. She had given up what she so deeply wanted. And I saw in her the recapitulation of African conversion, as it might have been her great-great-grandmother. They, as it happened, were almost unaffected by the Accident; the damage came on her European side. She looked so deeply sad that I could do nothing but say, with formal hate: "The Accident Makers."

"The Accident Makers," she answered. It is these occasional moments of ritual anger and intention of violence that are sometimes all that keep us steady and orientated toward life.

At my next checkup I had confirmation of something that I was beginning to suspect. The fetus was developing into something very broad. The shoulders would make a normal delivery impossible, especially for a primipara. A Caesarean was simple, but if I was anesthetized it was possible that the malformed—or rather experimentally formed—baby would be destroyed and I could not risk that. If only I could get hold of Hari! But he was now occupied with the fourth of the possible mothers and, as I knew, something beyond logical persuasion was necessary with each. I thought of getting one of them to stand in, but felt it might be too much of a shock and could induce them to terminate the experiment. One of them was an old friend, but less stable than I am. I knew that Hari had encouraged them all by telling them that I was the first experimenter, the leader of the team, and I have a good reputation as a biologist. He and I, discussing it, felt that six possible colonists might do for a start. It could be seen after a few years how they were developing and whether the same or a different type of genetic pattern should be used for the next batch.

However, I spoke to all those who were likely to be present, emphasizing that this was the first stage of an experiment in applied genetics. And then Motaba said that she would like to be present. She did not express it, but clearly she had the same fear as I had; and her loyalty to her friend was stronger than her loyalty to her moral feelings, if one could call the Better Humanity drive that. And I recalled a passage in one of those old letters about a lapsed convert who also, guiltily, was loved and helped. But would any of them, tangled as they were in the Better

Humanity principles—most doctors had become involved—be entirely trustworthy with—and now I said it to myself clearly—my child?

I went under the anesthetic with considerable latent fear. I dreamed of rushing along cliff roads, in and out of caves, under a treble moon. I knew this was the landscape of another planet. I knew that the air was unbreathable before I was plunging into prickly darkness, clutching for something—something. I woke and saw Hari's face upside down. "She sent for me," he whispered, sloping his head at Motaba, who was also there. "She could not trust herself. But how could you keep me from this stage of the experiment?"

"Where?" I said, "where?" For I could tell by the pain which was beginning to be apparent that the operation had been concluded.

Motaba picked up something with tight shut eyes. Hari said, "The first colonist."

"Is it," I asked, "male or female?" Obviously it would be incorrect to say boy or girl.

"Definitely male," said Hari. So I had been correct in my view of the chromosomes.

"And otherwise?" It dizzied me to move. Motaba pulled the wrapping back and her fingers were trembling; tears crawled down her cheeks. The head appeared thickened and slightly flattened; this was to be expected and need have no effect on brain volume or content; the outer ears were an odd shape, which might be the external sign of a useful modification of the eustachian tube and inner ear.

"Leg stumps," said Hari succinctly, "arms shortened, some digits absent, but can grip. Spine as decided. Shoulder and pelvic bones modified. Congratulations."

For a minute I swirled back into sleep. It had been a success. And disconcertingly I dreamed that I had borne a normal human baby and knew that this was what I wanted on one level, but could never have. Yet thinking that I had achieved it, I woke. And saw Motaba's face of grief and accepted the truth. "Give it to me," I said. I touched its pale brown, very delicate skin. "What do we call it?" I said to Hari. His eyes too filled with tears, in spite of our mutual success. I wanted to cheer him. "I know your sector calls their children for their favorite gods," I said, "but we can't call this one for Krishna. Clearly."

"Clearly," said Hari, with a shake in his voice. "Not Jaggernaut," he said, and I knew that we had both thought of the black, stump-legged god of Puri, "That was never—living. Make it Siva. Of the many avatars."

"Yes," I said as the first colonist opened blank bright eyes from under its heavy brow ridge. And then it opened its mouth and yelled: for me. And my heart turned over. It was my achievement. My child.

UTOPIAN

By Mack Reynolds

When he awakened the second time, there was more food and a larger portion. And after a while they had wheeled him out onto a porch. He recognized the scene. No other houses were in sight, but there was no doubt about it. He was within a mile of Cape Spartel, atop the mountain which rises above Tangier and looks out over Spain and the Atlantic.

There was precious little else he could identify. The architecture of the house was extreme. The chair in which he sat was wheel-less, but carried him at the gentlest direction of the hand of the one who had called himself Jo Edmonds.

The three of them—the girl's name turned out to be Betty Stein—accompanied him to the terrace, treating him as though he was porcelain. Tracy Cogswell was still weak, but alert enough now to be impatient and curious.

He said, "My elbow. It's no longer stiff. It's been stiff since . . . since 1939."

Academician Stein fluttered over him. "Don't overdo, Tracy Cogswell, don't overdo."

The younger one, Edmonds, grinned and said, "We had your elbow and various other, ah, deficiencies taken care of before we awakened you."

Tracy was about to say, "Where am I?" but he knew where he was. Something strange was going on, but he knew where he was. He was within a few miles of Tangier, and in the strangest house he'd ever seen and certainly the most luxurious. That fact came home to him. He was evidently in the hands of the opposition; only a multimillionaire could have afforded this sort of an establishment, and there were no such in the movement.

He considered Jo Edmonds' words and accepted them. But in the acceptance, he realized the implications. He'd had that arm worked on in London by possibly the world's outstanding practitioner in the field. He'd saved the elbow but let Tracy know it would never be strong again. Now it was strong, for the first time since the debacle on the Ebro.

By the third day, he was up and around, and beginning to consider his position. He kept his mind from some of the more far out aspects. Such explanations could come later. For now he wanted to evaluate the situation in which he found himself.

He didn't seem a prisoner, but that was beside the point. You didn't have to have steel bars to be completely under duress. The three oddly garbed characters who had him here were seemingly of good will, but Tracy Cogswell was old enough in world political movements to know that the same man who sentenced you to gas chamber or firing squad could be a gentle soul who loved his children and spent his spare time puttering happily in a rock garden.

He wondered about the possibilities of escape. No, not yet. For one thing, he'd never make it. Still too weak. For another, he had to find out what was happening. Perhaps . . . just perhaps . . . there was some explanation which would make sense to the Executive Committee.

He had made his own way out to the terrace again and had seated himself on a piece of furniture somewhat similar to a lawn chair. That was one of the things that got to him. Even the furniture, in this ultra-automated house, was so far out as to be unbelievable.

Jo Edmonds drifted easily onto the terrace and raised his eyebrows at Tracy. He was wearing shorts today, shorts and slippers that seemed somehow to cling to the bottom of his feet, although there wasn't even a strap on top. He was flipping, as though it was a coin, the flat green stone.

"How do you feel?" he said.

Cogswell said in irritation, "What the hell's that?"

Edmonds said mildly, "This? A piece of jade. Do you enjoy tactile sensation?"

Cogswell scowled at him.

Edmonds said, "The Chinese have been familiar with the quality of jadeite for centuries. They've developed its appreciation into an advanced art form. I have quite a collection. Make a point of spending at least two hours a day over it. It takes considerable development to obtain the sensual gratification possible by stroking jade."

Cogswell said, "You mean to say you've got nothing better to do with your time than pet a piece of green stone?"

Jo Edmonds flushed at the tone. "There are less kindly things to which to devote yourself," he said.

Walter Stein emerged from the house and looked worriedly at Tracy. "How are you feeling? Not overdoing, are you?"

A Paul Lucas type, Tracy decided. Paul Lucas, playing the part of an M.D.

Tracy said, "Look, I've got to the point where if I don't find out what's going on, I'll go batty. I realize that somehow or other, you rescued me from a crazy nightmare I got into. I must have had a complete nervous breakdown."

Jo Edmonds chuckled, good-naturedly.

Cogswell turned on him. "What's funny?"

Academician Stein held up a hand. "Jo's humor is poorly taken. You see, we didn't rescue you from yourself. It was we who put you into your predicament. Please forgive us."

Tracy Cogswell stared at him.

Stein said uncomfortably, almost sheepishly, "Do you know where you are, Mr. Cogswell?"

"Yes. That's Spain over there."

Stein said, "That's not exactly what I mean. Let's cut corners, Mr. Cogswell. If we were still using the somewhat inefficient calendar of your period, this would be approximately the year 2000."

Strange, Tracy told himself, *it doesn't seem to come as a surprise. I knew it was something like that.*

"Time travel," he said aloud. It was a field of thought in which he had never wandered but he was dimly aware of the conception; a movie or two, a short story or so, over the years.

"Well, not exactly," Stein said, scowling. "Well, but yes, in a way."

Jo Edmonds laughed softly. "You're not very definite, Walter."

The older man had taken a seat on the low stone parapet that surrounded the terrace. Now he leaned forward, elbows on knees, and clasped his hands together. "Time travel isn't possible, so far as we know."

"But you just said—"

"Actually, you've been in a state of suspended animation, I suppose you could call it."

Things were fitting into place quickly. There were a lot of loose ends, but the tangle was coming out. Tracy said, "But you had to travel back to my day to . . . to do whatever it was you did to me. To take over my actions."

Stein said seriously, "Not our physical selves, Mr. Cogswell. It is impossible to send matter through time. Except forward, of course, at the usual pace. However, the mind can and does travel in time. Memory is nothing more than that. In dream, the mind even sometimes travels ahead, although in such haphazard manner that it is all but impossible to measure, to gather usable data."

Jo Edmonds said, "In your case, it was a matter of going back into the past, seizing control of your mind and body and forcing you to perform yourself the steps that would lead to your, ah, suspended animation, as the academician puts it."

For some reason, the younger man's tone irritated Cogswell. "What's an academician?" he said.

Edmonds raised his eyebrows. "Oh, that's right. The degree evolved after your period. It was found that even the PhD. had become somewhat commonplace, so the higher one was created."

Tracy Cogswell's irritation was growing. The two of them, no matter how well intentioned, had a lot to answer for. Besides that, they were so comfortably clean, so obviously well fed, so unworried and adjusted. They had it made. It probably took a dozen servants to keep up this house, to wait hand and foot on these two so that they could look so comfortably sleek. And how many people did it take slaving away somewhere in industry or office, to provide the funds necessary to maintain this fabulous establishment?

Parasites!

Tracy said flatly, "So you figured out a way of sending back through time. Of providing my hypnotized body with information that allowed it to put itself into suspended animation. To accomplish this, you had me abscond with some twenty thousand dollars. Perhaps not a great deal in your eyes, but it was composed of thousands upon thousands of tiny donations—donations to a cause. An attempt to make the world a better place in which to live."

Stein was frowning worriedly and clucking under his breath, but Jo Edmonds had an amused expression on his face.

Cogswell snapped, "When I've got some of my strength back, I'd like to take a crack at wiping some of the vacant-minded amusement off your pretty face, Edmonds. But for now I'd like to know this: WHY?"

The girl, Betty, came out then and looked from one of them to the other. She said impatiently, "Good heavens, look at the state Mr. Cogswell is in. I thought you weren't going to discuss this project until he was suitably recovered."

Cogswell glared at her. "I want to know what the big idea is! I've been kidnaped. On top of that, in spite of the fact that seemingly I did it, actually you people are guilty of stealing twenty thousand dollars." He could feel the flush mounting his face.

"See?" she said indignantly to Stein and Edmonds.

The two looked embarrassedly at Tracy. "Sorry. You're right," Edmonds said to her. He turned on his heel and left.

Stein began bustling and clucking again, attempting to take Tracy's pulse. Tracy jerked his arm away.

"Damn it," he said. "Tell me what it's all about."

"Later, later," Stein soothed.

It was the girl who said, "See here . . . Tracy. You're among friends. Let us do it our way. Answers will come soon enough." She added, like a nurse to a child, "Tomorrow, perhaps, I'll take you for a pleasant ride over Gibraltar and up the Costa del Sol."

In the morning, for the first time, Tracy Cogswell ate with the rest of them in a small breakfast room, he supposed you'd call it. The more he saw of the house, the more he was impressed by its efficient ultra-luxury. Impressed wasn't quite the word. Cogswell's background hadn't admitted of this sort of life, even had he desired it, and actually he hadn't. The movement had been his life. Food, clothing, and shelter were secondary things, necessary only to keep him going. The luxuries? He'd seen little of them, and cared less.

He had expected to be waited upon by Moorish servants, or possibly even French or Spanish ones. However, evidently he was being kept under wraps. Betty served them, bringing in dishes and platters from the kitchen.

The food, admittedly, was out of this world. He wondered, momentarily, whether or not she had cooked it herself. No, of course not. Betty Stein was much too decorative to have any useful qualities.

The conversation was desultory, obviously deliberately so. However, there was still amusement behind Jo Edmonds' eyes.

Toward the end of the meal, Stein said, "How do you feel, Mr. Cogswell? Up to the little jaunt Betty suggested?"

"I don't see why not." The more information he gathered about his surroundings, the better prepared he'd be when and if he went on the run.

He was able to walk by himself to the garage, although

Stein bumbled worriedly alongside all the way.

Cogswell was settled into the front seat of a vehicle that didn't look so greatly different from a sedan of his own period, except for the lack of wheels, and Betty took her place behind the controls.

The difference came, Cogswell found, when they emerged from the garage, proceeded a few feet and then took to the air, without wings, rotors, propeller, jets, or any other noticeable method of support or propulsion.

She could see he was taken aback. "What's the matter?"

Cogswell said, "I hadn't expected this much progress in this much time. You needed wings in my day."

She was obviously a skilled driver—or rather pilot.

"I sometimes get my dates mixed up," Betty said, "but I thought you were beginning to get air-cushion cars, hovercraft, that sort of thing in your time."

Cogswell was looking down at the countryside beneath them. Tangier had changed considerably. It had obviously become an ultra-wealthy resort area. Gone was the Casbah, with its Moorish slums going back a thousand years and more. Gone was the medina, with its teeming thousands of poverty-stricken Arabs and Riffs.

Tracy Cogswell grunted to himself. He supposed that as Europe's and America's wealthy had discovered the climatic and scenic advantages of northern Morocco, they had zeroed in. They must have displaced the multitude of natives who had formerly made uncomfortable, by their obvious need, those few of the well-to-do who had lived here before. The rich hate to see the poor; it makes them uncomfortable.

There were quite a few of the flying cars such as he and Betty were in. That was one thing. With flight at various levels, it relieved the congestion. However, there were probably other traffic problems that had evolved.

Betty put on speed and in a matter of five or ten minutes, they were circling Gibraltar, perhaps the world's most spectacular landfall. Here, too, the signs of the military of his own period had given way to villas and luxury apartment houses.

Cogswell said, "Where are all the stores, garages, and other business establishments?"

Betty said, "Underground."

"Where you can't see them and be bothered by their unattractiveness, eh?"

"That's right," she said, evidently missing his sarcasm.

They flew north along the coast, passing Estepona, Marbella, and Fuengirola. Cogswell was impressed. Even in his own time, the area had been booming, but he had never expected to see anything like this.

"Too crowded," Betty commented. "I'm amazed that so many people gravitate to the warm climate."

Tracy said impatiently, "Everyone would, wouldn't they, given the wherewithal?"

"But why? Why not stay in areas where you have seasonal changes? For that matter, why not spend some seasons in the far north, and enjoy the extremes of snow and cold weather? Comfortable houses can be built in any climate."

Cogswell grunted. "You sound like that queen, what was her name— The one who said, 'Let them eat cake.' "

Betty frowned, not getting it. "Marie Antoinette? How do you mean?"

Tracy Cogswell said impatiently, "Look. You people with lots of dough don't realize what it can mean for somebody without it to spend some time in the sun. And—if possible, and it usually isn't—to finally retire in a desirable climate in old age. It's something a lot of poor working stiffs dream of—but you wouldn't know about that."

Betty looked at him. "Dough?" she said.

"Money," Cogswell said impatiently. "Sure, if you have piles of money, you can build swell houses even up in Alaska, and live comfortably. You can live comfortably anywhere, given piles of money. But for most people, who've probably lived the greater parts of their lives in some near-slum, in some stinking city, the height of ambition is to get into a warm climate and have a little bungalow in which to finish off the final years."

Suddenly, Betty laughed.

Tracy Cogswell froze up, his face went expressionless. Until this, he'd rather liked the girl.

Betty indicated the swank villas beneath them. They were flying over Torremolinos now. "Were you under the impression that those people down there had lots of money?"

That took a time to sink in.

Cogswell said, "Possibly not by your standards. By mine, yes."

Betty said, "None of them have any money at all. Neither have I."

That was too much. He gaped at her.

Betty said, "There is no such thing as money any more. There hasn't been for quite a while."

Cogswell figured he understood now. "Well, it's the same thing. Credit cards, or whatever the means of exchange."

Betty laughed again and there was honest amusement in her voice, not condescension. She said, her voice gentle, "Tracy Cogswell, in all those years you belonged to your movement, in all the years of dedication, did you really think, really inwardly believe, that someday it might come true? That someday the millennium would arrive, Utopia be achieved?"

The cold went through him.

He closed his mouth, but continued to stare his disbelief.

"Tracy," she said gently, "your movement was successful more than twenty years ago."

After a long time he said, "Look, could we go back to the house? I could use a drink."

They were amused by his reactions, but it was a friendly amusement and with a somehow wry connotation which Tracy Cogswell didn't quite get. So many things were bubbling through his head, so many questions to ask, he didn't have time for complete answers.

"And the Russkies?" he demanded. "What happened there?"

Jo Edmonds said, "About the same as everywhere else. Overnight, the contradictions that had built up through the decades of misrule and misdirection finally boiled over. It was one of the few places where there was much violence. The Commies had done too much to too many to have been allowed peaceful retirement."

Betty shook her head. "In some places, it was terrible."

Tracy Cogswell drew from his own memories pictures of members of the secret police hanging from lampposts by their heels. He had been in Budapest during the 1956 uprising. "Yes," he said, uncomfortably.

Then, "But countries like India, the African nations, South America. How do they stand now?"

Academician Stein was chuckling softly. "These things seem so long ago to us," he said. "It's almost unbelievable that they can be news to an intelligent adult. The backward countries? Why, given the all-out support of the most industrially advanced, they were brought up to the common level within a decade or two."

"It was a universally popular effort," Betty added. "Everybody pitched in."

"Yes, yes, of course," Cogswell blurted. "But, look—look, the population explosion. What happened there?"

Jo Edmonds, who was sitting relaxed in an armchair near the fireplace, a drink in one hand, his inevitable piece of jade in the other, said easily, "Not really much of a problem, given world government and universal education on a high level. If you'll remember, the large families were almost always to be found in the most backward countries, or among the most backward elements in the advanced countries. Education and efficient methods of birth control ended the problem."

"Look," Cogswell said happily, "could I have another drink? This must be the damndest thing that ever happened to a man. Why, why, it's as though St. Paul woke up in the year, well, say, 1400 A.D. and saw the strength of the Church."

All three of them laughed at him and Jo Edmonds went

over to the sideboard and mixed him another drink.

Tracy Cogswell said, "That reminds me of something else. How about servants? It must take a multitude of maids to run a house like this."

Betty made a *moue* at him. "Nonsense. You aren't very good at extrapolation. Why, even in your own day in the advanced countries the house was automated to the point where even the fairly well off didn't have domestic help. Today, drudgery has been eliminated. Anyone can have just about as large a house as they want, and keep it up by devoting only a few minutes a day to its direction."

It was still all but inconceivable to him. "And everybody, just *everybody* can afford a place like this?"

It was Stein's turn again. As they'd all been doing, he prefaced his explanation with a laugh. "Given automation and cheap, all but free, power and what is the answer? Ultra abundance for everyone. Surely the signs must have been present in your day. That was the goal of your organization, wasn't it?"

"Yes," Cogswell said, shaking his head. "Yes, of course." Then he added, his voice very low, "I'll be damned."

They all laughed with him.

Jo Edmonds brought the new drink and Cogswell finished it in one swallow. He considered for a minute. "Look," he said. "I don't suppose anyone remembers what happened to a fellow named Dan Whiteley."

"Whiteley," Stein scowled.

"He was a member of the organization."

"Dan Whiteley," Betty said. "I read something about him. Let me see, he was a Canadian."

"That's right. From Winnipeg."

"Did you know him?" Betty said, her voice strange.

He said slowly, "Yes, yes I knew him quite well." Unconsciously, he stroked his left elbow. The others had been in favor of leaving him behind. Dan had carried him, one way or the other, half the night. Toward the morning the police had brought up dogs and they'd been able to hear them baying only half a mile or so behind.

Betty said gently, "The Commies got him when he was trying to contact some of the intellectuals and get your movement organized in China. He succeeded, but later was caught and shot in, I believe, Hankow. He's now sort of a minor martyr. Students of the period know about him."

Tracy Cogswell took a deep breath. "Yeah," he said. "That's the way Dan would have ended. Could I have another drink?"

Stein said, "You're not overdoing, are you?"

"No, of course not. Look, how about cancer, and space flight, and how about interracial problems and juvenile delinquency?"

"Hold it!" Jo Edmonds laughed. Somehow there was a strained quality in the laugh that Cogswell couldn't quite put his finger on.

Stein said, "You can imagine how long any of the old diseases lasted once we began to devote the amount of time to them that our scientists had formerly put into devising methods of destroying man."

Betty said, "Oh, we have observatories and various laboratories on the moon. And . . ."

Jo Edmonds brought the drink and Tracy Cogswell took a long swallow and then shook his head.

Walter Stein was quickly on his feet. "See here," he said, "you're pale. We've allowed you to push yourself too far." He clucked unhappily. "Betty was premature this morning. We hadn't expected to allow you so much excitement for several days yet. Now, back to bed for you."

"I feel a little tired and a little tight," Cogswell admitted.

In bed, just before he dropped off, he gazed up at the ceiling. What did he feel like? Somewhat as he had when a kid, back there in Baltimore. When tomorrow was going to be Christmas.

He was drifting into sleep before a worrying thought wriggled up from below. He never quite grasped it all.

However, his subconscious worked away.

They were waiting for him when he emerged for breakfast in the morning. All three of them, dressed as usual in the most imaginative clothes possible. Cogswell had already come to the conclusion that fashions and styles were a thing of yesteryear; people dressed in the most comfortable way they damn well pleased. He supposed that when it had been followed, fashion had largely been a matter of sales promotion.

For the first time since his awakening, he felt really fit, both mentally and physically alert. After they'd exchanged good mornings and questioned him on his well-being, Tracy Cogswell got to the point.

"Yesterday, I was pretty well taken up in enthusiasm. I doubt if many men live to see their own idea of Utopia achieved. In fact, looking back I doubt I know of a single example. But anyway, now I'd like to get some basic matters cleared up."

Edmonds finished his coffee, leaned back, and began fiddling with his piece of jade. "Fire away," he said, but he, like the others, seemed to have a faint element of tension.

Cogswell said, "As I understand it, through a method devised by Stein, here, you were able to send his mind back to my time, hypnotize me, and force me to take the steps that resulted in my being—well, deep-frozen."

Walter Stein shrugged. He still reminded Cogswell of Paul Lucas, playing the part of an anxious scientist. "That's a sufficient explanation."

Cogswell looked at him questioningly. "What was all that about the monument, and the tomb beneath?"

Stein said, "We had to have some place to leave your body where it wouldn't be discovered for decades. A cave beneath a holy man's tomb was as good a bet as any. Even today, such monuments are respected."

"I see," Cogswell said. "I've got some mind-twisting questions I want to ask about what seem to me some strange paradoxes, but they can wait. First, what happened after I'd gone? What do the records say about my disappearance? What did the International Executive Committee do? What kind of a report was given out about me to the membership of the movement?" His voice tightened as he spoke.

Betty took up the ball. She said, "Remember, Tracy, when I told you yesterday that Dan Whiteley had become a minor martyr?"

He waited for her to go on.

"You are also so known. Tracy Cogswell, the dependable, the organization man *plus ultra.*" She spoke as though reciting. "Fought in Spain as a boy. Friend of George Orwell. Spent three years in Nazi concentration camps before escaping. Active in overthrowing Mussolini. Fought on the side of the revolutionists in the Hungarian tragedy of 1956. Helped Djilis get out of Yugoslavia. Finally, was given post of international secretary, coordinating activities from Tangier." She took a breath, then went on. "Captured by Franco police and smuggled into Spain. Died under torture without betraying any members of the organization."

Tracy Cogswell was on his feet. His voice was strained. "But . . . but Dan Whiteley was there, at the end. He knew that last wasn't true. I appropriated almost twenty thousand dollars of the movement's funds. It must have been practically the whole international treasury."

Edmonds said with sour humor, "Evidently, your organization needed a martyr more than it needed the money. You've gone down in history as Tracy Cogswell, the Incorruptible, the Dependable, the perfect organization man."

Cogswell slumped back into his chair. At least, that way, a hundred friends had never known his final act of betrayal. Beyond him to resist, but still betrayal.

He said, "All right. Now we come to the question that counts." He looked from one face to another. They knew what he was about to ask. "Why?"

Jo Edmonds, for once, slipped his piece of jade into a pocket. He opened his mouth to speak but Stein quieted him with a shake of his head. "Let me do this, Jo. How we put this now means success or failure of the whole project."

"What project, damn it?" Cogswell snapped.

"Just a minute," Stein said, flustered a bit. "Let me give you some background."

"I've been getting background for days. Tell me why I'm here!"

"A moment, please. Tracy, man was an aggressive, hardfighting animal from the time he emerged from the mists of antiquity. Physically weak, as predatory animals go, he depended on brain and cunning to subjugate his fellow beasts. Only those clever enough to outwit the sabertooth, the cave bear, the multitude of other beasts more dangerous than man, physically, survived."

"I don't need this," Cogswell growled.

"A moment, please. Even when his fellow beasts were conquered, man still had nature to combat. He still must feed, clothe, and shelter himself. He must free himself of the seasons. Of cold and the night, of flood and storm, of draft and pestilence. And step by step he beat out his path of progress. It wasn't always easy, Tracy."

"It was never easy," Tracy Cogswell said impatiently.

"All along the way," Stein pursued, "man fought not only as a species but as an individual. Each man battled not only nature, but his fellow man, since there was seldom sufficient for all. Particularly when we get to the historic period and the emerging of the priest and warrior, and finally the noble, man pitted himself against his fellows for a place at the top. There was room for only a fraction."

The academician shook his head. "Survival of the fittest," he said. "Which often meant the most brutal, the most cunning, the conscienceless. But it also meant the strengthening of the race. When a ruling class was no longer the most aggressive and intelligent element of a people, it didn't long remain the ruling class."

Walter Stein hesitated for a long moment. "In short, Tracy, all through his history man has had something to fight against—or for." He twisted his mouth in a grimace of attempted humor. "It's the nature of the beast."

"Isn't all this elementary?" Cogswell said. Some of the heat of his impatience was gone but he couldn't understand what the other was building up to.

Stein said, uncertainly, "I suppose the first signs of it were evident in your period. I recall reading of educators and social scientists who began remarking on the trend before the twentieth century was half through."

"What trend?" Cogswell scowled.

"In the more advanced countries of your period. The young people. They stopped taking the science and engineering courses in school, they were too difficult to wish to bother with. A youngster didn't have to fight to make his way, the way was greased. The important thing was to have a good time. Find an angle so that you could obtain the material things everyone else had, without the expenditure of much effort. Don't be an egghead. Don't stick your neck out. Conform. You've got cradle to the grave security. Take it easy. You've got it made."

Betty Stein, quiet for a long time, added softly, "And the most advanced countries—so far as social progress is concerned—had the highest suicide rates."

"That's the point," Stein nodded. "They had nothing to fight against and man is a fighting animal. Take away something to work for, to fight for, and he's a frustrated animal."

A horrible understanding was growing within Cogswell.

He looked from one to the other of them, all but desperately. "Why did you bring me here?" he said hoarsely.

Stein ignored him and pressed on. "Since the success of your movement, Tracy Cogswell, there has been world government. Wars have disappeared and racial tensions. There is abundance for all, crime is a thing of the past. Government is so changed as hardly to be recognized from the viewpoint of your day. There are no politics, as you knew them."

Jo Edmonds said bitterly, "You asked about space flight, yesterday. Sure, there's a small base on the moon, but nothing new has been done in the field for a generation. We have lots of dilettantes," he flicked his beautifully carved bit of jade, "lots of connoisseurs, lots of gourmets—but few of us can bother to become scientists, builders, visionaries."

"Why did you bring me here?" Cogswell repeated.

"Because we need your know-how," Jo Edmonds said flatly.

Cogswell's eyes went tired. "My know-how?"

Betty said gently, "Tracy, when we sought back through history for someone to show us the way, we found Tracy Cogswell the Incorruptible, the Dependable, the lifelong devoted organization man."

Tracy Cogswell was staring at her. "Who are you people? What's your angle?"

It was Academician Stein who answered, and he said what Cogswell now already knew. "We're members of the new underground. The human race is turning to mush, Tracy. Something must be done. For decades we've had what every Utopian through history has dreamed of. Democracy in its most ultimate form. Abundance for all. The end of strife between nations, races, and, for all purposes practical, between individuals. And, as a species, we're heading for dissolution. Tracy, we need your experience to guide us. To head the new movement."

Jo Edmonds leaned forward and put it in another way.

"You—you and your movement—got us into this. Now get us out."

ORGY OF THE LIVING AND THE DYING

By Brian W. Aldiss

The way his wife's voice came to Tancred Frazer was this way.

She visiphoned his world-code number from the cool hall in their country house situated in the depths of Hampshire, England. The vision and sound impulses were accepted by the local exchange and carried along coaxial cable to the Southampton main exchange, and from there broadcast to the transmitter at Goonhilly down in Cornwall. From Goonhilly, the signal went up to Postbird III, the communications satellite, which promptly bounced it back to Earth again.

The signal was accepted at Calcutta. Here came the first delay—a wait of four and a half minutes before the call could be accepted by the Allahabad office, in the province of Uttar Pradesh, in the heart of India. Finally, a relay clicked over on the automatic exchange, and the next link in the circuit was opened. After a brief delay, the call got as far as Faizabad, to the north of Allahabad.

At Faizabad, the automatic processes ceased. They were planned for installation there in 2001, the following year; but, since the official declaration of famine by the government, it looked as if the new exchange might have to wait. Meanwhile, the very pleasant operator on the board managed, after some minutes delay, to get the incoming call through to the village of Chandanagar, twenty miles away.

Chandanagar was small, and had remained insignificant for some thousands of years until the UN Famine Abatement Wing had arrived and set up its establishments in the semi-desert thereabouts. Chandanagar, in fact, could accept only the sound signal; it did not boast a micro-photo-diode bankage capable of handling vision calls. So Chandanagar shuttled the sound signal only forward to UNFAW HQ.

The very pleasant operator at UNFAW HQ read back the world-code number, checked with a list, and said, "Oh, you want the British Detachment! Tancred Frazer is with the British Detachment. They are about five miles from here, but I have a land-line. Hang on!"

He had a temporary line available. Leaning dangerously over on his stool, he plugged into an auxiliary board and cranked a handle with some vigor. A phone bell spluttered five miles away.

It rang in the front office of an air conditioned building around which, for many miles in all directions, lay the heatbaked plain of the Ganges. Heavy on the plain lay the death that drought brought in its wake.

Tancred Frazer himself answered the phone when it spluttered the

you suffer the malnutrition which brings all kinds of shadow

third time, and so was able to hear his wife's voice as she spoke from the cool lounge of their house in Hampshire.

For all the glad noises they made at each other, their conversation went haltingly.

"The daffodils were over by the end of the first week in April."

They seemed very soon to get down to unimportant things.

"Late for daffodils, wasn't it?"

the flower shall die and also the seed thereof but some

"No, darling, very early. There *is* something the matter, isn't there? Do please tell me if there is. You know I shall only worry. Is the sight of all those poor starving people getting you down?"

He held a hand to his brow and said, "No, I'm fine. Kathie—" But he could not bring himself to make any declarations of affection; that would have been too false, even for him, in the circumstances.

"I'm going to ring off and worry if you don't tell me, you know."

"I'm being bombarded by voices." Reluctantly.

"You're eating buns and what? This is a terrible line."

"I said I'm being bombarded by voices. I hear them in my head—your voice and all these pathetic people here."

"Poor darling! It's the heat, I'm sure. Is it awfully hot in Chandanagar now?"

That was safer; they were getting back to the weather. But as he eventually put the phone down, Tancred thought miserably, Of course she knows, she heard the admission in my voice as surely as I heard the knowledge in hers. After all, she's been through it enough times. What

daffodils were over by the end of the first week in April the

a bastard I am! But underlying it all he felt anger at Kathie, anger because she was innocent. He padded back into his improvised bedroom to Sushila, hitching the towel round his waist as he went.

Sushila Nayyer had covered herself with a sheet and reclined on his bed in the simple grandeur of her being. Sushila was now almost nineteen, a mature and strong-minded woman. She had stayed with Tancred and Kathie in England three years ago, when she was studying medicine at Guy's Hospital; he had conceived a most violent desire to sleep with her then. When his period of UN service brought him the chance of going to famine-struck regions of India, he had at once set about tracking Sushila down, which accounted for his presence in this dusty camp. He still could only marvel at his luck.

"Was it your wife?" she asked. "Phoning all the way from England?"

I don't think you often enjoy the luxury of hearing the real

"Yes. She wondered why I hadn't written. It's all right."

They looked at each other. He wondered just how much their inner selves understood from that glance.

"Do you want to come back on the bed with me?"

"You bet I do!"

As he took off the towel, so she turned back the sheet. Because she was a modest Muslim woman, the gesture was curiously modest, a confidence between them. Her body, the flesh built onto fine Asiatic

O Babi Babi will the children remember me their mother

bones, was an oasis compared with the deserts of starved bodies outside, the famine-clad mothers who walked a hundred miles to find water for

and in the well only a smell of old bones the rotted carcass

their children. Tancred tried to dismiss the tiresome voices and images that punctuated his being, and climbed beside that beautiful creature, prepared even before he touched her to possess her again. Kissing her belly, he could almost ignore the disruptive and fragmentary voices. As he buried his face in her strange-smelling black hair, the phone convulsed itself into life again.

"Sod it!" he said.

monsoon's breaking at last according to the weather station

This time, the interruption was more permanent. When he had put the phone down, he went back to Sushila.

"Sorry, lover girl! I'll have to get dressed. That was Frank Young. There's an emergency call out. Bad floods at Bhagalpur, and HQ want as much as we can give. I have to go and see Young. Where the hell is Bhagalpur, anyway?"

He was glad to see she was going to take this interruption without one of her displays of temper; there was only a slight trace of sulkiness in her voice as she said,

"It's a small town about fifty miles north of here, towards the Nepal border. Will you have to go?"

Oh I don't blame you you couldn't be faithful however hard

"I hope not. It depends on Young. He says he is going."

Dressing, Frazer went through the office and out into the road outside. As he lost the protection of the air conditioning, he felt the monstrous heat of the plains engulf him. But the air conditioning system had three vents, one on either side of the office block and one at the front, and it was possible to stand in the road so that one took advantage of the cooler air voided from the ugly front grill above the office door. Even so, he felt strangely ill, as he often did when standing here looking at the desolation about him.

The detachment had wired itself off from the rest of the world; its several acres were surrounded by barbed wire. The hospital was the only considerable building in the encampment: a big square gray building down the road, already full to overflowing. All about it stood the wretched bivouacs of the refugees, a sagging village of bamboo poles and tattered sacking and plastic sheets.

The office block was nearer the gate. It was a new building, already showing signs of decay. Next to it, a new storehouse had just been completed and was already having to be repaired—part of the wall looking onto the office block had collapsed. Although it was

to stare out through the window at the blackness of the

the stifling afternoon hour when most people except adulterers rested, building women were at work repairing the wall, walking slowly with dignity, bare feet gray, loads of homemade bricks in baskets on their heads, up and down the scaffolding, hardly speaking, a fold of their saris over their heads as a marginal protection against the heat.

The road straggled in front of office block and store. On the other side of the road were the old lath-built warehouse, several times robbed and now almost empty, and the light huts used as living quarters by the UN medical team. Nearer the gate was the transport section, the guardhouse, and other offices. That was all. It seemed a poor little incursion to make on the vast monotony of the plain.

Although Frazer took all this in, for he never shed his horrified fascination with the harshness of the view and the sight of the famine victims, some of whom now squatted or stood, as he did, outside the offices, his gaze was drawn chiefly to the sky.

Toward the north, the plain died in purple haze. Above the haze, stormy rain clouds piled into the sky, distorted, compressed, angry, here

you see passion and violence are a very integral part of the

black, there brilliant, as if atomic fires stirred within them. There rode the monsoon, bringing blessed rain. It looked as if the rain would fall on Chandanagar: but so it had looked for the last five nights. Instead, the rain had fallen to the north; while the wells in Chandanagar offered only a smell of old bones as the ground rotted in the three-year-

in the well only a smell of old bones as the rotted carcass of

old drought, the river above Bhagalpur flooded and washed away the inhabi-

In my pot only broken crumbs of water only broken crumbs

tants.

An old woman called to him, extending an arm like an old broken umbrella. He crossed to Young's hut.

Frank Young was already on the move. He was in his sixties, a slaggy choleric man with sparse hair covering his skull, as heavy-jowled as he was heavy-buttocked, but still a swift-moving man when action was required of him. He had brought this UNFAW detachment into being, seen it through numerous crises, including a cholera scare, and showed no signs of giving up yet. Equally, he showed little sign of liking Frazer, although his position of command inhibited him from showing this more than necessary. His two under-officers, Garry

You had your orders you had no damned business leaving

Knowles and Dr. Kisari Mafatlal, a plump Bengali, were with him. Knowles was moving out, saying "I'll get the hovers ready," as Frazer entered.

Mafatlal gave Frazer an uneasy smile. He had thick well-oiled hair and beautiful manners, both of which attributes made him appear out of place beside Frank Young. "I was trying to explain to Mr. Young what an unpredictable river our Ganges is, and always has been throughout the entire historical times, with one branch simply entirely dry while another branch may be—"

"Yes, never mind that now, Mafatlal," Young said brusquely. He treated the long-winded little man as a figure of fun; under Young's influence, most of the other doctors did likewise. "Frazer, you have the picture? Severe floods in the Bhagalpur Area. Galbraith at HQ has just radioed me asking for full support. Over a thousand believed drowned in Bhagalpur itself, and a severe landslide threatening villages a few miles from Bhagalpur. I'm going to take both hovercraft and all UNFAW personnel, except the hospital staff and Mafatlal. Mafatlal and you will be in charge here. We'll radio you when we get to the other end. Okay?"

"I can hardly officially take charge, sir. I'm only a visitor here. If I came with you and Knowles—"

"I want Knowles with me. Garry knows this kind of work. You sit here and hold Mafatlal's hand—and that woman doctor's, of course. It's all routine. Just remember we have valuable stocks of grain in the new store, and keep the guards up to their duties."

"How long do you plan to be gone?"

Controlling his exasperation, Young drew tight the

straps on his sleeping bag, which he then slipped into his pocket, and said. "That depends on the monsoon, not me, doesn't it? Damned silly question to ask, Frazer, if you don't mind my saying so."

"Just now, I am telling Mr. Young that we may also have the flooding here also within twenty-four hours—" Mafatlal said, but Young nodded curtly and ushered them out of the room.

"Pleasant fellow," Frazer commented sarcastically, as he stood outside with Mafatlal and watched Young's baggy figure move among the huts, calling to the other members of the team.

"Yes, he is a very pleasant fellow at heart," said Mafatlal. "First, you have to see to his heart. Also, his heart responds to action and then he likes to assume a very authoritarian pattern of behavior, perhaps ingested mentally from his father at some early age—I believe his father was a military man. Don't you find, Mr. Frazer, that on the whole the man of inaction is an easier psychological type to get along with in everyday pursuits?"

"I never considered it." Christ, was he going to have to listen

you try to hide that you are unsure of your own psychological

to Mafat's philosophizing all the while the others were gone?

"You are a man who considers more than he cares to reveal, Mr. Frazer, are you not?"

Frazer screwed up his eyes and stared at Mafatlal. Perhaps

the flower shall die and the seed but some flowers never die

he should confide in the doctor, tell him about the voices; sometimes they seemed oddly precognitive; as if they might be more than the signs of an inner sickness.

"I'm worried, Kisari, to tell you the truth. I just don't want to go into the matter."

"Of course, I understand. It's good of you to tell me. But maybe I can be of more help to you than you think, because I have always made

my child child child this poor old sack that is thy mother

it my business—"

"I don't want to go into it now." He wanted to function well here, make himself useful. A little knot of refugees was closing in on him and Mafatlal. They were given a bowl of rice gruel each per day; it was sufficient to keep them living but not properly alive. Their eyes were a torment to him. They knew already a crisis centered on the camp and feared that it threatened their shadowy existence. They were talking earnestly to Mafatlal in supplication; he was answering them

to stare out through the window at the blackness of the

curtly, as if he also had temporarily become the man of action. Between the well fed and the starving was drawn the most rigid line of all.

Sushila appeared at the door of the office block, dressed in her neat authoritative dress. Glad to see her, Frazer crossed to her side and explained the situation.

"The people tell me that the rain will break here this evening," she said quietly. "If it does, the fit ones will attempt to go back to their villages to see if the wells have water again. Shall you let them go?"

"We do not want to stop them. There's plenty of rice and flour in the new store, but we don't know when fresh supplies will arrive, so the fewer mouths to feed here the better."

"But you will shut the camp tonight and double the guard?"

"Yes. But there can be no danger, surely?"

"Already in Allahabad they will know this camp is almost empty of UN personnel. There are unscrupulous people about during bad times."

He smiled. "Sushila, you are so splendidly beautiful. But you are overanxious. How about getting back to the hospital and seeing nobody gets jittery down there? I'll come and collect you for a drink at sundown."

They looked at each other. He was aware that a slight breeze stirred about them. She appeared reassured by what he said, and smiled slightly.

"Perhaps if things go well I will take you on a little expedition tomorrow, Tancred," she said. "If you are a good boy." She turned and walked in the direction of the hospital.

The two big hovercraft were revving their engines; dust eddied about

my dust loud with the living dust singing like flies dear Siva

their gray flanks. It streamed down past the women now lethargically ceasing the day's work on their wall, blowing away toward the hospital and the ragged encampment. It streamed past the ten men of the UNFAW team as, packs on backs, they moved toward the air-cushion vehicles. They waved a salutation to Frazer and Mafatlal as they went.

try to get back before my birthday Tancred you know it

Frazer and Mafatlal stood in the roadway until the machines moved off. They watched as they moved slowly across the stricken plain, two whirling pillars of dust blowing with them. By that time, the building women had climbed down from their wooden scaffolding and were trailing back toward their quarters. But the refugees still sat or lay listlessly in the shade, or stood where the grill of the inefficient air conditioner poured a cooler wind out of the office block.

In the sky, the granite clouds puffed and flattened themselves,

the roses need the rain although it's lovely to have the spell of

denying rain. Cold and desolation took hold of Frazer; he thought with

es liegt der heisse Sommer while in my heart the winter is

melancholy of his betrayed wife. I can't damned help it, Kathie; I'm a victim of lust or something—maybe I never had enough breast-feeding as an infant. Probably Mafat could explain it to me. . . .

He did not need explanations but he needed a drink. Desiring company, he asked Mafatlal in for one as well.

The little doctor would have only a small whisky, well diluted, and with sugar in. He admitted he preferred it diluted with champagne, but only water was available. As he toyed with the drink, he made polite conversation, to which Frazer gave random answers. Finally, he said, "Mr. Frazer, may I make a personal statement?"

"Go ahead."

"I am always wondering why I find it very very difficult to strike up a confidence with English and American men. Would you say that that might be because of certain possibly faulty qualities in my own character which repel them?"

"God, I don't know, Kisari! Personally, I find all these personal questions pretty embarrassing, and so do a lot of people."

"Ah, but should you find them embarrassing? Should there not be fewer barriers between people? Perhaps the old saying is true that Englishmen are reserved and want only to live within themselves."

Slightly irritated, Frazer said, "Actually, I am not English at all. I am Swiss. It just happens I've lived in England most of my life, and my wife is English."

Mafatlal put his head on one side inquiringly. "I see! Well, I would not say that that invalidates my thesis. You may have picked up the habit of shutting yourself away from your fellow men and so you can perhaps talk only to women, isn't it?"

Frazer got up and poured himself another whisky. Annoyed though he was, he could not help seeing the funny side of this interview.

if you are a good boy I will take you on a little expedition

"Kisari, I know you have a degree in psychoanalysis. Why not turn it against yourself? You really want to talk about Sushila, don't you? You're just eaten up with jealousy because you think I'm lying with her every day, aren't you?"

"Any man might envy you the body of Sushila Nayyar, Tancred, indeed, yes!—though I have other fish to cook with my lady loves of the hospital nursing staff. But I know why you feel so guilty about your enjoyment of Sushila."

"Guilty! I do not feel guilty! It's not a question— Look, as I've said before, I find these personal discussions very unpleasant indeed. If you have finished your drink, perhaps you wouldn't mind leaving me in peace, damn it!"

Mafatlal set down his glass and gestured sadly. "May I say that you would be better perhaps if you also took the sugar lump in your whisky?

may I say that you ease your conscience by confessing to your

Totally no offense, of course. Life is sour enough for all of us. . . ."

He stood up, for once leaving a sentence unfinished. Nodding, he walked out of Frazer's temporary apartment, through the office, and out into the road. Very dignified, Frazer thought. Very dignified, if a pain in the neck. He did not feel guilty about Sushila. Well, not in

the habit of shutting yourself away from your fellow men and

the way Mafatlal meant. But it might have been worth hearing what the long-winded little blighter had to say on the subject. . . . Mafatlal was no fool; Sushila thought highly of him.

He sat down and drained his glass, suddenly miserable. Dusk was swooping in. The rain was not coming to Chandanagar this evening. No doubt it was plastering down on Bhagalpur instead. He genuinely sorrowed for the wretched famine victims. At the same time, the sight of all that malnutrition, all those starving children, filled him with so much unease that he could hardly tolerate the thought of any more refugees. Often it seemed to be their voices that he heard in his head. Anxiously he thought, It's a deep spiritual sickness from which I suffer. My stomach churns all the time. And the air conditioning plant growled at him.

a lover and his beloved came together in the evening when

As the night gathered, he went out to collect Sushila from the hospital. A family was admitted through the main gate just before it closed for the night. The man walked in front, white-haired, hollow-eyed, carrying a child; the woman followed, an iron cooking pot on her head and two boys walking beside her. An older girl walked behind; she also carried a child. All the children looked near death; the boys mere walking skeletons, every rib showing; the girl looked like a little old woman. Their skins were furry with dust. An orderly, a plump Bihari girl with a diamond glinting at one nostril, led them down toward the kitchens.

Frazer followed them slowly. Now, at the dawn of the twenty-first century, most of the world was eating factory-made foods, and enjoying them. In India, people refused to touch them, just as they still refused fish. In the nineteen-eighties, events seemed to have taken a progressive turn, and a contraceptive pill had at last gone some way toward being accepted; then had come the big Bombay Chemicals scandal, when over two thousand women had died from a wrongly made-up consignment of the pills, and matters had slipped back again. There had followed a religiously inspired revolt against the climate-control which, while it always had to rob Peter to pay Paul, had at least gone some way to eliminate droughts; and now the subcontinent was sliding back to where it had been in the fifties and sixties of the twentieth century. Currently, the standard of living was higher in the equatorial belt of Mars than it was in Uttar Pradesh.

All about the hospital, where the disgraced bivouacs clustered,

and the daffodils were almost over by the end of the first week

in the failing light, spirals of smoke drifted up from glowing *sigris* and oil lamps gleamed here and there. No breeze stirred now. Again the monsoon had turned its back on this section of the pitiless plain. On this further night, the orgy of the living and the dying could take place undisturbed by hope.

that's it rub it against me darling your fabulous briny juices

Frazer spent next morning industriously touring and inspecting the camp. All was in order, as far as order went. Nobody was dying; everyone was currently getting one bowl of rice and one bowl of gruel per day. If there was no real famine in camp, equally there was no infectious disease. What there was was suffering, the long attrition of semi-starvation that brought stupidity and indifference, and welcomed in any number of physical defects. Frazer believed in the body; he hated to see this large-scale wastage of it. Especially he hated to see the cadaverous women bringing forth babies and nestling them to dry dugs. It was a travesty of the life process.

Beyond the camp perimeter stretched the baked land, patches of scrub standing out vaguely, like the discolored patches on the skin of a tertiary syphilitic. Here and there, he could see cattle standing on the *maidan*; some had followed people to Chandanagar, hoping for water. The beasts were hollow and rotten. One fell over sideways as Frazer looked. The vultures who sat about the camp moved over to its carcass, walking slowly over the ground like shabby Calcutta clerks with their

the stinking bastards pull the guts out of the ass first of all

hands behind their backs. They never flew in the Chandanagar area unless you ran up and tried to kick them, as Frazer did; death could be tackled at walking pace in Uttar Pradesh.

Delhi has had enough sir Delhi is tired of other people's

"I've had enough of this place," Frazer said to Sushila over lunch. He was eating in the cool hospital staff dining room, taking a fresh lime juice and gin with his artificial rump steak. "Can't we get out of here and drive into Faizabad for the evening? Young just radioed that they're going to be away all week, as far as he can see."

"Whom will you leave in charge?"

"Kisari Mafatlal, of course. He's senior to me."

You're eaten up with jealousy because you think I'm lying

With her magnetic eyes fixed on his, she said, "The people will be very distressed to see you go; you know that, don't you, Tancred?"

"Oh, what nonsense!" But he was conscious of a slight feeling

and from the love we've built let's go out and love and help

of guilt. "They care nothing about me. They're too busy with their own preoccupations to be interested in anything I do."

"That is not so. However, if you are happy. . . ."

"I am happy. The bright lights and madding crowds of Faizabad, then?"

"Darling, you forget I told you yesterday I have a little expedition to take you on."

"No. Oh, yes, of course! Have I been a good boy? Where do we go?" He felt sick again as she began to explain. He wanted to get out of camp; but when the chance came to go, he could think only of the heat and the death waiting outside.

There was no trouble about their commandeering a truck. As Frazer walked over to the offices, wretched groups of refugees still waited where the cool air gushed out on them, the laboring women still moved in dream time up and down their scaffolding. He left word with a *chuprassi* to tell Mafatlal where he was going.

a very pleasant fellow at heart but his heart responds to action

Sushila was wearing a short stiff skirt which contrasted piquantly with a white blouse buttoning high on her neck; it lent her a comic and misleading air of primness. She took the seat beside Frazer, gave him directions as they rolled out of the main gate, and leaned back to light a cigar when he switched the truck on to automatic.

"I'm taking you to see my parents' house, Tancred. I thought that would be very pleasant for you. There are some clothes I wish to collect."

"I thought you had quarreled with your father."

"My father is not there. He has moved to the hills where there is no drought. There is only an old family *chokidar* guarding the house. He has been instructed not to admit me, but he will."

"*Shabash!* Sounds like a great homecoming!"

"Anyhow, it's a lovely afternoon for a drive, darling."

"Oh, yes, bloody great! Lovely scenery, too!"

He felt uneasy and irritable. An emotion was coming from her which he could not analyze; of recent months, he had become so confident of interpreting what other people were feeling that to be baffled worried him.

They were now entering the land of the dead, where the only color was the color of cow dung. The camp had fallen behind and was swallowed into the heat haze. The rutted track they followed led from nowhere into nowhere under the gilt dome of sky, never deviating

from another century this enormous luxurious lugubrious

even when they passed through villages. The villages stood petrifying,

and I only an old cup of clay that fills only with the bitter

without motion, moribund, as if time had turned to jelly in the wrath of the sun. Occasionally, a paper-thin cow stood arrested in a doorway,

how can you be starved for sex I give you all I've got don't

occasionally a mangy dog ran from the truck, occasionally an old man or woman died at their leisure in a patch of shade. The beaks

you've always been sheltered what do you know of suffering

of well arms pointed up to the sky. The desolation seemed less outside the

privileged idle life shut away from knowledge of the real

villages.

Gradually, villages grew more frequent. The road became increasingly broken, turning downhill in uneasy rushes. It emerged on a riverbank.

This was one of the many streams of the Ganges. Distantly, water could be seen, bracketed between miles of sand and dried mud. Dirty shacks had been built on the mud flats, life had been contrived; suddenly one evening would come the foaming floods and sweep that pitiful contrivance away—it could be tonight.

They drove along the track that followed the riverbank. Flies buzzed in the cab with them. A few coarse trees grew here, desiccated and gray; only palm trees appeared to flourish in the drought. Vultures and kite hawks sat in the low trees, meditative. A scarecrow walked along the road, burdened under a dripping water skin. He walked on for six minutes before Frazer's hooting dislodged him from the crown of the road.

"Silly old sod! Where is this house of yours, anyway? How much further do we have to go through this god-blasted desert?"

She pointed ahead. "Behind those trees there." Leaning forward eagerly, she threw her cigar butt out of the window.

The Nayyer family house was walled round with white walls and guarded with huge wooden gates. Through cracks in the timber, they spied an aged Sikh, snoozing on a *charpoy* in the shade of a wizened mango tree. By dint of much calling and whistling, he was roused and eventually let them through the gate, grumbling at the nuisance of it all.

The house was large, girt with verandas and balconies, smothered with dying vine. It had been pretty in better days. To one side, overlooked by giant pines, lay a cracked brown area where a pleasant pool had once lain. A *chokidar* in a faded green tunic appeared, making *salaam* to Sushila.

He let them in a side door, an old gray unshaven man in slippers, chewing *betel.* All doors and shutters in the house were tightly closed. A scent hung in the corridors which seemed compounded of the world's nos-

where forgotten things belong you keep coming back like a

talgia, flowers and dust and wood smoke and the dress of human lives.

the daffodils will be out when you return and we'll still be

She left him to wander round as she went up to her old room. The *chokidar* brought a warm bottled grapefruit juice for Frazer to drink; he walked about, sipping at the tumbler, curious to see everything. The furniture was heavy and dark; secrets were wardrobed into every shadowy room; the house waited. Frazer experienced a strong sense of intrusion, and of excitement. Suddenly, he wanted Sushila and hurried up the wide stone stairs to find her.

Sushila was in her bedroom; she had opened one shutter, so that an angle of sun burned into the room by the window, lighting everything by reflection. She was bending over a trunk, pulling out lengths of sari. When Frazer entered she turned, her face lit from below, seeing instantly

you dirty swine you're at her all the time aren't you won't

what he wanted.

She twiddled fingers on a level with her ear, in a gesture of disapproval.

"No, Tancred, no sex! We ought to get back. Now that we're here, I'm anxious to get back to the camp, in case there is trouble there." She slammed down the trunk lid.

"To hell with camp! I want you here in your own surroundings, not in a concentration camp!" He grasped her fiercely, thrusting one hand round her shoulders and the other between her legs, pulling her, fighting

the rosy glow of summer is on thy dimpled cheek awhile in

with her to get her onto the bed. She always responded to violence,

while in thy heart the winter is lying cold and bleak es liegt

wonderful girl, strong as a panther considering how fragile she was, spirited, savage, the savage always there ready to wake again. . . .

They fell onto the bed, raising a cloud of dust. She was slapping him about the neck, cursing him.

"Oh, you sod, you dirty Swiss sod, you lecherous dirty Swiss sod!"

"Let up, you bitch, *dekko chute!*"

you're like all the Europeans you're just a spoiler I just can't

On the white counterpane under the drapes of muslin mosquito net, they struggled, he dragging and tearing at her clothes until, bit by bit, her body was revealed. She was still struggling—with him now.

It was quick and brutal for him, soon over.

Afterward, she was furious again. She marched up and down the room as he lay on the bed, grabbing up her torn clothes and cursing him, damning him for ruining her possessions.

"Go back to camp in a sari, then! You've got a mass of them here!"

"You bloody Europeans, you're all the same! You're just a spoiler, spoil this, spoil that, spoil everything, don't care! Oh, I warn you, honestly, Tancred, I hate you, I hate you so stinking much, you raping swine, I just can't tell you possibly!"

He had already heard her say it all in his head. He was sick with precognition.

Suddenly, she flung a brass vase at Frazer. It struck the wall above him and bounced away. He jumped off the bed and grabbed her wrist, squeezing it until she sank to the floor, gasping with pain.

"Don't you fling things at me, you little wild cat! Get a sari on, and let's be getting back to camp! *Jaldhi jao!*"

stocks of grain and remember to keep the guards up to their

She selected a magnificent twelve-yard sari, all copper and brown and crimson, and wound it slowly about her body, saying, "I will never lie with you again; I prefer fat Kisari Mafatlal to you. You are so common! You have a wife at home, you common man! Wouldn't you be ashamed if she knew you were going with a colored woman?"

He put his shoes on and went over to the balcony, looking out over the dying garden. A parakeet with red head and green wings swooped down onto a veranda. It landed almost at the feet of an old woman standing motionless at the veranda rail, only to dart off again immediately. Perhaps the old woman was the *chokidar's* wife. Frazer was happy to think that she probably did not understand English. When she looked up at him, he retired into the bedroom. Sushila was arranging her hair, her brows heavy.

so shall the flower die and the seed and some flowers shall

"You're beautiful, Sushila. I love you!"

"You do not love me! And I know why you want me, because Mafatlal told me."

Angrily, he said, "Let's get on, woman! The sky's clouding up. If the monsoon came on, we'd be stuck here."

Her hand flew to her mouth. "Oh, my confounded Christ! Then there'd be real trouble! Us marooned here and Young coming back to Chandanagar and finding you'd cleared off and stolen his best lady doctor and left his flock!"

Her words made him even angrier. The bitch was getting at him! He marched downstairs and into the garden, revving the truck impatiently as she stayed on the terrace to talk to the *chokidar,* who was now joined by the old woman Frazer had seen from the window. This old woman carried Sushila's suitcaseful of belongings and placed it reverently in the back

while in my heart the winter is lying cold and bleak the rosy

of the truck.

As they drove along by the shrunken river's bank, he sang an old song of Heine's which his mother had taught him long ago, back in the Lauterbrunnen days: *"Es liegt der heisse Sommer,"* keeping it going as they roared through the fossilized villages.

His head ached. Finally he said, "I'm giving up, Sushila. I'm going back home as soon as possible. I'm no good out here—I haven't the dedication the job requires."

She was still angry and said nothing. To draw her out, to

flatter her, he said, "Your country is too harsh for me, Sushila. You survive in it, fragile as a flower, but it's killing me. I've felt ill ever since I came to Chandanager. Perhaps you're right and I'm a common man."

you are so common wouldn't you be ashamed if she knew you

Adamant, she said, "You're a spoiler, Tancred, like all your race. That's all I have to say to you."

"That's all, eh? No deep Indian wisdom to give to the disappearing white man! There's a myth in Switzerland—and in England too—that India is a land of ancient wisdom, where eventually a man will come face to face with the knowledge of himself. Have you nothing like that to offer, eh, except catty remarks?"

She laughed. "You often come face to face with yourself, Tancred, but you will not acknowledge it."

"Tell me, then! Give me a piece of your wisdom, the immemorial wisdom of the East! What does go on inside that brain of yours, anyway, sex apart?"

She began to light a cigar, and only then looked at him through the smoke.

"I will tell you, then. I will tell you something, something to keep stored among the funny voices in your head. Perhaps you will strike me, but I don't care! I don't think you often get the luxury of hearing the real truth about yourself, do you? You have come to Chan-

Mutti Mutti I didn't mean it really I didn't mean it don't cry

danagar and the famine because it represents a state of mind to you from your childhood, I don't know what. And there you have come to me to torment me because I also represent to you something other than what I really am. You see, you cannot understand famine as famine, because it is a thing alien to your part of the world, and so for you it can be believed only as a famine of love. That you can experience! It is the common experience of Europe and

America, the famine of love. Your lands are deserts in that sense. Your famine of love is your big neurosis that drives you to live among machinery."

"You're joking, of course!"

"And you suffer the malnutrition of the soul, which brings all kinds of shadow-diseases to your soul. You have been pushed to me to seek comfort in my bosom because you have to respond in that way to the hunger all round you, as the psychic forces of Chandanagar bear down on you. But even to my bosom you have to bring your deeper discontents from other times. Even my bosom you make your battleground! Your dirty common adulterous battleground! You are slowly dying, even as the people in the UNFAW enclosure."

He had not expected to hear it, rattling in the truck with death's landscape leaden under the storm clouds. Her words were a terrible torment for him; no precognition prepared him for her judgment. It took away his defenses of anger, so that he could only look away from her sullen eyes, knowing their relationship was at an end and that she had killed it as deliberately as one chops off a snake's head. He wished he could have wept.

"And that wisdom comes mostly not from me, Tancred, but from Kisari Mafatlal. He understands about all the matters people do not care to

you try to hide that you are unsure of your own psychological

reveal."

"Do you have to discuss me with him?"

"Don't sound so much like an old beaten dog! When we spoke of you, we hoped only that we could help you."

That little figure of fun! Mafatlal, that windbag, talking seriously with, sharing confidences with, Sushila! It might be wondered what else they shared! These Indians, they were so treacherous. . . .

the tulips were over by the end of the last week in April with

Even a girl educated in England. . . .

The long afternoon was tiring visibly over the immense bowl of plain when they sighted the camp. Neither spoke to the other as the truck bumped forward. Again the monsoon clouds were gigantic in the sky although not a drop of moisture spilled from their purple lips.

She said, "The gate's shut already!"

He peered forward, instinctively accelerating the truck.

The gate was indeed closed. Flipping off the automatics, he steered the truck forward until its nose was thrust hard against the wire-shielded pole. He jumped out, shouting in Hindu as he did so for the guards to lift the barrier.

Two men ran forward, very black and in filthy clothes. Frazer had never seen them before. Both were armed. They fired at him. As he flung himself down, he heard the windshield shatter behind him and a bullet go screaming into space. Diving behind the truck, he climbed up and fumbled in the tool box for a weapon. There was not enough time: the men were on him. Frazer flung himself at one of them, but the man whipped up his rifle, so that Frazer ran against it. The other man clamped his weapon round Frazer's throat.

"Don't make struggle, *sahib!*"

He had little chance of struggling. They had him tight. Another man had run up, shouting. He hauled Sushila out of the front of the truck: she stood unconcernedly brushing shattered glass off her sari. As she and Frazer were led past the guardhouse, he saw the guards lined up against a wall inside, their palms to the wall and their trousers down, as a bandit with a rifle stood over them.

"This is all your fault, Frazer!" Sushila said.

Two strange trucks were inside the camp. One stood outside the new store. One was further down, covering the hospital.

He knew what they were after, of course. The grain! The store was full of rice, plus large quantities of wheat and flour, as well as canned goods.

The bandits marched him and Sushila roughly down the

road. They stopped by the store, the doors of which were shut, and one of them shouted something, evidently to a superior inside. The store door opened and a ferocious face peered out. It belonged to a large Indian

the very glow of summer is on thy dimpled cheek cold and

with a thatch of lank hair. He was eating. In an angry-sounding exchange, he gestured to the office block next door, and gave Frazer's captor a key.

Frazer and Sushila were then dragged to the offices. The door was unlocked, and their captors told them to stay inside and keep quiet adding that they were lucky to get away so lightly. They were pushed in and the door slammed and locked on them.

"Oh God, they are robbing the store!" Frazer said.

"And having a good feed first! The bosses sit in there having a good feed while the underlings keep peace! They will have cut all communications with the outside world. There is nothing we can do! They are desperate! They will take everything!" She began to wail with her face in her hands; he was glad to ignore her.

"What a fool I was to leave! . . . Even if they have rounded up the doctors at the hospital, won't the refugees do something to save the food stocks?"

"What can those poor people do? When *can* they do? They will do nothing."

Of course it was true. Some of them had even been standing about outside, waiting in the cool ejected air from this building, as if nothing was happening that could possibly concern them.

A frightened clerk appeared on the stairs. The bandits had shut the clerks in the office block too, under pain of instant death if they attempted to get out.

"We'll barge the door down! How many of you are there? We can rush them while the pigs are still eating."

There were ten clerks upstairs. Shame-faced, they revealed why they could venture nothing: the bandits had a napalm gun. They were threatening the hospital with it at the moment, but they would turn it on anyone who made any trouble.

"That's why they are so confident! Sushila, we *must* do something!

you had your orders Frazer you had no business deserting

I'm not just going to stand here while they fill their stomachs!"

Furious and frustrated, he ran into the room he was using as a bedroom. Kisari Mafatlal lay on his camp bed, a clerk tending him and bathing his forehead. The plump little doctor had been badly beaten about the face; he peered at Frazer out of an enormously puffed eye.

Through painful lips, he told Frazer and Sushila how the bandits had arrived at the gate in their two trucks, claiming to be bringing stores from Allahabad. The gate guard had been suspicious and had called Mafatlal. Mafatlal had been wary enough to ring through to UNFAW HQ and warn them that, if he did not ring through again in five minutes, it would mean trouble at the camp. Then he had gone bravely to the gate, asked to see the stores that the bandits claimed they were bringing, and had been clobbered.

"How long ago was this?"

"It only just happened, as you can see. I was thrown in here to die!"

"Thank God the HQ police will soon be along!"

"It will take them one hour at the earliest to arrive here. Then these pigs will all be escaped across the *maidan*."

you had your orders Frazer and I hold you entirely responsi-

"There must be something we can do! Sushila, look after Kisari; I'm going to look around."

He needed—he did not know what. He unlocked the door into the basement and hurried down the crude concrete steps, seeking a weapon. The self-powered air conditioning plant was here, laboring

your deeper discontents from other times even my bosom

away, its semi-audible note creating a pain in the teeth, as always. Apart from the plant, the cellar was bare. He skirted it, prepared to

shadow-diseases even my bosom by the first week of April

go, stopped.

Stuffing his handkerchief into his mouth to hinder the vibrations, he rolled an empty oil drum over to one wall, rammed it there with a brick, and climbed onto it. The voices in his head tormented him.

By pushing aside the clumsy metal ventilator that spewed out used air, he could look through the grill onto the store where the bandits

to stare again out through the window at the blackness of the

were feasting. The wooden scaffolding was in place, although the women

will the little ones remember me their mother an old withered

laboring to repair the wall had been sent away. Even the new wall showed

no milk but dust and in my bowl only these broken grains

cracks. The wall round the ventilator grill against which Frazer stood

tender mouths tender mouths you are slowly dying tender

was also a maze of cracks.

"All that vibration . . ." he muttered. He was trembling, almost delir-

all that vibration April is the cruelest month bringing Christ

ious.

As he checked over the unwieldy machine, throbbing to itself, memories stirred. It was a primitive machine, with the legend "Made in Bombay" and a patent number and the date "1979" proudly displayed on its flank. Over twenty years old! But, of course, it wasn't the vibration as such. . . .

Hastily, he followed the circuit through the refrigeration plant, saw the air ducts snake out through the cavity walling. It would be possible to switch off most of the circuit, and concentrate the output of the machine through the one grill. . . . Suddenly, he knew what he wanted, and was running back upstairs to Sushila.

"Sushila, help me lift Kisari enough to get the blankets from under him. I need the blankets. Then . . . that's it! . . . then, I want to borrow your sari. . . ."

Before she could flare up, he explained his plan.

In the end, she shrugged and unwound the flaring material from her body until she stood there in brassiere and panties. Gratefully, he passed her a clean shirt from his trunk. With her help, he swathed himself in the blankets, and she bound them to him and over his head with the sari. When he was completely muffled from head to foot, he fumbled his way downstairs again.

Hastily, he switched off power, then went round ripping off connections. Soon, the giant ventilator would concentrate all its output through the one ventilator overlooking the new store.

Gritting his teeth, Frazer switched on again.

He could hear very little now. But he could feel the waves of sound. He knew he was right, even as he felt his stomach quivering. This was infrasound. The plant was emitting slow air vibrations at less than ten hertz—the human ear would only register sound from sixteen hertz up. The compressions were radiating outward, mostly in one direction only, like a primitive death ray. Even the voices in his head were silenced.

Peering through the fringes of his blankets, and through the fine silk of the sari, Frazer looked anxiously toward the ventilator. He could hear secondary vibrations setting up in the steel grill, a low moan rising and fading, almost like the monsoon wind coming in over the plains. How long should he give it? He could not see out—

A curiously pulsating roar reached his ears. It could only be— He dashed forward and switched off his deadly machine. The roar took on a steadier note and became identifiable as masonry falling. Panting, Frazer dragged the sari and blankets from his head, feeling as sick as a dog. Staggering over to the wall, he knocked the vent aside and looked out. Nothing could be seen for a great billowing cloud of red dust!

Calling, shouting incoherently, he made his way upstairs.

"Help me get this padding off, Sushila, and we'll go outside!" As she unwrapped him, he thought that, although the blankets had saved him from some of the vibrations, the infrasound had given his body a thorough shake-up. He was feeling brittle and cold right inside his bones; a continuous whine seemed to have set up in the coils of his intestines.

With Sushila following, dressed in his shirt and a pair of his shorts, Frazer marched into the front office and hurled himself at the door. On his third charge, one of the wooden panels broke; he pushed it away and climbed outside, helping the girl out after him.

you're just a spoiler spoil this spoil that spoil everything

"How did you do it?" she asked. She grasped his hand, staring at the great reddish cloud of dust now clearing.

Through the cloud, they could see that the near wall of the store had collapsed, carrying the plastic roofing with it. The store was otherwise still more or less standing, although cracks marked the whole facade of it. The contents should not have suffered too much damage.

"I'm just a spoiler," Frazer said. "I spoil everything—but

in this case, you might add that the spoiling had been going on for a long while. That's why they always had trouble with the wall. Our air conditioning was permanently beaming low-power infrasound at it; all I did was step up the power."

"I don't understand at all. You did this with sound?"

"Yes, infrasound. Sound you can't hear: slow air vibration, in fact." He had to hold on to her shoulder to stand steady. "It creates a sort of pendulum action, which can quickly build up a deadly reverberation in solid objects or in human beings. Can't you still feel your stomach and heart vibrating?"

"I feel sick, yes. It's just excitement, I think."

"It's infrasound. Maybe infrasound is a source of emotional excitement. Maybe I owe the voices I hear in my head to the faulty air conditioner. Ever since I've been here, I've had a low-powered death

hunger all around you as the psychic forces of Chandanagar

ray turned on me all the time. What you said was right— I was slowly

you have been pushed to seek comfort in my bosom because

dying."

"But you switched the machine off now?"

He nodded.

They looked at each other cautiously. To cover all that he was feeling, Frazer said, "Let's go and see what's happened to the bandits."

"Will they be dead?"

"I hope not." He started shouting to the guards in the gatehouse. The bandits who had been keeping the guards quiet were now standing by the front of the ruined store; with the initiative taken out of their hands, they made no attempt to stop Frazer as he went up and opened the store door.

Dust swirled out of the interior. He stepped back,

choking. In a minute or two, the bandits emerged, sorry and sick, all but one crawling on hands and knees. Frazer had an idea of what they would be feeling; their invisible injuries would include an intense irritation internally, as if their various organs had been set rubbing against each other by the low-pitched sound. They would have recovered by tomorrow. And, by then, they would be in the lockup in Allahabad. The doctors down at the hospital were already rounding up the bandits with the napalm weapon; the calamity to their leaders had robbed them of the will to fight.

Still the monsoon did not break, still the reinforcements from UNFAW HQ which Mafatlal had alerted did not arrive; perhaps the very pleasant man operating the switchboard had forgotten all about the detachment and its problems. It was a very Indian situation.

Mafatlal's wounds had been treated and he was resting in his own room. Sushila and Frazer sat by him, drinking. Although Frazer was the hero of the hour, Mafatlal was the invalid of the hour and enjoying the situation to the full.

"You see, Tancred, passion and violence are a very integral part of the Indian scene. But they come and then they are gone, as also applies

he understands about all matters people do not care to reveal

to humanity. But the things they represent are always a permanency, which we must tolerate in the most philosophical way. The flower shall die and the seed and some flowers shall never die, as Krishna says, stating the paradox of life. It is, you will agree, somewhat of a rather Indian situation from your point of view, perhaps . . . ."

Frazer doubted if Sushila was listening. At the present moment, the characters of the three of them were in equipoise; but that would not last. The dynamics of the girl's life were unfolding, even in these stagnant surroundings, inevitably to work against any stability.

And he. . . . He wondered if it might be possible to resume those happy intimacies with her. Both she and Mafatlal were slightly in awe of him

you have been pushed to seek comfort in my bosom just

at the moment, since he had played so actively his role of the Westerner, the spoiler; so the time might be propitious for him to try his luck with her again. Or should he wait till Young returned, face the trouble of that encounter, and then inaugurate his return to England and Kathie? He would do what he would do; what others said or thought about him could make no difference to him, could it?

Tomorrow, he would decide. He would see how he felt. That also was

the flower shall die and the seed and some flowers shall

a very Indian situation.

die and the seed and some flowers shall never ever die

SEA CHANGE

by Bertram Chandler

John Willis sat uneasily on the hard bench that ran along one wall of the Federal Employment Bureau. Now and again he tried to read the newspaper that he had bought (and could he afford the fifty cents? he had asked himself) on his way to the bureau from the Transients' Hostel. A colony on the Moon. . . . Men on Mars. . . . A manned laboratory in orbit about Venus—and none of it front page news. The big headlines had been reserved for the Fourth Test Match between Australia and the U.S.A., currently being played in Melbourne. And rightly so, he thought with wry humor. Americans taking up cricket, of all games, was far more fantastic than the facts of the astronauts.

Somebody was calling his name, "Captain Willis!" He got to his feet, bundling up the morning paper. He walked to the counter. He found it hard not to look at the firm, fully exposed breasts of the girl who had summoned him.

"Yes?" he said. "Yes?"

"Your personal data has been processed, Captain. It so happens that there is a vacancy for a master in one of the paper pulp tankers operated by the Ministry of Timber Products. You will report to their Dock Office at 1045 hours this morning."

"But, Miss. . . ." He looked down at the little sign on the polished surface of the counter in front of her. "But, Miss Vitelli, there must be a mistake."

"The Computer never makes a mistake," she told him severely.

"But, damn it all, I'm nearly eighty years old."

"Legally speaking," she said, "you're forty-five."

Legally speaking—and biologically speaking. He could see his reflection in the mirror-like finish of the counter. He looked just as he had when, having won the first prize in the Opera House Lottery, he and Jane, his wife, had decided to make another gamble. The doctors had told him that he had only a year to live. But, in the U.S.A. there were already the facilities for stasis, the so-called Deep Freeze. Jane had accompanied him—to America, and then into the cold and dark that might well be eternal. But it had been only a little more than thirty years.

He looked younger now than he had when the decision had been made. His face was still rugged, but the wrinkles had vanished from about the blue eyes, which had lost their faded quality. His hair was still dark—and, in fact, the first streaks of gray had disappeared.

Even so. . . .

"But you don't understand," he told the girl. "I passed for master way back in 1945, during the Second World War. Even at the time when I was . . . suspended, in 1967, there was so much new, electronic navigation and the like, that was not covered by my certificate."

"Nonetheless," she stated, "you were sailing as master then, in 1967. And your qualifications were valid. And still are. And if the Computer says that there is nobody else immediately available for this job—that's all there is to it. Of course, if you don't really want it . . ."

"I'm afraid that I do. The first prize was a lot of money back in 1967—but it was whittled away. Storage charges for two—*and* the operation. We aren't quite paupers—but we're not far from it."

"And this is the only sort of job that you're likely to get." The girl handed Willis his papers in a big, plastic envelope and said, very definitely, "Good morning, Captain."

Back in the cramped, temporary apartment that would have to do until he and Jane found something better he unpacked, bringing out from the suitcases the clothes and other possessions that, like their owner, had been in cold storage for a third of a century. The clothing was useless, most of it, although he put to one side the uniform cap with the golden laurel leaves on the visor. He would have to change the cap badge—but the dull, well-weathered artificial foliage would be preferable to something glaringly new. Then there was his sextant. He would want that. And his reduction tables . . .

"I must go down to the sea again . . ." quoted Jane, rather bitterly. She was a tall girl, slim, darkly auburn, with a mouth too wide and features too strong for conventional prettiness. But, even in her discontent ("I should have known," she had said, shortly after their arrival back in Sydney, "I should have known! All of our friends either dead or with one foot in the grave! And everything changed! And the fashions!") she was rather beautiful.

"It's a job," he said. "And not a badly paid one. I've skimmed through this newfangled Award of theirs. Four weeks on, rather hard running. Then two weeks off. And annual leave on top of it."

"I thought that it was temporary appointment."

"At the moment, yes. But the permanent master of *Pulpster* is going on *his* annual leave and it's not certain that he'll be returning."

"Retiring?" she asked.

"No. Bettering himself. The bright young men don't want to spend their lives crawling around the coast at fifteen knots, not even in the *big* bulk carriers. The hovercraft, roaring across the Tasman at ten times that speed, are the glamor ships these days."

"And I suppose the pay is higher, and the conditions better."

"Yes."

"Do you think that you . . . ?"

"No," he told her regretfully. "They'd be out of my class. I've a ten knot mentality, although I should be able to cope with fifteen."

"Still," she said a little more cheerfully, "you've got a fresh start. And you haven't got to begin again at the bottom."

"Insofar as rank is concerned, no," he agreed.

He rose early the following morning, showered, shaved (this newfangled depilatory cream was a blessing) and dressed. He said good-by to Jane. She had wanted to come down to the ship with him, and he would have liked her to have done so, but he knew that he would be far too busy in the brief hours between arrival and departure. He carried his baggage from the bed-sitting room to the elevator, rode down to the lobby in solitude. The sleepy night clerk ordered him a cab.

The driver, during the ride down to the harbor, was talkative. The breed had changed little, if at all, over the decades. Willis made a pretense of listening.

The first daylight was coming in when the cab drew up off *Pulpster*'s berth. Her new captain paid off the driver, wincing inwardly as he parted with notes that, in the old days, would have represented a day's pay. He realized that his own salary was big only on paper. He stood beside his little pile of baggage, shivering slightly in the morning chill. He noticed that the linesmen were waiting along the edge of the wharf. A man in uniform—Willis recognized the Maritime Services Board cap badge—walked up to him. "Joining her?" he asked.

"Yes."

"Shouldn't be long now. She's just passed under the bridge."

"Good."

"And you're the new skipper?"

"Yes."

"Haven't seen you around, Captain."

"No. I've . . . been away."

The official gave Willis a curious look, then turned his head. "Here she comes now. Just rounding Miller's Point."

Yes, here she came—low in the water, rust-colored from truck to water line, with a high mast, sprouting antennae, that was a logical upward extension of the bridge superstructure a little forward of amidships, a green funnel (the one touch of color) protruding from a low house on the poop. She stood in through the wide opening where the Pyrmont Bridge had been in Willis' time—and then, just abaft her raking stem, there was a flurry of foam and another, more violent turbulence under her cruiser stern. Full astern and transverse thrust, thought Willis. Not having any more to rely on tugs which, sometimes, did as they were told and which, all too often, thought that they knew best. He was looking forward to handling this ship.

She came alongside beautifully, swinging short round under the influence of her propulsive and maneuvering screws, seeming, at the finish, to be moving laterally through the water. Weighted heaving lines were thrown from fo'c'sle and poop; that technique, almost as old as ships themselves, had not changed. But the mooring ropes that the linesmen manhandled ashore, casting the eyes over the bollards, were fantastically light. And so was the manning. An officer on the fo'c'sle head, with one rating only, and another rating on the foredeck to handle the forward backspring. An officer aft, with one man for the stern line and another for the after spring. With self-tensioning winches—and no featherbedding—that was all that was required.

He watched the hands coming off stations—making all fast fore and aft was no longer a time-consuming operation—saw the gangway mechanically extruded as somebody, somewhere, pushed a button, looked with interest at the connecting up of the shore pipe lines without all the fussing with nuts and bolts and flanges that he had been used to thirty years ago.

He picked up his briefcase and his sextant case—he hoped that the A.B.s of this day and age did not consider it beneath their dignity to carry the master's gear on board—and walked up the metal gangway, the self-adjusting threads rattling ever so slightly under his feet.

Captain Harlow was a tall man, dark of hair and complexion, neat in his sharply creased khaki, possibly in his mid-thirties, if not younger. "Welcome aboard, Captain Willis," he said. "Old Dalby condescended to let me know that I was being relieved this time in. Sit down, Captain. Make yourself at home. After all, this *is* your home now."

Willis seated himself in one of the two easy chairs, looked around the day cabin. It could have been worse, much worse. The bulkheads were textured plastic paneling, the uncarpeted deck was covered with softly resilient tiles in contrasting and complementing colors. On the desk stood a small-screen television set. And on the low coffee table, between the two chairs, was the inevitable silver tea service, with a large plate of hot buttered toast. This had been brought up by one of the two stewardesses—a pleasant young woman whose uniform, rather to Willis' relief, did not leave her breasts exposed. He had never liked women aboard a ship—and if he had to have them he preferred them decently covered.

"Sorry I've no time to show you around properly," Harlow said. "But it's always a mad rush in Sydney. And at the other end. By the time that we've taken care of the legal side of the hand-over it'll be sailing time. But the mate'll show you what lives where, and what it does."

"Captain Dalby put me in the picture," said Willis. "Two hundred and seventy feet over-all. Fifty-foot beam. Three thousand tons deadweight—but a couple of dracones just in case they want us to tow a few tons extra. Turboelectric drive. Nuclear power. . . ."

"You *have* been doing your homework."

"When one has been away from the job for thirty years, Captain Harlow, one has to."

"Thirty years? You're joking."

"I'm not."

"Then . . . then you're a resurrectee?"

"I'm afraid so."

"Cheer up. You'll find this job a piece of cake. There's precious little new in the way of navigational equipment—this isn't, after all, one of the trans-Tasman fliers. And the officers all have *recent* certificates—the chief officer has his mate's, and the second and third both have second mates'. They'll put you wise to anything you aren't sure about. And now I'll get showered and changed, and then we'll have breakfast."

During the meal Willis met his officers. There was Darryl, the mate, who looked to be about Willis' own biological age, a short, swarthy man with lank, thinning hair and a perpetual scowl. Taylor and Brown, second and third officers respectively, could almost have been twins; both were tall, thin-featured, and with almost white hair. Carter, the engineer, pale-skinned and black-bearded, looked more physicist than mechanic. Miss Wendover, the electrician, was a rather bulky and brawny brunette, who, Willis guessed, would look and feel more at home in her overalls than either in uniform or a civilian dress.

These were the only officers, and apart from them the crew was a small one. There was the plump, motherly Mrs. Livermore, the chief stewardess, and the neither plump nor motherly Miss Lewisham, her blond assistant. There were no cooks; the ship was well stocked with deep-freeze meals. As for the rest—there was a leading hand, three general purpose ratings and a deck boy. There was little work to be done aboard this automated ship, not even the perpetual scraping and painting that had kept the hands busy when Willis had been last at sea. The steel from which *Pulpster* was built had been allowed to rust while she was still on the stocks—and that rust was the protective coating against further corrosion.

Harlow was anxious to get off the ship and to sign clear. Willis accompanied him ashore and, after his name had been put on the register at the customs house, wás driven round to the shipping office to sign the articles of agreement and to make the necessary entry in the official log. Then, with these documents in his briefcase, he returned to the vessel. It was almost sailing time. He changed hastily into his new khakis, picked up his binoculars, and then climbed the companionway to the combined wheelhouse-chartroom. He overheard the tail end of a conversation before his three officers were aware of his presence.

"What gripes *me,*" the chief officer was saying, "is that *my* certificate, although it's only a first mate's ticket, is worth a damn sight more than *his*. He passed for master way back in Captain Cook's day, before electronic navigation had been dreamed of. But *his* precious piece of paper is still valid—and I'm qualified to sail only as mate . . . ."

Willis backed quietly down the companionway, and then made quite a deal of unnecessary noise coming back up.

Willis managed. His Sydney pilotage exemption was still valid, and the renewal of his Hobart exemption—which expired after five years if not used in that period—presented no great problems. And there had been no major changes in either port, looking at them as seaports, since his withdrawal from circulation. Sydney still handled conventional vessels—although most of them were either container ships or bulk carriers. Bate Bay, to the south of the oil tanker port of Botany Bay, was the hovercraft port for New South Wales, and there the traffic from "the farm," the islands that were now called North Zealand and South Zealand, roared inland with hardly a diminution of speed.

But the hovercraft were no concern of Willis', neither were the huge bulk carriers nor the big container ships. He shuttled back and forth in his little *Pulpster,* with his long pilotage at the Port Huon end and his short, but rather more wearing, pilotage at the Sydney end. But this was far easier than it had been when last he had worked the port. Now there was a television screen in the wheelhouse, and on it was presented an over-all aerial picture of the harbor. Now he could see what was on the other side of every corner before he started to turn it.

Insofar as the other electronic gadgetry was concerned he was reasonably happy. Radar he was already familiar with, and gyro compass, and automatic steering, and echo sounding. He liked the met. screen in the chartroom that, at the push of a button, would show either an up-to-the-minute meteorological chart of any selected area or—but this, although fascinating, was of little practical value—a TV picture of the Earth's atmosphere transmitted from whichever satellite was best sited to provide the coverage. He was rather sorry that his ship, being only a coaster, was not fitted with the equipment required for navigation by artificial satellite—he would have liked to have been able to play around with it—but yet he sneered at the Decca Navigator as a useless luxury. (That, of course, had been in existence before he was put into his cold sleep, and he had been one of those opposed to the establishment of a chain of Decca stations around the Australian coast.) "You're just putting yourself at the mercy of a single fuse. . . ." he told his officers and, rather to their distress, insisted on doing his own navigation, the old-fashioned way, with sextant, chronometer, ephemeris, and reduction tables, when crossing the stretch of open water between the mainland and Tasmania.

The ship handled well, very well, and it had not taken him long to get the feel of her. The only fly in the ointment was the unavailability of any other master to relieve him for time off when he had his four weeks in. Officers came and went and returned, as did ratings, but for Willis it was watch on and stay on. With a discharging time of only six hours he rarely saw his wife, especially after she returned to her old trade as a designer. He did see the apartment which she had taken for them, but was never able to sleep there, was rarely able to enjoy a meal there.

But, as she pointed out, it was a job, and a reasonably well-paid one, and the time off not taken was accumulating.

And then it happened.

It was in the small hours of the morning, and the ship

was fifty miles south of Gabo on her northbound voyage. It was the alarm bells that awakened Willis—but if they had not done so the cessation of engine hum would have aroused him. He had pulled on his dressing gown and was on his way up to the bridge when he heard his telephone buzzing. He ignored it. It would only be the second mate trying to tell him that the engines had stopped.

The combined wheelhouse-chartroom was in pitch darkness. Everything was dead—steering compass repeater, the dials of the Decca Navigator, the radar display unit, the clock of the Chernikeeff Log, all the pilot lights that had reminded Willis, more than once, of Christmas tree decorations. He saw the second mate, a shadowy figure standing by the intercommunication telephone. But that had worked. It should have done, anyhow. The system, like the alarm system, was battery-powered.

"What's wrong?" he asked.

"I . . . I don't know, sir. The engines have stopped. . . ."

Willis bit back a sarcastic rejoinder. Ask a silly question, get a silly answer. All that he said was, "Don't ring the chief. It always annoys engineers to be pestered by the bridge when they're up to the neck in trouble. He'll let us know, in his own time. But where are we?"

The second officer found a torch, and by its light Willis examined the lattice chart. The ship was in no danger, and the rising westerly wind would blow her out into open water. But, now that she had lost her steerage way, the motion was becoming uneasy.

The intercom telephone buzzed. Willis groped his way to the instrument, pulled the handset from its clip. "Master here."

"Chief here, Captain. I needn't tell you that she's stopped."

"You needn't. How long before you get her going again?"

"You'll have to call for a tug."

"As bad as that?"

"Yes. As bad as that. Damn it all," the engineer swore, "you wouldn't read about it! A modern, nuclear-powered ship buggered by the sort of breakdown that used to happen in the very first turbine steamers!"

"What *is* the trouble?"

"A leaky condenser, that's all. Salt in the feed water. The turbo-generators have had it, in a big way."

"What about some lights? And some power—we shall need that for the radio."

"That shouldn't be long. Lecky's on her way up to start the emergency jenny. . . ."

From the after end of the accommodation there came an irregular mechanical coughing that suddenly steadied to a healthily rhythmical beat. Lights came on throughout the ship—not all of them, only those on the emergency circuit. Then, shockingly, they flared explosively, flared and died. From the radio telephone console there sputtered an intense blue flash; from the second mate, who had just switched the set on, there was a startled curse. There was a woman's scream from the after part of the boat deck, a metallic crash and clatter.

Willis waited for his eyes to become accustomed to the fresh onset of darkness. The acrid stench of smoldering insulation made him sneeze. He heard the watch officer say, "It must have been the governor. She was tinkering with it yesterday. The jenny just ran away with her. . . ."

"Go down and see if she's hurt," ordered Willis.

He recalled his amusement when the chief had referred to the electrician as "passion fingers. Everything she touches, she fucks up." It didn't seem so funny now.

She wasn't hurt, luckily. And the diesel generator wasn't damaged badly, not so badly as to be beyond repair.

"Come daylight," promised the chief, "and we'll get right on with it. Then you'll have power for the radio."

"And can the radio be fixed?" Willis asked the second mate, who had been working on it by the light from an electric torch.

"I don't think so, sir. All twelve transistors seem to be burned out."

"We have spares, surely."

"Yes. But only six."

"Why didn't the safety devices, the cutouts, function?"

"*She* has been working on them," admitted the engineer.

Willis grunted. "So we just sit here," he said coldly, "until such time as somebody realizes that we're overdue, and sends out aircraft to look for us. . . ."

And of course, he thought, *we can use the hand-powered transceiver from the life raft to make a call. But I'll just wait and see if one of my bright young gentlemen thinks of it. And if nobody does, then . . .*

And if nobody does . . .

He walked out to the weather wing of the bridge. There was more wind than there had been earlier, but it would not be a violent blow—he hoped. He visualized the weather chart that he had studied on the met. screen before writing up his night orders—the extensive low to the south'ard, the isobars not unduly crowded, moving slowly east across the Tasman Sea toward South Zealand.

The mate was up now. (Had he slept through the alarms, or had he just ignored them?) Willis heard him complaining bitterly because the second mate hadn't made the pot of tea with which he always started his watch. Then, when he finally realized what was amiss, he muttered, "This ship's been jinxed ever since that bloody ancient mariner joined her. . . ."

"Too right, Mr. Darryl," Willis told him, walking up to him in the darkness. "And I should have brought my albatross with me, shouldn't I? But never mind. By the looks of the weather we shan't meet the same fate as the original Ancient Mariner did."

The mate said nothing, but his silence was more eloquent than speech.

Willis went on. "It will be light by six. Get all hands out—and set sail."

"Set *sail,* sir?" Darryl's voice was an outraged squeal. "Are you *mad?"*

"No, Mr. Darryl. I'm not mad. And if *you* don't know how to go about it, I'll take over."

"And put that in your pipe and smoke it, Mr. Christian," murmured the second mate.

It is one thing to say, "Set sail,"—it is another thing to do it. Willis probably would never have thought of it himself if, just about the same time that he had won first prize in the Opera House Lottery, a motor ship of about the same size of his present command hadn't sailed into port after a major breakdown. Her captain had used tarpaulins, awnings, even boat covers. *Pulpster* had no tarpaulins and no boat covers, and her awnings were permanent fiberglass fittings. But there were the dracones, two of them, great nylon sausages, in the after storeroom. There was the huge, versatile sewing machine owned by Mrs. Livermore, whose paying hobby was dressmaking. Willis had commented on it while making rounds, and the stewardess had told him that it would sew *anything*. She also had with a good stock of thread, and though it was intended only for seaming female garments its tensile strength was equal to that of the sail twine of the sixties.

And *Pulpster* might almost have been designed with the possibility of her proceeding under sail in view. The block of accommodation, with the tall but sturdy mast rising from the bridge, was one third of the ship's length from forward. The deck between stem and bridge face was uncluttered, as it was from the after end of the midships house to the funnel. There was ample room to spread the dracones broken out from the lazaret, space to measure and mark and cut, to range and to feed the nylon sections into and through the stewardess's machine. There was a careful measurement and planning, to cut the amount of stitching required to a minimum. But the stock of thread held out.

There was power now. The diesel generator was thudding away, little the worse for its freak breakdown. There was power for the winches, and for the steering gear—when it would finally be required—and for the gyro compass. There would be enough for the met. screen—the one newfangled gadget that an old-time windship master would really have appreciated—and for the Chernikeeff Log, but not enough for the other navigational aids. However, one man in the ship was used to doing without radar, Decca, and all the rest of it.

There was power for the portable welding plant that was part of the engine-room equipment—and, using it, the chief engineer (far more enthusiastic and useful than the mate) was able to convert a length of piping into a boom of sorts for the mainsail, with a shoe that fitted around the heel of the mast. The rig, when it was finished, was a queer one—"A sort of a kind of a bastard ketch . . ." said Willis. It was not until the afternoon of the second day that the self-tensioning winches fore and aft were brought into service and the sails hoisted, the metal hanks rattling up the travelers that had been welded to the mast. Willis didn't dare to ask what had been cannibalized for these necessary fittings, but he gained the impression that the chief engineer had been quite ruthless in his ripping out of all sorts of piping that was not in use with the main engines out of commission. Yes—cannibalization, improvisation; that was how it had been in the old days before the all-powerful unions said, "You may do *this*, but you must not do *that*."

Engine-room bits and pieces, mooring lines and spare mooring lines, odd snatch blocks, and handy billies that had been loafing in the stores for years unused—everything and anything was pressed into service. The decks, at first glance, were a cat's cradle of cordage. The mooring lines, with the spares shackled to them for extra length, led aft from the forward winches—one, the halyard, to a snatch block at the masthead, one, the downhaul, through a lead block that took it clear of everything to another lead block at the foot of the mast. There was a similar arrangement aft. Then there were the sheets, the hauling parts of which had been led to the winches not otherwise in use. It was a great pity, thought Willis, that those machines could not be controlled directly from the bridge—if this had been the case he could have claimed that *Pulpster* was a fully automated sailing ship. . . . in any case, shorthanded as he was by windjammer standards, he would have to put her on automatic steering whenever possible.

Now his sails, such as they were, had been hoisted. He felt a pang of disappointment; they were not as he had envisaged them. They sagged and they bagged—but they drew. And, after all, he was not a professional sailmaker. The wind, luckily, had dropped to a comfortable Force 4—even so, Willis was glad that he had stayed the mast. The lee shrouds were slack, and the weather ones were bar taut. He was glad, too, that those mooring lines that had been used for stays were at least half wire; there was too much elasticity in the artificial fibers.

He stood on his bridge, looked forward, looked aft, looked aloft. Everything seemed to be holding, and nowhere were there any signs of chafe. The sheet of the mainsail, though, needed adjustment. He gestured to the second mate, who hove on it with the weather winch until ordered to belay. Bates, the leading hand, was at the wheel. Willis told him, "Port easily. Bring her round to 015. . . ." He heard the clicking of the steering repeater. "015 it is, sir," reported the helmsman. "Good. Hold her at that." She was sailing as closehauled as she ever would be, seven points from the wind. She must be making leeway—just how much could be determined later. But she was sailing, and although she heeled over it was not at a dangerous angle, and with the weight of the sails holding her she was as steady as a rock, in spite of the sea and swell almost on the beam. There was another faint clicking, this time from the chartroom. It was the Chernikeeff Log. She was beginning to make way through the water.

"Mr. Taylor," Willis told the second mate, who had come back to the bridge, "you can put her on automatic. Unless there's any shift of wind we'll leave her on that, although we may have to alter course once we find out where we are. . . ."

"And how shall we do that?" demanded Darryl, who was standing beside Willis but carefully avoiding playing any part in the proceedings. "How shall we do that?" he repeated, looking up at the mast, which had been shorn of all the antennae that would have interfered with the setting of the sails.

"Don't worry about it," Willis told him. "I'd teach you how—but I've always made it a rule never to lend my sextant to anybody." He added generously, "You can watch me." It would soon be time for evening stars, and the sky was clear.

But there was something that he had to do first. Jane would be worrying by this time. "Mr. Darryl," he ordered, "have the life raft transceiver brought up here. We'll tell the world where we are and what we're doing."

"We could have done that before!" snarled the mate. "We could have sent out a distress call and been taken in tow, two days ago!"

"Yes, Mr. Darryl. We could have done. Why didn't *you* suggest it?"

The mate was silent—and so was the speaker of the transceiver when, several minutes later, it was brought up to the bridge and the leading hand set to vigorously cranking the handle. On its way along from the raft it had been dropped. . . .

So I'm really on my own, thought Willis. He hoped that Jane wouldn't worry too much.

He was really on his own—even though the following morning an aircraft found the ship, a relatively slow propeller-driven plane. It circled them and then, realizing that radio communication was for some reason impossible, tried to signal with an Aldis lamp. Willis himself picked up the ship's Aldis; his officers were not used to such archaic methods of signaling. He flashed *OK* several times. The airmen must have read it eventually; at last they dipped a wing in salute then flew away to the northwest.

He was really on his own when, during the afternoon, the wind freshened to gale force, and above. With the exception of Darryl his officers and crew were willing enough—but they were so inexperienced, they knew so little. It was not their fault. Over the years the examination room emphasis had been on technology rather than old-fashioned seamanship. As for Willis—he was realizing that he didn't know enough, not nearly enough. He had ridden out many a blow in this very part of the world—but not in a sailing vessel, a juryrigged sailing vessel at that. He had been able to put the ship's head to wind and sea so as to minimize their effects, to avoid violent, dangerous rolling, to protect his vulnerable hatches. But with no engines obedient to his command he could not do this now.

Even so, with his long experience of Bass Strait weather, he should have known better than to have made his sails with neither reef points nor any other means of reefing them. He could have taken in sail altogether—but unless he kept going he would have to ask the next aircraft to find them to send for assistance. Already the last deep-freeze meal had been heated and served and eaten, and the emergency stock of canned provisions would not last for long—and neither would the fresh water.

He stood on the bridge, balancing himself against the occasional heavy lurch, the increasing list. He looked up at the sails, the two triangles of seemingly flimsy fabric, full they were, and taut, too taut, reminding him of a toy balloon overinflated, on the very point of bursting. And how long would it be before they did burst?

He looked down and to wind'ard, flinching as the spray whipped from the wave crests slashed his face. Under the gray sky, the ragged, gray, harried clouds, the water was gray too, white-capped and streaked with foam. It was a short sea, steep and vicious. There wasn't much swell as yet, but it was building up.

The crew was ready now to carry out his orders. He had explained everything carefully, in minute detail. He had been honest with them, telling them that if he took in sail altogether—or if the sails were blown to useless tatters—probably nothing worse would happen to them than being driven, out of control, into mid-Tasman, where help was almost sure to arrive before the food and the water gave out. After all, a tanker, unless holed, is virtually unsinkable. He had pointed out the risk that the volunteer who went up the mast would be taking.

Then, with all necessary gear assembled, Willis gave the helm order that would bring the ship up into the wind. She carried her way even when the sails ceased to draw; her design, with bridge well forward, made it all too likely that she would fall off again, but as long as the foresails were brailed in smartly the mainsail should keep her steady. Donaldson, one of the younger hands, a man proud of his athletic prowess, went up the mast like a monkey—like a monkey climbing a coconut palm in the teeth of a hurricane. The end of yet another sacrificed mooring line was fast about his waist. He made it—and still the ship showed no inclination to fall away from the wind. He clung there for a while and then, at last, working awkwardly with only one hand, contrived to get a bight of the line over the sail, and then another bight, and then another. It was slow work, and hazardous, and working those bights down to the required positions was even slower and more hazardous. But at last it was finished, and the end of the line taken to a winch and the sail brailed in.

The brailing in of the mainsail was accomplished in less time, but none too soon. After hanging in stays *Pulpster* decided, quite suddenly, that she would be happier with the wind on the beam. Had she come round the wrong way Willis would never have been able to get her back on to her northerly course, but his luck held.

Even so, even with sail shortened after a fashion, the crisis was far from over. The wind was still rising—*Where's it all coming from?* Willis asked himself—the sea was steeper and the swell now short and heavy rather than moderate. With each gust the ship lurched over to leeward—and each time it seemed that she was never coming back. There was only one thing to do.

"Ballast!" he ordered, shouting to make himself heard above the screaming of the gale. "Put in . . . numbers two and three . . . double bottoms!"

"No!" bawled Darryl, his mouth an ugly hole in his fear-contorted face. "She's like a . . . bloody submarine . . . already!"

"Put them . . . in! Or we . . . capsize!"

"It's *your* . . . orders, Captain!"

"Yes. It's my . . . orders!"

"I . . . refuse. . . ."

But Taylor, the second mate, was already on the telephone to the engine room.

As the tanks filled the situation worsened, until Willis managed to turn the ship away from the wind, running free, his untidy apologies for sails goose-winged. He had been frightened, badly, by the free surface effect, knew that it had been the cause of the loss of more than one vessel. But with the gale astern she handled well, rolling easily. He kept her on this easterly course until the chief rang up to say that, according to the gauges, both tanks were now full. Willis brought her round then, slowly and carefully, until once again she was on an approximation to a port tack.

She was stable now, and the weight of the wind was no longer pushing her over. She was stable, but she was far too low in the water. The seas were breaking over her very superstructure, solid battering rams of water. Somehow the windows of the wheelhouse, to which the officers had retreated, were still holding. (The glass, of what Willis regarded still as his own time, would have shattered long since.) The funnel was gone, and nobody had seen it go. Miraculously the sails, together with their standing and running rigging, were surviving the beating they were taking.

Willis went to the telephone. "Chief," he said, "is there any way that you can pump diesel oil overside? On the weather side preferably?"

"Is there any way that you can stop water coming down the funnel? The engine room's damn nearly flooded!"

"That's what I'm trying to do, Chief."

"I see. But we've not all that much left, Captain, and we must have fuel for the jenny. . . ."

"Lube oil, then. . . . It might be better. . . . Just a trickle from the weather discharges. No more than a trickle. . . ."

A good vegetable oil, such as linseed, would have been better still, best of all, but there was none in the ship.

Still, the lubricating oil was better than nothing. Finally

the seas in *Pulpster*'s immediate vicinity were no longer breaking, were subjugated by that thin, very thin glistening film, heaving sullenly under the liquid integument. She staggered ahead, sluggish, low in the water, far too low in the water—but, as a tanker, she was safer than a dry cargo carrier would have been in like circumstances. She was making headway, and apart from an occasional slop with no weight to it she was shipping no water, and although the sails were showing signs of wear and tear they were still holding.

She made headway, and toward midnight the wind moderated and the ballast tanks were pumped and the sails unbrailed.

For the rest of the voyage there was what Willis referred to as his "air umbrella." And then there was the tug, fussily efficient, which came roaring up over the horizon, whose skipper told Willis that he had been ordered to take *Pulpster* in tow. Willis replied that he was the only one who gave orders aboard his ship, and at last the tug went away.

And the wind backed, west to southwest, and finally to south, and as it came round so did Willis, keeping the ship on the port tack, bringing her back in toward the coast. With the shift of wind the sky cleared again and he was able to obtain good astronomical fixes. At last he raised Macquarie Light at its maximum range, allowing for his height of eye, of thirty miles.

He stood in confidently. He knew that he would make the Heads by daylight. The life raft transceiver had been repaired and he made contact with Harbor Control. He said, "My E.T.A. at the Heads is 0600 hours. I require tugs to assist me in berthing. I have no main engines. Please tell tugs to meet me off the Fairway Buoy."

"I have instructions for you, Captain, from your owners. The tug *Kurraba* will meet you off the Fairway Buoy and take you to an anchorage on the bank. You are to remain there until you are in a fit state to come alongside. Shore labor will be sent out to you."

"In that case," said Willis, "please instruct *Kurraba* only to stand by me. I shall sail in to the anchorage."

"Good on yer, mate," said Harbor Control.

Darryl groaned.

"Our lords and masters," said Captain Dalby, the old marine superintendent, "are displeased with you. Very displeased, Captain."

"I did what I thought best, sir. After all, the cost of a deep sea tow—"

"—is not much compared with the loss of your ship's services for several days." The old man started to tick items off on his fingers. "Then there are two nylon dracones—ruined. Four mooring lines—likewise. *And* the damage done by your engineer in his mad search for metal fitting for your sails. Oh, yes. *And* your collision with that ferry in the West Channel."

"She shouldn't have come so close, sir. She could see that I was under sail."

"Nonetheless, you are far from popular—except with the press and the various newsreels. It is lucky for you that your fantastic voyage—one of them called it that—coincided with a shortage of *important* news."

"I was certainly surprised at the audience I had to watch me come in."

"Even so, I strongly advise you to write out your resignation."

Willis got to his feet. He felt sorry for himself—and sorrier for Jane. He had been given a chance—and because of his stubborn pride had muffed it. He would never be able to make a living in this brave, new, automated world in which ships were nothing but machines and their masters only drivers.

"Good-by," he said stiffly. "I'd better be getting along to the Employment Bureau."

"Not so fast, Captain Willis."

"Does the general manager want to fire me in person?"

Dalby smiled grimly. "He'd like to, but he daren't. There's been far too much press coverage. Romance isn't quite dead, you know." He looked at Willis over his steepled, bony fingers. "Don't you want to know about your next job?"

"Admiral, I suppose. At the main entrance to the Hilton-Australia."

Dalby laughed. "You'll still be 'captain'—but your starting pay will be better than what you've been getting with us."

"Not the trans-Tasman hovercraft?"

"No. But the pay and conditions of chief seamanship instructor at the Captain Cook Nautical Academy aren't to be sneezed at. And—this will please you—there's talk of building a training schooner. . . ."

"Thank you," said Willis at last.

"Don't thank me," Dalby told him. "Thank yourself. And your luck."

BLACK IS BEAUTIFUL

By Robert Silverberg

my nose is flat my lips are thick my hair is frizzy my skin is black
is beautiful
is black is beautiful
I am James Shabazz age seventeen born august 13 1933 I am black I am afro I am beautiful this machine writes my words as I speak them and the machine is black
is beautiful

Elijah Muhammad's *The Supreme Wisdom* says: *Separation of the so-called Negroes from their slave master's children is a MUST. It is the only SOLUTION to our problem. It was the only solution, according to the Bible, for Israel and the Egyptians, and it will prove to be the only solution for America and her slaves, whom she mockingly calls her citizens, without granting her citizenship. We must keep this in our minds at all times that we are actually being mocked.*

Catlike, moving as a black panther would, James Shabazz stalked through the city. It was late summer, and the pumps were working hard, sucking the hot air out from under the Manhattan domes and squirting it into the suburbs. There had been a lot of grinding about that lately. Whitey out there complained that all that hot air was wilting his lawns and making his own pumps work too hard. Screw Whitey, thought James Shabazz pleasantly. Let his lawns wilt. Let him complain. Let him get black in the face with complaining. Do the mother some good.

Silently, pantherlike, down Fifth Avenue to Fifty-third, across to Park, down Park to Forty-eighth. Just looking around. A big boy, sweat-shiny, black but not black enough to suit him. He wore a gaudy five-colored danshiki, beads from Mali, flowing white belled trousers, a neat goatee, a golden earring. In his left rear pocket: a beat-up copy of the new novel about Malcolm. In his right rear pocket: a cute little sonic blade.

Saturday afternoon and the air was quiet. None of the hopterbuses coming through the domes and dumping Whitey onto the rooftops. They stayed home today, the commuters, the palefaces. Saturday and Sunday, the city was black. Likewise all the other days of the week after 4 P.M. Run, Whitey, run! See Whitey run! Why does Whitey run? Because he don't belong here no more.

Sorry, teach. I shouldn't talk like that no more, huh?

James Shabazz smiled. The identity card in his pocket called him James Lincoln, but when he walked alone through the city he spurned that name. The slave master name. His parents stuck with it, proud of it, telling him that no black should reject a name like Lincoln. The dumb geeps! What did they think, that great-great-grandpappy was owned by Honest Abe? Lincoln was a tag some belching hillbilly stuck on the family a hundred fifty years ago. If anyone asks me today, I'm James Shabazz. Black. Proud of it.

Black faces mirrored him on every street. Toward him came ten diplomats in tribal robes, not Afros but Africans, a bunch of Yorubas, Ibos, Baules, Mandingos, Ashantis, Senufos, Bakongos, Balubas, who knew what, the real thing, anyway, black as night, so black they looked purple. No slave master blood in them! James Shabazz smiled, nodded. Good afternoon, brothers. Nice day! They took no notice of him, but swept right on, their conversation unbroken. They were not speaking Swahili, which he would have recognized, but some other foreign language, maybe

French. He wasn't sure. He scowled after them. Who they think they are, walking around a black man's city, upnosing people like that?

He studied his reflection for a while in the burnished window of a jewelry shop. Ground floor, Martin Luther King Building. Eighty stories of polished black marble. Black. Black man's money built that tower! Black man's sweat!

Overhead came the buzz of a hopter after all. No commuters today, so they had to be tourists. James Shabazz stared up at the beetle of a hopter crossing the dull translucent background of the distant dome. It landed on the penthouse hopter stage of the King Building. He crossed the street and tried to see the palefaces stepping out, but the angle was too steep. Even so, he bowed ceremoniously. Welcome, massa! Welcome to the black man's metropolis! Soul food for lunch? Real hot jazz on 125th? Dancing jigaboo girls stripping at the Apollo? Sightseeing tour of Bedford-Stuyvesant and Harlem?

Can't tell where Bedford-Stuyvesant ends and Harlem begins, can you? But you'll come looking anyway.

Like to cut your guts up, you honkie mothers.

Martin Luther King said in Montgomery, Alabama, instructing the bus desegregators:

If cursed, do not curse back. If pushed, do not push back. If struck, do not strike back, but evidence love and good will at all times.

He sat down for a while in Lumumba Park, back of the Forty-second Street Library, to watch the girls go by. The new summer styles were something pretty special: Congo Revival, plenty of beads and metal coils, but not much clothing except a sprayon sarong around the middle. There was a lot of grumbling by the old people. But how could you tell a handsome Afro girl that she shouldn't show her beautiful black breasts in public? Did they cover the boobies in the Motherland? Not until the missionaries came. Christ can't stand a pair of bares. The white girls cover up because they don't got much up there. Or maybe to keep from getting sunburned.

He admired the parade of proud jiggling black globes. The girls smiled to themselves as they cut through the park. They all wore their hair puffed out tribal style, and some of them even with little bone doodads thrust through it. There was no reason to be afraid of looking too primitive any more. James Shabazz winked, and some of them winked back. A few of the girls kept eyes fixed rigidly ahead; plainly it was an ordeal for them to strip down this way. Most of them enjoyed it as much as the men did. The park was full of men enjoying the show. James Shabazz wished they'd bring those honkie tourists here. He'd love a chance to operate on a few of them.

Gradually he became aware of a huge, fleshy, exceedingly black man with grizzled white hair, sitting across the way pretending to be reading his paper, but really stealing peeks at the cuties going by. James Shabazz recognized him: Powell 43X Nissim, Coordinating Chairman of the Afro-Muslim Popular Democratic Party of Greater New York. He was one of the biggest men in the city, politically—maybe even more important than Mayor Abdulrahman himself. He was also a good friend of the father of James Shabazz, who handled some of Powell 43X's legal work. Four or five times a year he came around to discuss some delicate point, and stayed far into the night, drinking pot after pot of black coffee and telling jokes in an uproarious bellow. Most of his jokes were anti-black; he could tell them like any Kluxer. James Shabazz looked on him as coarse, vulgar, seamy, out of date, an old-line pol. But yet you had to respect a man with that much power.

Powell 43X Nissim peered over the top of his *Amsterdam News,* saw him, let out a whoop, and yelled, "Hey, Jimmy Lincoln! What you doin' here?"

James Shabazz stood up and walked stiffly over. "Getting me some fresh air, sir."

"Been working at the library, huh? Studying hard? Gonna be the first nigger president, maybe?"

"No, sir. Just walkin' around on a Saturday."

"Ought to be in the library," Powell 43X said. "Read. Learn. That's how we got where we are. You think we took over this city because we a bunch of dumb niggers?" He let out a colossal laugh. "We *smart,* man!"

James Shabazz wanted to say, "We took over the city because Whitey ran out. He dumped it on us, is all. Didn't take no brains, just staying power."

Instead he said, "I got a little time to take it easy yet, sir. I don't go to college for another year."

"Columbia, huh?"

"You bet. Class of '05, that's me."

"You gonna fool with football when you get to college?"

"Thought I would."

"You listen to me," said Powell 43X. "Football's okay for high school. You get yourself into politics instead up there. Debating team. Malcolm X Society. Afro League. Smart boy like you, you got a career in government ahead of you if you play it right." He jerked his head to one side and indicated a girl striding by. "You get to be somebody, maybe you'll have a few of those to play with." He laughed. The girl was almost six feet tall, majestic, deep black, with great heavy swinging breasts and magnificent buttocks switching saucily from side to side beneath her sprayon wrap. Conscious that all eyes were on her, she crossed the park on the diagonal, heading for the Sixth Avenue side. Suddenly three whites appeared at the park entrance: weekend visitors, edgy, conspicuous. As the black girl went past them, one turned, gaping, his eyes following the trajectory of her outthrust nipples. He was a wiry redhead, maybe twenty years old, in town for a good time in boogieville, and you could see the hunger popping out all over him.

"Honkie mother," James Shabazz muttered. "Could use a blade you know where."

Powell 43X clucked his tongue. "Easy, there. Let him look! What it hurt you if he thinks she's worth lookin' at?"

"Don't belong here. No right to look. Why can't they stay where they belong?"

"Jimmy—"

"Honkies right in Times Square! Don't they know this here's our city?"

Marcus Garvey said:

The Negro needs a Nation and a country of his own, where he can best show evidence of his own ability in the art of human progress. Scattered as an unmixed and unrecognized part of alien nations and civilizations is but to demonstrate his imbecility, and point him out as an unworthy derelict, fit neither for the society of Greek, Jew, or Gentile.

While he talked with Powell 43X, James Shabazz kept one eye on the honkie from the suburbs. The redhead and his two pals cut out in the direction of Forty-first Street. James Shabazz excused himself finally and drifted away, toward that side of the park. Old windbag, he thought. Nothing but a Tom underneath. Tolerance for the honkies! When did they tolerate *us?*

Easy, easy, like a panther. Walk slow and quiet.

Follow the stinking mother. Show him how it really is.

Malcolm X said:

Always bear in mind that our being in the Western hemisphere differs from anyone else, because everyone else came here voluntarily. Everyone that you see in this part of the world got on a boat and came here voluntarily; whether they were immigrants or what have you, they came here voluntarily. So they don't have any real squawk, because they got what they were looking for. But you and I can squawk because we didn't come here voluntarily. We didn't ask to be brought here. We were brought here forcibly, against our will, and in chains. And at no time since we have been here, have they even acted like they wanted us here. At no time. At no time have they ever tried to pretend that we were brought here to be citizens. Why, they don't even pretend. *So why should we pretend?*

The cities had been theirs for fifteen or twenty years. It had been a peaceful enough conquest. Each year there were fewer whites and more blacks, and the whites kept moving out, and the blacks kept getting born, and one day Harlem was as far south as Seventy-second Street, and Bedford-Stuyvesant had slopped over into Flatbush and Park Slope, and there was a black mayor and a black city council, and that was it. In New York the tipping point had come about 1986. There was a special problem there, because of the Puerto Ricans, who thought of themselves as a separate community; but they were outnumbered, and most of them finally decided it was cooler to have a city of their own. They took Yonkers, the way the Mexicans took San Diego. What it shuffled down to, in the end, was a city about eighty-five per cent black and ten per cent Puerto, with some isolated pockets of whites who stuck around out of stubbornness or old age or masochism or feelings of togetherness with their black brothers. Outside the city were the black suburbs, like Mount Vernon and Newark and New Rochelle, and beyond them, fifty, eighty, a hundred miles out, were the towns of the whites. It was apartheid in reverse.

The honkie commuters still came into the city, those who had to, quick-in quick-out, do your work and scram. There weren't many of them, really, a hundred thousand a day or so. The white ad agencies were gone north. The white magazines had relocated editorial staffs in the green suburbs. The white book publishers had followed the financial people out. Those who came in were corporate executives, presiding over all-black staffs; trophy whites, kept around by liberal-minded blacks for decoration; government employees, trapped by desegregation edicts; and odds and ends of other sorts, all out of place, all scared.

It was a black man's city. It was pretty much the same all across the country. Adjustments had been made.

Stokely Carmichael said:

We are oppressed as a group because we are black, not

because we are lazy, not because we're apathetic, not because we're stupid, not because we smell, not because we eat watermelon and have good rhythm. We are oppressed because we are black, and in order to get out of that oppression, one must feel the group power that one has. . . . If there's going to be any integration it's going to be a two-way thing. If you believe in integration, you can come live in Watts. You can send your children to the ghetto schools. Let's talk about that. If you believe in integration, then we're going to start adopting us some white people to live in our neighborhood. . . .

We are not gonna wait for white people to sanction black power. We're tired of waiting.

South of Forty-second Street things were pretty quiet on a Saturday, or any other time. Big tracts of the city were still empty. Some of the office buildings had been converted into apartment houses to catch the overflow, but a lot of them were still awaiting development. It took time for a black community to generate enough capital to run a big city, and though it was happening fast, it wasn't happening fast enough to make use of all the facilities the whites had abandoned. James Shabazz walked silently through silence, keeping his eyes on the three white boys who strolled, seemingly aimlessly, a block ahead of him.

He couldn't dig why more tourists didn't get cut up. Hardly any of them did, except those who got drunk and pawed some chick. The ones who minded their own business were left alone, because the top men had passed the word that the sightseers were okay, that they injected cash into the city and shouldn't be molested. It amazed James Shabazz that everybody listened. Up at the Audubon, somebody would get up and read from Stokely or Malcolm or one of the other black martyrs, and call for a holy war on Whitey, really socking it to 'em. Civil rights! Equality! Black power! Retribution for four hundred years of slavery! Break down the ghetto walls! Keep the faith, baby! Tell it how it is! All about the exploitation of the black man, the exclusion of the Afros from the lily-white suburbs, the concentration of economic power in Whitey's hands. And the audience would shout amen and stomp its feet and sing hymns, but nobody would ever do anything. *Nobody would ever do anything.* He couldn't understand that. Were they satisfied to live in a city with an invisible wall around it? Did they really think they had it so good? They talked about owning New York, and maybe they did, but didn't they know that it was all a fraud, that Whitey had given them the damn city just so they'd stay out of *his* back yard?

Someday we gonna run things. Not the Powell 43X cats and the other Toms, but *us.* And we gonna keep the city, but we gonna take what's outside, too.

And none of this crap about honkie mothers coming in to look our women over.

James Shabazz noted with satisfaction that the three white boys were splitting up. Two of them were going into Penn Station to grab the tube home, looked like. The third was the redhead, and he was standing by himself on Seventh Avenue, looking up at Uhuru Stadium, which he probably called Madison Square Garden. Good boy. Dumb enough to leave yourself alone. Now I gonna teach you a thing or two.

He moved forward quickly.

Robert F. Williams said:

When an oppressed people show a willingness to defend themselves, the enemy, who is a moral weakling and coward, is more willing to grant concessions and work for a respectable compromise.

He walked up smiling and said, "Hi, man. I'm Jimmy Lincoln."

Whitey looked perplexed. "Hi, man."

"You lookin' for some fun, I bet."

"Just came in to see the city a little."

"To find some fun. Lots of great chicks around here." Jimmy Lincoln winked broadly. "You can't kid me none. I go for 'em too. Where you from, Red?"

"Nyack."

"That's upstate somewhere, huh?"

"Not so far. Just over the bridge. Rockland County."

"Yeah. Nice up there, I bet. I never seen it."

"Not so different from down here. Buildings are smaller, that's all. Just as crowded."

"I bet they got a different looking skin in Nyack," said Jimmy Lincoln. He laughed. "I bet I right, huh?"

The red-haired boy laughed too. "Well, I guess you are."

"Come on with me. I find you some fun. You and me. What's your name?"

"Tom."

"Tom. That's a good one. Lookee, Tom, I know a place, lots of girls, something to drink, a pill to pop, real soul music, yeah? Eh, man? Couple blocks from here. You came here to see the city, let me show it to you. Right?"

"Well—" uneasily.

"Don't be so up tight, man. You don't trust your black brother? Look, we got no feud with you. All that stuff's ancient history! You got to realize this is the year 2000, we all free men, we got what we after. Nobody gonna hurt you." Jimmy Lincoln moved closer and winked confidentially. "Lemme tell you something, too. That red hair of yours, the girls gonna orbit over that! They don't see that kind hair every day. Them freckles. Them blue eyes. Man, blue eyes, it turn them on! You in for the time of your life!"

Tom from Nyack grinned. He pointed toward Penn Station. "I came in with two pals. They went home, the geeps! Tomorrow they're going to feel awful dopey about that."

"You know they will," said Jimmy Lincoln.

They walked west, across Eighth Avenue, across Ninth, into the redevelopment area where the old warehouses had been ripped down. Signs sprouting from the acreage of rubble proclaimed that the Afro-American Cultural Center would shortly rise here. Just now the area looked bombed out. Tom from Nyack frowned as if he failed to see where a swinging night club was likely to be located in this district. Jimmy Lincoln led him up to Thirty-fifth Street and around the hollow shell of a not quite demolished building.

"Almost there?" Tom asked.

"We here right now, man."

"Up against that wall, that's where," said James Shabazz. The sonic blade glided into his hand. He studded it and it began to whir menacingly. In a quiet voice he said, "Honkie, I saw you look at a black girl a little while ago like you might just be thinking about what's between her legs. You shouldn't think thoughts like that about black girls. You got an itch, man, you scratch it on your own kind. I think I'm gonna fix you so you don't itch no more."

Minister James 3X said:

First, there is fear—first and foremost there is inborn fear, and hatred for the black man. There is a feeling on the part of the white man of inferiority. He thinks within himself that the black man is the best man.

The white man is justified in feeling that way because he has discovered that he is weaker than the black man. His mental power is less than that of the black man—he has only six ounces of brain and the Original Man has seven-and-a-half ounces. . . . The white man's physical power is one-third less than that of the black man.

He had never talked this long with a honkie before. You didn't see all that many of them about, when you spent your time in high school. But now he stared into those frightened blue eyes and watched the blood drain from the scruffy white skin and he felt power welling up inside himself. He was Chaka Zulu and Malcolm and Stokely and Nkrumah and Nat Turner and Lumumba all rolled into one. He, James Shabazz, was going to lead the new black revolution, and he was going to begin by sacrificing this cowering honkie. Through his mind rolled the magnificent phrases of his prophets. He heard them talking, yes, Adam and Ras Tafari and Floyd, heard them singing down the ages out of Africa, kings in chains, martyrs, the great ones, he heard Elijah Muhammad and Muhammad Ali, Marcus Garvey, Sojourner Truth, du Bois, Henry Garnet, Rap Brown, rattling the chains, shouting for freedom, and all of them telling him, go on, man, how long you want to be a nigger anyhow? Go on! You think you got it so good? You gonna go to college, get a job, live in a house, eat steak and potatoes, and that's enough, eh, nigger, even if you can't set foot in Nyack, Peekskill, Wantaugh, Suffern, Morristown? Be happy with what you got, darkie! You got more than we ever did, so why bitch about things? You got a city! You got power! You got freedom! It don't matter that they call you an ape. Don't matter that they don't let you near their daughters. Don't matter that you never seen Nyack. Be grateful for what you got, man, is that the idea?

He heard their cosmic laughter, the thunder of their derision.

And he moved toward Tom the honkie and said, "Here's where the revolution gets started again. Trash like you fooling with our women, you gonna get a blade in the balls. You go home to Nyack and give 'em that message, man."

Tom said lamely, "Look out behind you!"

James Shabazz laughed and began to thrust the blade home, but the anesthetic dart caught him in the middle of the back and his muscles surrendered, and the blade fell, and he turned as he folded up and saw the black policeman with the dart gun in his black fist, and he realized that he had known all along that this was how it would turn out, and he couldn't say he really cared.

Robert Moses of SNCC was questioned in May 1962 on the voter registration drive in Mississippi:

Q. Mr. Moses, did you know a Herbert Lee?

A. Yes, he was a Negro farmer who lived near Liberty.

Q. Would you tell the Committee what Mr. Lee was doing and what happened?

A. He was killed on September 25th. That morning I was in McComb. The Negro doctor came by the voter registration office to tell us he had just taken a bullet out of a Negro's head. We went over to see who it was because I thought it was somebody in the voting program, and were able to identify the man as Mr. Herbert Lee, who had attended our classes and driven us around the voting area, visiting other farmers.

Powell 43X Nissim said heavily, folding his hands across his paunch, "I got you off because you're your daddy's son. But you try a fool thing like that again, I gon' let them put you away."

James Shabazz said nothing.

"What you think you was doing, anyway, Jimmy? You know we watch all the tourists. We can't afford to let them get cut up. There was tracers on that kid all the time."

"I didn't know."

"You sit there mad as hell, thinking I should have let you cut him. You know who you really would have cut? Jimmy Lincoln, that's who. We still got jails. Black judges know the law too. You get ruined for life, a thing like that. And what for?"

"To show the honkie a thing or two."

"Jimmy, Jimmy, Jimmy! What's to show? We got the whole city!"

"Why can't we live outside?"

"Because we don't *want* to. Those of us who can afford it, even, we stay here. They got laws against discrimination in this country. We stay here because we like it with our own kind. Even the black millionaries, and don't think there ain't plenty of 'em. We got a dozen men, they could *buy* Nyack. They stay."

"And why do you stay?"

"I'm in politics," said Powell 43X, "You know what a power base means? I got to stay where my people are. I don't care about living with the whites."

"You talk like you aren't even sore about it," James Shabazz said. "Don't you hate Whitey?"

"No. I don't hate no one."

"We all hate Whitey!"

"Only you hate Whitey," said Powell 43X. "And that's because you don't know nothin' yet. The time of hating's over, Jimmy. We got to be practical. You know, we got ourselves a good deal now, and we ain't gon' get more by burning nobody. Well, maybe the Stock Exchange moved to Connecticut, and a lot of banks and stuff like that, but *we run the city*. Black men. Black men hold the mortgages. We got a black upper crust here now. Fancy shops for black folk, fancy restaurants, black banks, gorgeous mosques. Nobody oppressing us now. When a mortgage gets foreclosed these days, it's a *black* man doin' the foreclosin'. Black men ownin' the sweatshops. Ownin' the hockshops. Good and bad, we got the city, Jimmy. And maybe this is the way it's meant to be: us in the cities, them outside."

"You talk like a Tom!"

"And you talk like a fool." Powell 43X chuckled. "Jimmy, wake up! We all Toms today. We don't do revolutions now."

"I go to the Audubon," James Shabazz said. "I listen to them speak. They talk revolution there. They don't sound like no Toms to me!"

"It's all politics, son. Talk big, yell for equality. It don't make sense to let a good revolution die. They do it for show. A man don't get anywhere politickin' in black New York by sayin' that everything's one hundred per cent all right in the world. And you took all that noise seriously? You didn't know that they just shoutin' because it's part of the routine? You went out to spear you a honkie? I figured you for smarter than that. Look, you all mixed up, boy. A smart man, black or white, he don't mess up a good deal for himself, even if he sometimes say he *want* to change everything all around. You full of hate, full of dreams. When you grow up, you'll understand. Our problem, it's not how to get out into the suburbs, it's how to keep Whitey from wanting to come back and live in here! We got to keep what we got. We got it pretty good. Who oppressing you, Jimmy? You a slave? Wake up! And now you understand the system a little better, clear your rear end outa my office. I got to phone up the mayor and have a little talk."

Jimmy Lincoln stumbled out, stunned, shaken. His eyes felt hot and his tongue was dry. The system? The *system?* How cynical could you get? The whole revolution phony? All done for show?

No. No. No. No.

He wanted to smash down the King Building with his fists. He wanted to see buildings ablaze, as in the old days when the black man was still fighting for what ought to be his.

I don't believe it, he thought. Not any of it. I'm not gonna stop fighting for my rights. I'm gonna live to see us overcome. I won't sell out like the others. Not me!

And then he thought maybe he was being a little dumb. Maybe Powell 43X was right: there wasn't anything left worth fighting for, and only a dopey kid would take the slogans at face value. He tried to brush that thought out of his head. If Powell 43X was right, everything he had read was a lot of crap. Stokely. Malcolm. All the great martyrs. Just so much ancient history.

He stepped out into the summer haze. Overhead, a hopterbus was heading for the suburbs. He shook his fist at it; and instantly he felt foolish for the gesture, and wondered why he felt foolish. And knew. And beneath his rebellious fury, began to suspect that one day he'd give into the system too. But not yet. Not yet!

time to do my homework now

machine, spell everything right today's essay is on black power as a revolutionary force I am James Lincoln, Class 804, Frederick Douglass High School put that heading on the page yeah

the concept of black power as a revolutionary force first was heard during the time of oppression forty years ago, when

crap on that, machine we better hold it until I know what I going to say

I am James Shabazz age seventeen born august 13 1983 I am black I am afro I am beautiful

black is beautiful

let's start over, machine
let's make an outline first
black power its origin its development the martyrdoms and lynchings the first black mayors the black congressmen and senators the black cities and then talk about black power as a continuing thing, the never-ending revolution no matter what pols like 43X say, never give in never settle for what they give you never sell out
that's it, machine
black power
black power
black
black is beautiful

TAKE IT OR LEAVE IT

By David I. Masson

2000. 223. 08,42. Out of bed wrong side today. Trouble was, drier was cold. Following my shower, a freezing gale. Called up the man but took two hours to get through, and when I did get his ugly face on the screen he said it'll be ten days till they can show up. Maggy says why not use the holiday wraps—toweling should absorb enough moisture if you rub and pat a bit—and pep the washroom up to 30. Suppose that'll do. Have to. Then meanwhile the hairstyler got a bit cranky and aligned my second lock in front of my shoulder instead of the sine curve I've been used to, sod it. Johnny had to open his pharynx about it, too, young bug: "Your hair's skew, Dad!" Denise kidded me it was the sparrows. Maggy says I must have moved. One of these days *I* can tell, this is going to be. I hope *you're* functioning anyway, sodding tape-set; play you back and see. . . . Good. And then when I pressed the news button I thought, I bet this'll be black and so it was; this is, as black as they ever leak. As usual, the British news was cushy, only the exter news leaked much. Thousands dead in American riots, some of them fried by the cops and feds. (Our only rinse, never heard of frying here.) Same thing in Japan and China and Russia, more or less. Between the lines, inter looked bad too: "The disorganization in Beata is under active control. Prospective traffic from other megalopolises is advised to contact the police by prior call, during the next ten days." I've heard that one before. No motivation to visit in Beata, luckily. Then the weathercast: why they have to keep the rain off the south and west and let it chuck it down all over Midlandia and the north I don't know. I suppose the agric zones have to have their sun, but why at our expense? Depressing, I call it. All very well for the uppercrust with their ion fountains and their sunlighting.

Another day. Looks like showers. Feels like showers, too, from the ache in my bones. Sun's still up in the north at the day-ends, shouldn't be summer's end for a month or two. How you feeling, Maggy love?

Well, stir the kids and see if they can't find some hips. In spite of that cat last night, my innards are grumbling, dunno 'bout yours. . . .

Look sharp, John. That hedge'll have something on it by now. Watch out for the Gibsons, though. Now they've settled in the old helicopter, their Larry goes prowling early, and he's grown up real strong. I've seen him down that far. Couple of stones set him off last time, but it won't always, and if you and him was to meet up there suddenly on your own, I wouldn't back you, boy. Take the big catapult and four-five stones, do for a cat as well if you see one. The old fence post'll come in handy too. We'll be OK. with the aerial and the branch.

Wish my father had bought me a non-wind waterproof watch. It would have lasted through the river, and I'd know where we were so to speak. I think Mike Gibson must have one. Seen him looking at his wrist.

Have to look out a new battery if it gets much colder. You don't know how to start a fire properly, do you, Jane? Denise'll show you next time. First cool day after a dry stretch, we'll have one; some of the doors and chairs'll burn nicely, on the drive. Keep the bugs away too; if we leave a bit smoldering on the porch; too many in already. So long as we can keep the ants out. Plug the crack in the door with clay, Denise, and open the other door if it gets hot.

09,10. Johnny and Denise "blasted off" to the schoolab. Never guess they were fraternal twins if I didn't know. The pre-inductee center's only five hundred meters off, but I worry sometimes. Jane's infant center doesn't operate since the barons wrecked it the other night, but she looks in on edscreen here instead. Just now she's working on her "tartriper." This is what she used to call her talkwriter. She needs motivationing, though. According to Maggy it's correctioning she wants; Maggy's too hard on her.

Maggy's set the clensomat and called up the instruction program she's on about now—what is it? light-sculptation. I suppose this means she'll be on at me to get her a lightsculptor for Christmas. It's time I called up supplies, not to mention the programing for the old megastore. This batch has to be a bugged sample. Which reminds me: I have to check up again for bugs on our own cartons; I don't fancy guinea-pigging for other firms. Maggy doesn't know all their little dodges yet. Then I'll have to mission the megastore this afternoon, I suppose.

I do hope Denise and Johnny are all right. . . . No one would take them for fraternals, she images at least a year older; so we get all these disapproving stares when we're togethering, from people that don't have big families. Maggy decisioned to have Jane prior to her implant skinpill (she was getting allergic to the sniff method)—she said a third would keep the twins from fighting, when it grew up a bit, and it's true they don't resonate. . . . Someone actually propositioned Denise by paternoster three the other day. It's these eyes, this height, this sexational hair. Took her for an inductee, shouldn't wonder. Better than sexmurder, anyway.

Time for calling the megastore. My sight-aid? Here. . . .

That ceiling's leaking. The rafter's rotten above, I think. What say we look around for another pad? House-hunting's hopeless I know; places standing all occupied. Still, search around might turn up something. Don't say anything to Jane, I'll just have a wander, soon as John gets back.

Isn't that Mike Gibson up the hill? Coming through the old gap? Hope he hasn't seen John. Denise, climb upstairs and have a look round. Give that whistle if you want me up—Hell, there goes another meal; I'd have hit it if I hadn't been looking after Gibson; cats always shoot past the gate now. Try and get that thrush, Maggy, your aim's better.

10,05. Mail buzzer. First for six days. It was from Jim. A bit cagey, but clear Jessie's not herself and *something* shorted with Bill. Jim never got this tape of mine, day 205, it seems. It was the mail strike, I bet. I'll try a remake. Reach him in five days, say. Or shall I just call him up?

10,31. No good. Been trying half hour now. Half the channels are this way nowadays. I wonder, now, would it be quicker just to transportation it and visit with him? Let's see: the block; the transir—say half hour; the integrator, say twenty min; the H.V.T., one hundred fifty kilometers, say half hour with acse and dece; at his end it's multimode—say another half. Half-hour visiting—or say hour with lunch. Be back mid-afternoon, look in the megastore, O.K. Maggy. . . .

10,41. She thought she could negative-pressure me, huh. No, I must mission him. Two-legs better. Calling-up's hopeless, this channel. So long as he's in. Can leave a notation, if he's out. Take my notation-set, in case. Or get a spare one at a store his way: I'm not a nupe-watcher, if I'm shedding all this credit another nine pound won't sink me. Even get a cassette and leave a tape after all. What'll I get into? The yellow has this hole the time the barons—Maggy forgot to put it in the automend. No negentropy, this ma has; place is like a disability home. The old green, then. The red waywear, and carry floorwear, because he likes his floor cold. And sod it, I'll take *you;* might want to record something while it's hot, in transit. But Jim's I'll buy, if necessary. Set the responsomat for the megastore, in case. Be off in a micro.

Got him! . . . Give it to Ma, Jane. Well you hit it, you eat it; you can pick it too!—Hey, was that—? . . . What-is-it, Denise? See something? . . . Yes, working round the back he is. Maybe it's a dog he's seen. Or a fox. Well, I wouldn't whistle; never hear us through the pane, catch is all rusted up, and I don't want to smash the glass just yet; besides, John's blocked by those two buildings, he'd never hear anyway. Still, might turn Gibson. You run downstairs and scream through the doorway—just once. Then if I whistle scream again. Quick now—he's creeping back.

Whhh!!

Too sharp he is, give me that aerial and a cata. Run up and lookout till one of us comes back.

11,17. Ran up against Mike Gibson from the next block; he was queuing for the transir. Why don't you visit with us more often, he said. Says Larry's doing fine. Told him I was off to Jim's, but the transir intervaled us too far to finish the story. This higher-pigment type had slid between us, what Maggy's programs call a real overtan—h'mhm. . . . Mike, as I was saying—oh here comes the terminal.

11,38. This must be a hill over there. Wonder where it is. It's all cultured, too, and the lumimobile gives it panash. Sodding rain, you *need* a splash of color. . . . Travel broadens the mind. . . . Should've brought the instruxopak . . . . I'll turn on the woosic.

12,11. This auto method's fine. Last time it was self-drive waycars all the way. Of course you can personalization this kind, too. Nice and low-volume, too.

Do you know, I could have sworn this ma in the integrator called me a garnet, under her breath. Just because of this lot re the higher-pigment type. . . . How about the car woosic, now?

What the hell are you skulking up there for? . . . Mind your own business and I'll mind mine! . . . You move a step and I'll murder you, you thug! . . . You dare move another step and I'll bash your face in! . . . Keep off our manor you thieving bastard or I'll bash your head in! . . . Don't you dare come down any further! . . . You come past that house and I'll lay your face open! . . . And you're another! . . . Scared are you, got to have your bloody brat to face me out, have you? Ya, Larry, that's right, come rushing down, two against one, that's right! . . All right, don't you two come any further! You keep to your own manor, let me stay in mine! . . . Attack women, would you? Threaten a woman, eh? Maggy's worth two of you. Give it 'em, Maggy! . . . By hell, this is our house and the man that lays a finger on the hedge'll be the last thing he ever does! . . . Go home you bastards! Ya! Home! Ya!! Home!! Ya!!! Home!!! Virus get you, you bastards!!!

Hell, that was a near thing. I'm hoarse—aren't you. Maggy? Thank you for turning up. I think John got away. Here he is, round the back. My, we drew 'em off OK, didn't we? Lucky they hadn't any catas. Johnny my son, you made it. What, you got a—two hedgehogs, by hell! Smashing! Did they see you really, do you think? Who cares anyway, we're all safe and sound and two hedgehogs to the good. John, you're a master! No, Denise, they won't dare come right down. I think it was your mother that really put the fear of hell into them. Now what do you say to a fire and clay bake? Johnny can keep a lookout at the front, just in case. Denise, you can be cook.

13,02. I'm at Jim's. I'm putting *you* on, so's we can have a record of our visit. Jessie's off to rest, but we can dialogue.

"You saw what she's like. It started over Bill."

What happened?

"They beat him up. Bill. Barons. Working for the estate mafia *and* having a bit of fun on their own this time, I opinion. Last winter. Left him for dead near the lift shaft. Health squad got him in. Ended up in a cereb forty kilometers out—"

How's this?—where did you say?

"A cereb—a casualty home. He's not classified for

rehabilitation, only minimal prosthetics. So he's there for good. I've been businessing all on my own ever since. Jessie visitationed twice: *this* set her back. Then she started thinking the mafia were after Juju—and him no more than an infant. Besides, I've always kept right side of them—monster gifts from the store, forgetting to program debits, exetra. And I'm all right with the block king too. A J.C.O. he is—Junior Cleansing Officer. He's all right if you stand dead still when he passes by, and stand him a drink at the drinkateria. It's the ones with sexational wives and daughters need to worry. . . . No, the block king and the mafia are on my side. No fear there. Couldn't get Jessie to see it, though.

"Then she started saying she was a wicked woman, she'd neglected Bill, been the cause of it all, wasn't worthy to live. By spring, I couldn't do anything with her, she wouldn't take any telemedication, or even let me connection the diagnosticator. In the end I hooked the doctor (twenty thousand to care up onto, he's hard to get) and he got her certified for temporary care. I was at my wit's end re Juju; even when she was here I was scared she'd do something to him; but in the end I got Cousin Amy to mission up and care onto him. I only managed to visitation Jessie once, prior to the H.V.T. engineers' strike. Then she came back around day 180, but she's still to be sedationed. They say she classificationed against metapsychic drugs, otherwise she'd have been rehabilitationed long ago. Agitated depression, they call it. Juju's picked up a mob of fears from her kinky ways."

But she'll reclamation in time, with you, I expect?

"A year or two, they said. And then things aren't ideal here. The block alarm is pooff. Someone smashed it. If the corridor T.V.'s haven't registered the trouble, you have to call up the cops yourself—if the channel's functioning. Takes ten minutes to get through, average. And they won't act if they think it's a mafia job."

Sod it, I've left it fine. Got to get back and take in the megastore today. Your wall-chron's slow by my wrist-chron. Listen, try and call me up every five-ten days. You might get better luck than I did on the channel. I'll just look in on Jessie and off.

Maggy, I think I've found it. About an hour from here. It's an old garage block, top of a hill. The house is fallen in, but the garages are O.K. Faces southeast. Good view all round. Marshy below the hill. That'll keep 'em off. Woods, old orchards, on the slope. Nettles, badgers, birds, cats, berries, apples, pears, snails, owls. No good hanging on here. Set off now. In twos, Johnny in the rear, keep each other just in sight. Whistle and we'll freeze. . . . I don't care if the Gibsons do think they've scared us out, Virus get 'em. Get moving now.

23,17. It was so late when I got away, I decisioned a detour via the megastore. Found Pete missioning there. He was saying the mail was so slow and the set so blinky, he was considering tabling purchase of a private lascercom just to liaise with Droffield's and Willenhausen's. They're both in eyeline, all three being so high. I said right, go ahead, peg in my name with it. The versionizer hasn't come yet, how we're going to cope with the Jap mergees I don't know; they aren't in resonance with Commart English.

When I homed in on the unit Maggy was connectioning her matebureau business. Jane was culturing the creepers. A sparrow shot past me. . . . Time Jane initiated tapping a non-talk write-set. Must call up one her size keys.

Anyway I was glad to shed my wear and relax. Maggy had a horror story, though. "You know a man got caught today," she said, "in a paternoster, a vertipater, not a horipater, crushed, killed? Well, what they're saying at the salebox is, it wasn't an accident. They say the block mafia are running a transplant supply, undercover."

"How do they calculate it could have been done?" I said.

"Someone pushed in with him," she said, "staged the rest, they say. They say they've a health squad in their pocket, zipped him off. Been a crop of 'accidents' like that. Always young, healthy ones, ideal for transplant donors."

"They're fictioning!" I said; but all the same . . . Then to cheer her up, I asked re her horoscope. I'd just missed out on the horocast. It was a bright one for her *and* fair for all of us, as it happens, so we dialogued this-ward a bit. The twins came in, so *this* was all right. Then there was a screen-and-button 'puterpoll for Midlandia parliament on the alternatives for the new airport site. Maggy and I voted for the Northsea platform and new H.V.T. links. Johnny and Denise griped it isn't fair, they should poll too; serious. The rest of the evening we had educasts and spottoquiz. The color was a bit blinky, though. Have to file a mendation order. Time for bed.

See what I mean. Got possibilities. No ants either. We'll use this big one for us, see, the front rolls up and down, and there's a peephole in the roller. Next one for stores. This one here for wood and such. Escape staircase'll do for lookouts, over by the house. Salvage some things there, chairs exetra. Might manage to knock a hole from one garage to the next, in case of trouble. Soom get dark now—you settle in, I'll have a quick butchers round the house, what's left.

2000. 224. 23,35. Must have been religion day or something. First a Jove's Witness, then an Anglican Methodist, then a Yogist called up. Made short work of the A.M.; but the Witness and the Yogist persistented. The Yogist call must have been a computerized interview—you could tell from the pauses. Clever how the 'puters analyze your vocabulary and switch in the right reply. Only this must have been pitched for high persistence, it wouldn't take no for an answer. Endwise I had to operate the control and fade him out in mid-gesture. Then sod it if a neo-Marxist didn't screen up. He was personalized but even more persistent. Had to control him out, too. Following this an Ortho-Catholic who was easy stuff, especially as he called just following an aggressive redecoration rep who brain-rinsed me to exhaustion; to rehabilitation, I'd just ingested a pep with a real kick, when the O-C. screened up.

Next thing was, a door call. Imagine our surprise when Uncle Ned and Aunt Olga screened up. When they came in they said they were transiting and could they visit a couple of days with us. I had to miss my hour's exercise at the autosquash court, sod it. Aunty said, My, wasn't Denise a "sexy" bird already; she's going to be quite sexational, I opinion, and she imaged this then, with some jewelry that really resonated. They're all in bed now. Uncle's aged up, really in the higher-succession bracket, you'd opinion: at sixty-odd he images well over seventy; almost ready for a gerry, a retiring home. Aunt Olga actually wears wear indoors now—to act parallel with him. I suppose—although she's only forty-five; brought a shift and footwear with her. First news we watched, Uncle started on his usual gripe re the news being anesthetized, not like in his young days. Thank goodness this is only a couple of days they're staying. I was hoping to see the musical of Kafka's *Castle,* but now they've come we had to switch to another channel and see the underwater ballet of *West Side Story*. Maggy doesn't even *like* underwater ballet. The sparrows didn't either, they kept nuisancing around during it. One positioned momentwise on Aunt's head. The block's infested with them. The twins fed their predecessors when they were infants and now they're triple-hardened.

Uncle keeps on boring us re he used to roar round Brands Hatch when he was young, or how there used to be woods where our blocks stand, or recalling back to the rationing when he was an infant, in the Welsh mountains because grandmother was evacuated there in the 1939—45 war. Aunt Olga isn't on the same wave length: edgy and never announces. She was a great free-sexer for years, prior to settling down with Uncle. I suppose that's why she doesn't interface with infants or pre-inductees—Jane especially just emigrates when she's around—and why she images so dehydrated.

Following the children had "blasted off" to bed, though, she told us she had it on the salebox grapevine that the Heyns-Suit Babies are demanding *all* the key positions in forecasting, industry, and government, otherwise they'll organize a braindrain. Where would they go, I said, to the U.S.? No, she said, to Scandinavia apparently, Japan, and N.Z. Seems the Panpacific Alliance has them drooling. These H.S.B's think they've got it made, as Uncle would say, but who wants all these brains around? I wouldn't give a nupe for them. We'll outvote them a thousand to one at next week's centregov screen referendum, anyway.

Living off the fat of the land, we are. Oh my stomach. Acorns. Truffles. Garlic. A thrush and a pheasant. Not to mention these dogs . . . Maggy, come here. Maggy, come on now, yes, come on. . . .

2000. 225. 19,45. My hairstyler's off the blink now, thank goodness. . . . That cartoon of *Moby Dick* was a riot. Went on too long though. The whale had some funny numbers. Something more serious, though. I didn't tell Uncle and Aunt—they're next door just now—but I saw Larry Gibson on my way back from the megastore where I'd missioned to get away from *them* for a bit. Larry was in a crowd of all pigments, all queuing for the vertipater. Quite a sexational low-pigment bird in partywear was standing in front of him—and the wear was more minus than plus, of course. I was orbiting and trying to get through transit. The crowd pushed him and he just about knocked the bird down. He turned round—there was a higher-pigment type just in rear of him—and shouted "Get back you!" A neon-dearth-al-looking lower-pigment type close by, who I think was trying to make the bird, shouted out something, and Larry ripped out some object, rammed him in the diaphragm, and pulled twice. It was all over so quickly. The neon-dearth-al collapsed, blood all over the place, screams everywhere, the cops homed in in microseconds (the corridor T.V.'s will have picked it up), and there's Larry standing shaking over the corpse. What he'd done was use an instapeg wall-hook gun. One peg must have cut a big blood vessel, the second must have targeted on the vagus nerve or something. Says he,

"Bastard called me a racist!" Cops quizzed me. I said, yes, it sounded just like this. Course, this would be justifiable homicide. But I knew sodding well he was sodding well errored—it was only "rapist." Anyway they took my word for it. By good luck, the bird had stayed grounded, and she relayed me to the *n*th. The 'puter'll never convict, now.

I had to tell somebody or something, so now I told *you*. Shaking, I was, had to have a pep when I got in. Just told Maggy quietly Larry had killed a man up the corridor, and I hoped it would be O.K.

> *Denise shouldn't have gone off like that, even with the fence post with her. Been all day now and she'll never make it in the dark. I'll sit up a bit and wake you later, Johnny. Let Ma have some sleep till dawn. Might hear something, perhaps.*

2000. 226. 13,18. The supply-tube milk's changed. The flavor's queer and it's more green. Have to try with natural cow milk for a bit, if we can call it up. Anyway, this is something, the old couple are gone. I opinion, if it wasn't for the drier being cold they'd have stayed much longer. I put in ninety minutes autosquash to make up for yesterday exetra.

The lunch time edscreen is on early literature. Maggy likes it, but me-wise it's a drag. I could never understand these great historical novels like *The Sotweed Factor* and *The Spire,* and I don't make much interface with socio-philosophy ones like *Ulysses* or *The Trial.* Anyway I'd sooner call up my lunch and ingest it in peace. I don't mind listening to a magazine in parallel of course.

Maggy keeps impacting with Johnny for saying "followings" instead of "afters." Personally I don't mind what a pre-inductee says. Anything for peace at meals. It's different with Jane, she's still an infant. This lark re speaking right, it's all alf garnet, I don't resonate with it.

The megastore held a telecommittee this morning. We decisioned to production several new lines. They agreed to the lasercom, too. In the middle in came Jane and started announcing. I had to alarm Maggy to come and incentive her off. As Maggy was calling over for the matebureau, Jane wasn't very popular.

I was going to visitation my cousin Michael at his disability home. He's an LSD Baby, his parents used the stuff. Born too early to get classified for prostheses. But when I called up the "spa" they said his viability had diminished and he wouldn't survive long; he was sedationed and wouldn't be worth seeing now. That's what they *said,* anyway. *I* opinion they've initiated culling the inmates.

I know why Denise ran off like that: you were trying to mate with her; last night in the garage after that blowout we had. I didn't realize then, but I know now. Don't say no, your face gives you away. Trying your own sister, you—you—I've no words. . . . I bet she was a match for you, anyway, for all she's no older than you. I'm right, aren't I? I heard the roller door in the middle of the night. She must have gone then to hide in one of the other garages. Or else that's when she went off for good.

2000. 226. 22,51. Denise has sprung it on us that she's going on this world nature tour. It's in thirty days, and durates a hundred days. She'd connectioned it herself without asking us, and showed us her classification card today, so it was all fixed. Most on these tours are inductees, say thirteen to twenty-two, and handpicked too. Many of them are Heyns-Suit Babies. She's only twelve and no H.S.B. All the same she was classified OK. It struck me it might be a kidnap syndicate forgery, so I connectioned a recall from the original 'puter, but the data were OK. Recall systems are spoofproof, so this is final, I suppose. And as things are, there's no appeal unless we can incentive her to reverse. I don't think this is worth it, nor does Maggy. But I must say it's a trauma.

Come here boy. This bloody leg's broken, I'm sure. Virus take that bloody bird's nest. Wish I'd never gone after those eggs. If Denise had been here I'd have sent her up, she was nimbler. If I could have brought myself to ask you, John; but we weren't on speaking terms. It'll never heal. You three ought to've left me there, instead of heaving me back. You'll never thrive with me lying here. Don't say anything to Ma and Jane. Let them sleep.

2000. 227. 12,10. We have to evacuate this unit. It came on the screen, early. The whole block's being traded in for a new gerry, a retirement home. And the next block's being switched for a reciddy, a psychopathology home. We've all been given fifteen days to move. Maggy fed our requirements by call-up into the 'puter system, to integrate onto our classification. Including the desired move radius, which we settled at two hundred kilometers. It turned up only nine units within a range of sixty-to-seventy per cent on the desirability scale, and this is the best it could do. Six were filled units with families leaving inside four days, three were new units. Two of the three were pods in pod-batteries, the third was an unbooked unit in a new block. I spent the rest of the morning trying to call them up for teleview. I got five: the two pods and three filled block units. We visitaped the views and tonight we'll run them through for the twins, but I think we'll take one of the pods. (One of them's in the state of Yorkshire, but their laws aren't too tough.) It'll be a change, the only thing is, a lot of the facilities and supplies are only piped to the battery center. And they say these centers have pigeons the way we have sparrows. But we're sick of the block life, maybe the pod-batteries won't be so mafia'd and kinged, and we might resonate well with community life.

We'll have to try and call up the other four by the end of tomorrow. Then we'll have to get the schoolab facilities confirmed. *Then* we'll have to decision on which unit. *Then* we'll have to trade off our immobiles exetra locally against replacements in target. *Then* we'll have to fix goods transportation. *Then* we'll have to lodge all the addresses for readdressment-service, friends, firms, unaymit. I can hardly face these fifteen days. And Denise off fourteen days following then. Have to recall confirmation that her route's been recast. The cold drier'll stay cold now, sod it.

Now they're all gone: Maggy to milk that cow with the calf they found, with the old bucket; Johnny to hunt; Jane to look for berries. Parked me out on the cobbles. My innards must be busted, keep passing blood, can't keep anything down. I thought we'd make it, after Maggy and me lasting through the Virus, but it was too good to last. I hope you're all right somewhere, Denise, I hope nothing happened to you. . . . Just a drag I am, lying here. . . . Those bloody rats in the ruin, I can hear them, they won't get me either. Here goes. Bit of window glass here. Left wrist. Ahhh! Ahhh! Ahhh! Done it! Done it! Good-by Maggy. Aaah.

THE LAWGIVER

By Keith Laumer

"You're no better than a murderer," the woman said. "A cold-blooded killer." Her plump face looked out of the screen at him hot-eyed, tight-mouthed. She looked like someone's aunt getting tough with the butcher.

"Madame, the provisions of the Population Control Act—" he started.

"That's right, give it a fancy name," she cut in. "Try and make it sound respectable. But that don't change it. It's plain murder. Innocent little babies that never done anybody harm—"

"We are not killing babies. A fetus at ninety days is less than one inch long—"

"Don't matter how long they are, they got as much right to live as anybody!"

He drew a calming breath. "In five years we'd be faced with famine. What would you have us do?"

"If you big men in Washington would go to work and provide for people, for the voters, instead of killing babies, there'd be plenty for everybody."

"As easy as that, eh? Does it occur to you, madame, that the land can't support the people if they're swarming over it like ants?"

"See? People are no more to you than ants!"

"People are a great deal more to me than ants! That's precisely why I've sponsored legislation designed to ensure that they don't live like insects, crowded in hives, dying of starvation after they've laid the countryside bare!"

"Look at you," she said, "taking up that whole fancy apartment. You got room there for any number o' homeless children."

"There are too many homeless children, that's the problem!"

"It says right in the Good Book, be fruitful and multiply."

"And where does it end? When they're stacked like cordwood in every available square inch of space?"

"Is that what you do? Heap up all them little bodies and set 'em afire?"

"There are no bodies affected by the law, only fertilized ova!"

"Every one's a human soul!"

"Madame, each time a male ejaculates, several million germ cells are lost. Do you feel we should preserve every one, mature it *in vitro*—"

"Well! You got your nerve, talking that way to a respectable lady! You! A divorced man—and that son of yours—"

"Thank you for calling, madame," he said, and thumbed the blanking control.

"I'm no madame. . . ." the voice died in a squeal. He went to the small bar at the side of the room, dispensed a stiff shot of over-proof SGA, took it down at a gulp. Back at the desk, he buzzed the switchboard.

"Jerry, no more calls tonight."

"Sorry about that last one, Senator. I thought—"

"It's all right. But no more. Not tonight. Not until I've had some sleep."

"Big day, eh, Senator, ramrodding the enabling act through like you did. Uh, by the way, Senator, I just had a flash from Bernie, on the desk. He says there's a party asking for you, says they claim they have to see you—"

"Not tonight, Jerry."

"They mentioned your son Ron, Senator. . . ."

"Yes? What about him?"

"Well, I couldn't say, Senator. But Bernie says they say

it's pretty important. But like you said, I'll tell him to tell them not tonight."

"Wait a minute, Jerry. Put this party on."

"Sure, Senator."

The face that appeared was that of a young man with a shaven skull, no eyebrows or lashes. He gazed out of the screen with a bored expression.

"Yes, what is it you want?"

The youth tipped his head sideways, pointing. "We've got somebody with us you ought to talk to," he said. "In person."

"I understand you mentioned my son's name."

"We'd better come up."

"If you have something of interest to me, I suggest you tell me what it is."

"You wouldn't like that. Neither would Ron."

"Where is Ron?"

The boy made a vague gesture. "Spy, zek. We tried. It's your rax from here on—"

"Kindly speak standard English. I don't understand you."

The youth turned to someone out of sight; his mouth moved, but the words were inaudible. He turned back.

"You want us to bring Rink up or no?"

"Who is Rink?"

"Rink will tell you all that."

"Very well. Take my car, number 763."

He went to the bar, dispensed another stiff drink, then poured it down the drain. He went to the window, deopaqued it. A thousand feet below a layer of mist, glowing softly from the city lights beneath it, stretched all the way to the horizon fifty miles distant.

When the buzzer sounded he turned, called "come in." The door slid back. The boy he had talked to and another came through, supporting between them a plump woman with a pale face. The men were dressed in mismatched vest-suits, many times reused. The woman was wrapped in a long cloak. Her hair was disarranged, so that a long black curl bobbed over the right side of her face. Her visible eye held an expression that might have been fear, or defiance. The men helped her to the low couch. She sank down on it heavily, closed her eyes.

"Well? What's this about Ron?" the senator asked.

The two men moved toward the door. "Ask Rink," one of them said.

"Just a minute. You're not leaving this woman here . . . ?"

"Better get a medic in, Senator," the shaved lad said.

He looked at her. "Is she ill?" She opened her eyes and pushed her hair out of her face. She was pale, and there were distinct dark hollows under her eyes.

"I'm pregnant," she said in a husky voice. "Awful damn pregnant. And Ron's the father."

He walked slowly across to stand before her. "Have you any proof of that remarkable statement?"

She threw the cloak open. Her body looked swollen enough to contain quadruplets.

"I'm not referring to the obvious fact of your condition," he said.

"He's the father, all right."

He turned abruptly, went to the desk, put his finger on the vidscreen key.

"I'm not lying," she said. "The paternity's easy to check. Why would I try to lie?" She was sitting up now; her white fingers dug into the plum-colored cushions.

"I assume you make no claim of a legal marriage contract?"

"Would I be here?"

"You're aware of the laws governing childbirth—"

"Sure. I'm aware of the laws of nature, too."

"Why didn't you report to a PC station as soon as you were aware of your condition?"

"I didn't want to."

"What do you expect me to do?"

"Fix it so I can have the baby—and keep him."

"That's impossible, of course."

"It's your own grandson you're killing!" the woman said

quickly. "You can talk about how one of your compulsory abortions is no worse than lancing a boil—but this"—she put her hands against her belly—"this is a baby, Senator. He's alive. I can feel him kicking."

His eyes narrowed momentarily. "Where is Ron?"

"I haven't seen him in six months. Not since I told him."

"Does he know you came here?"

"How would he know?"

He shook his head. "What in God's name do you expect of me, girl?"

"I told you! I want my son—alive!"

He moved away from the desk, noting as he did that the two men had left silently. He started to run his fingers through his hair, jerked his hands down, rammed them in the pockets of his lounging jacket. He turned suddenly to face the girl.

"You did this deliberately—"

"Not without help, I didn't."

"Why? With free anti-pregnancy medication and abort service available at any one of the thousand stations in the city, why?"

"Not just free, Senator—compulsory. Maybe I think the government—a bunch of politicians and bureaucrats—has no right to say who can have a child. Or maybe the pills didn't work. Or maybe I just didn't give a damn. What does it matter now?"

"You're not living naked in the woods now. You're part of a society; and that society has the right to regulate itself."

"And I have a right to have a baby! You didn't give me—or anybody—the right to live! You can't take it away!"

He took a turn up and down the room, stopped before her. "Even if I wanted to help you, what is it you imagine I could do?"

"Get me a birth permit."

"Nonsense. You don't even have a contract; and the qualifications—"

"You can fix it."

"I believe this whole thing is no more than a plot to embarrass me!"

The woman laughed. She threw back her head and screamed laughter. "Ron was right! You're a fool! A coldblooded old fool! Your own grandson—and you think he's something that was just thought up to annoy you!"

"Stop talking as though this were a living child instead of an illegal embryo!"

Her laughter died away in a half titter, half sob. "It's a funny world we've made for ourselves. In the old days before we got so goddamned smart a man would have been proud and happy to know he had a grandson. He'd look forward to all the things he'd teach him, all the things they'd do together. He'd be a little part of the future, that he could see growing, living on after he was dead—"

"That's enough!" He drew a controlled breath and let it out. "Do you realize what you're asking of me?"

"Sure. Save my baby's life. Ron's baby."

His hands opened and closed. "You want me to attempt to deliberately circumvent the laws I've devoted my life to creating!"

"Don't put words to it. Just remember it's a baby's life."

"If I knew where Ron was . . ."

"Yes?"

"We could execute a marriage contract, predate it. I could manage that. As for a birth permit—" He broke off as the girl's face contorted in an expression like a silent scream.

"Better hurry up," she gasped. "They're coming faster now. . . ."

"Good God, girl! Why did you wait until now to bring this to me?"

"I kept hoping Ron would come back."

"I'll have to call a doctor. You know what that means."

"No! Not yet! Find Ron."

"None of this will help if you're both dead." He keyed the screen, gave terse instructions. "Handle this quietly, Jerry. Very quietly," he finished.

"Damn you! I was a fool to come to you!"

"Never mind the hysterics. Just tell me where to start looking for Ron."

"I . . . I don't have any idea."

"Those friends of yours: what about them? Would they know?"

"I promised Limmy and Dan I wouldn't get them mixed up in anything."

He snorted. "And you're asking me to break my oath to the people of this country."

The girl gave him an address. "Don't put them in the middle, Senator. They were pretty decent, bringing me here."

"The obstetrician will be here in a few minutes. Just lie there quietly and try to relax."

"What if you can't find him?"

"I suppose you know the answer to that as well as I do."

"Senator—do they really—kill the babies?"

"The embryo never draws a breath. Under the legal definition it's not a baby."

"Oh, Senator—for God's sake, find him!"

He closed the door, shutting off his view of the frightened face.

Red light leaked out through the air baffles above the bright-plated plastic door. At the third ring—he could hear the buzzer through the panel—it opened on a shrill of voices, the rattle and boom of music. Acrid, stale-smelling air puffed in his face. A tall man with an oddly-trimmed beard looked at him through mirror-lens contacts. A tendril of reddish smoke curled from the room past his head.

"Uh?"

"I'd like to have a word with Mr. Limberg, please."

"Who?"

"Mr. Limberg. Limmy."

"Uh." The bearded man turned away. Beyond him, strangely costumed figures were dimly visible in the thick crimson fog, standing, sitting, lying on the floor. Some were naked, their shaved bodies decorated with painted patterns. A boy and girl dressed in striped tunics and hose undulated past arm in arm, looking curiously alike. The youth with the shaved head appeared, his mouth drawn down at the corners.

"I need to find Ron in a hurry. Can you tell me where he might be?"

"Rink had to blow her tonsils, uh?"

"This is important, Limmy. I have to find him. Seconds may be vital."

The boy pushed his lips in and out. Others had gathered. listening.

"Hey, who's the zek?" someone called.

"It's Eubank. . . ."

The youth stepped out, pulled the door shut behind him. "Look, I want no part, follow?"

"All I want is to find Ron. I'm not here to get anyone in trouble. I appreciate what you did for the girl."

"Ron's a pile, as far as I'm concerned. When I saw Rink meant to go through with it, I sent word to him. I didn't know if it reached him or not. But he screened me about half an hour ago. He's on his way here now from Phil."

"On the shuttle, I suppose. Good. I can contact him en route?"

"With what for fare? I heard you kept him broke."

"His allowance—never mind. If he's not riding the shuttle, how is he getting here?"

"Car."

"You must be mistaken. His license was lifted last year."

"Yeah. I remember when—and why. . . ."

"Are you saying . . . suggesting . . ."

"I'm not saying anything. Just that Ron said he'd be at your place as quick as he could get there."

"I see." He half turned away, turned back to thank the boy. But the door had already closed.

"Please try to understand, Lieutenant," Senator Eubank said to the hard, expressionless face on the screen. "I have reason to believe that the boy is operating a borrowed manually controlled vehicle on the Canado autopike, northbound from Philadelphia, ETD forty minutes ago. He's just received some very shocking news, and he's probably driving at a very high speed. He'll be in an agitated condition, and—"

"You have a description of this vehicle, Senator?"

"No. But surely you have means for identifying a car that's not locked into the system."

"That's correct—but it sometimes takes a few minutes. There are a lot of vehicles on the 'pike, Senator."

"You understand he's under great stress. The circumstances—"

"We'll take him off as gently as we can."

"And you'll keep me informed? I must see him at the first possible instant, you understand?"

"We'll keep you advised—" The police officer turned his head as if looking at someone off-screen.

"This may be something, Senator," he said. "I have a report on a four-seater Supercad at Exit 2983. He took the ramp too fast—he was doing a little over two hundred. He went air-borne and crashed." He paused, listening, then nodded. "Looks like paydirt, Senator. The ID checks on the hot-list out of Philly. And it was on manual control."

The officer used his screamlight to clear a path through the crowd to the spot where the heavy car lay on its side under the arches of the overpass. Two men with cutting torches were crouched on top of it, sending up showers of molten droplets.

"He's alive in there?" Senator Eubank asked.

The lieutenant nodded. "The boy will have him out in a couple of minutes. The crash copter is standing by."

The torches stopped sputtering. The two men lifted the door, tossed it down behind the car. A white-suited medic with a bundle under his arm climbed up and dropped inside. Half a minute later the crane arm at the back of the big police cruiser hoisted the shock-seat clear of the wreck. From the distance of fifty feet, the driver's face was clay-white under the polyarcs.

"It's Ron."

The medic climbed down, bent over the victim as the Senator and his escort hurried up.

"How does it look?" the lieutenant asked.

"Not too good. Internals. Skull looks OK. If he's some rich man's pup, he may walk again—with a new set of innards—" The man broke off as he glanced up and saw the civilian beside the officer. "But I wouldn't waste any time taking him to the hospital," he finished.

The duty medtech shook his head. "I'm sorry, sir. He's on the table right at this moment. There's no way in the world for you to see him until he comes out. He's in very serious condition, Senator."

"I understand." As the tech turned away he called after him: "Is there a private screen I could use?"

"In the office, sir."

Alone, he punched his apartment code. The operator's face appeared on the screen. "I'm sorry, no— Oh, it's you, Senator. I didn't know you'd gone out—"

"Buzz my flat, Jerry."

The screen winked and cleared. After fifteen seconds' wait, the image of a small, sharp-eyed man appeared, rubbing at his elbows with a towel.

"About time you called in, John," he said. "First time in thirty years I've let myself be hauled out of my home in the midst of dinner."

"How is she?"

The elderly man wagged his head. "I'm sorry, John. She slipped away from me."

"You mean—she's dead?"

"What do you expect? A post-terminal pregnancy—she'd been taking drugs for a week to delay the birth. She'd had no medical attention whatever. And your living room rug doesn't make the best possible delivery table! There was massive hemorrhaging; it might have been different if I'd been working in a fully equipped labor room—but under the circumstances, that was out of the question, of course, even if there'd been time."

"You know . . . ?"

"The woman told me something of the circumstances."

"What about the child?"

"Child?" The little man frowned. "I suppose you refer to the fetus. It wasn't born."

"You're going to leave it inside the corpse?"

"What would you have me do?" The doctor lowered his voice. "John—is what she said true? About Ron being the father?"

"Yes—I think so."

The little man's mouth tightened. "Her heart stopped three and a half minutes ago. There's still time for a Caesarian—if that's what you want."

"I . . . I don't know, Walter."

"John, you devoted thirty years of your life to the amendment and the enabling act. It passed by a very thin cat's whisker. And the opposition hasn't given up, not by a damn sight. The repeal movement is already underway, and it has plenty of support." The doctor paused, peering at the senator. "I can bring the child out—but John—a lot of this is already in the record. There'd be no way of keeping it out of the hands of the other side: *your* law—violated by you, the first week it was in force. It would finish you, John—and Population Control, too, for a generation."

"There's no hope of resuscitating the mother?"

"None at all. Even today people sometimes die, John."

"I see. Thank you, Walter. You did your best."

"About the child . . . ?"

"There is no child. Just an illegal pregnancy."

"You may go in now," the nurse said. Ron was on his back, his shaven head protruding from the bloated cocoon of the life-support tank. His eyes opened as his father bent over him.

"Dad—I was a damned fool. Knew I was going too fast. . . ."

The senator leaned closer to catch his whisper.

"I had to try . . . to get back in time. . . ." He paused and his eyelids flickered. "Limmy told me . . . she went to you. I knew . . . you'd take care . . . my wife."

"Easy, Ron, easy. No need to talk now—"

"When Rink told me . . . about the baby . . . I ran out on her. She handed me a contract, all made up. But I couldn't see it, bringing a child into this mess. I thought . . . when I left she'd go in and have it taken care of. Then I heard . . . she didn't. It . . . did something to me. I still had the papers. I registered 'em in Phil. I used your name to get the birth permit. You don't mind . . . ?"

"Ron. . . ."

"I wanted to be there. Too late; damned fool. I always was a damn fool, Dad. It'll be different, now. A lot different. Being a father . . . not so easy, eh, Dad. But good. Worth it. Worth everything. . . ." The boy's voice faded.

"Better to let him rest now, sir," the nurse whispered.

The senator rose stiffly. At the door, he looked back. Ron seemed to be smiling in his sleep.

"Did you say something, sir?" the nurse asked. He looked down at her bright face.

"What is there to say?"

Her eyes followed him as he walked away down the brightlit corridor.

TO BE A MAN

By J. J. Coupling

As he came out of the plane Peter saw them waiting just a few feet away, the four of them. That was what Jim Evers would do. As president of Synthetronics he had started with a small invention and his partner's money. By driving and inspiring a smart staff he had pulled ahead in a fast field. Today he could get through any NO ENTRANCE barriers, and he had no compunction about doing so. Now he did it to greet a returning employee. This meant, Peter realized, that Jim really wanted him back—that he needed him.

Maybe that explained why Jim had brought his daughter, Betty Lou, cuter than ever. He knew that Peter would like that. And there, representing management no doubt, was Tom Everhart. Jim's partner and vice-president of the firm. Jim's secretary, Kitty, was there, too. As he walked toward them, Peter wondered if this was completely by accident. He and Kitty had been more than friends for years, though they hadn't advertised the fact.

Betty Lou managed to get ahead of the rest to hug him, as she always had, and he hugged and kissed her before he realized that after three years she wasn't a little girl any more.

Jim gripped his hand and arm and said, "You're looking great, boy." Tom wrung his hand, slapped him on the back, and said, "It's swell! Just swell! I bet you gave those Commies hell. Expedited them right into their graves, I bet.

And those Pandas. I bet you had something for them, too," he winked.

Kitty, whom he had never quite got around to marrying, gave him their sign, and he returned it. They'd see each other later, after the party.

"I guess you can take Betty Lou home, and Kitty back to the plant, can't you, Tom?" Jim said rather than asked. Jim treated Tom like a brother—a younger brother. Tom had put up the money to found Synthetronics, but Jim had the drive.

When they were in the car by themselves, Jim said, "It's been hell without you, Pete. Those expediters I've had were no damn good. I fired the last one this morning. Snafus and red tape—why, I've had a government inspector here, right on the premises in person, all over a thousand-dollar foul-up. How a man can stay in business these days—say, how did you do it, Pete?"

Peter thought of pleasant days before his console, calling this agency and that, unraveling revised and rerevised regulations on the viewscreen, keying in requests, amendments, and disclaimers. He thought of relaxed hours chatting with other expediters, face to face on the viewscreen. Especially, he thought of Sandra Stevens, the Monolith expediter. Sandra had helped him when he was green on the job. She had continued to help him in her cool, clever way. Now that he was back he looked forward to talking with her again, not just for the help, but because he enjoyed it.

"Oh, it isn't very hard," he replied to Jim.

Jim let it go at that.

"That what you were doing in Panda?" he asked. "I know how classified everything is, of course."

Peter nodded. "Pretty much," he said. "I had quite a setup there, too."

He thought of the immaculate office, the immaculate computer room, with the steaming jungle right at the door. Lines by cable and microwave to every nearby hamlet. Beams via satellite to the computers of the whole country and the whole free world.

That had been after the indoctrination period. Even a top expediter had to go through the motions of becoming a soldier, before he settled down to his real job. Peter thought of the muggy trips into the retaken villages—territory was continually changing hands in Panda as the Russians and the Chinese and the Americans outmaneuvered one another, according to rules that even Peter did not understand.

If America lost, jeeps and halftracks would take everything out in a hurry. But, it was a fine thing to drive into a retaken village, even in the steamy weather. Everyone lined up in their yellow or red pajamas (yellow was for China, red for the Soviet Union), bowing and scraping.

Then he would haul down the flag and raise Old Glory. At his order, the Pandas would strip off the enemy pajamas, fold them neatly, and lay them on the ground. He would give them all blue pajamas, one by one, inspecting the liberated population as he did so. The girls were really quite attractive. Not friends, like Kitty, of course, but they understood enough English to be obliging and funny. When the pajamas had been put on, and the enemy food and equipment burned, and new food and equipment issued, he'd move on—or retreat. That sort of thing had had its rewards, but he really liked it better at the expediting outpost.

"Is that where they got you?" Jim asked.

Peter remained physically calm, but there was still a shudder somewhere in his mind.

"Yes," he said. "Wild Pandas."

"God!" Jim said. "I thought they'd cleaned those up years ago."

"So did I," Peter said, "but there they were."

He'd been immersed in an intricate problem of supplies for the patientless hospital next door. He surmised that they were for Doc Scragmore's pet research, and from the trouble he was having getting them, he concluded that someone was finding this out.

"There was a snap, and the screen went blank," Peter

told Jim. "Then there was another snap, and I realized it was a shot. I looked out, and there was this crazy mob of little men in *black* pajamas. I'd never seen any before. I thought I'd forgotten that I had a gun, but I grabbed it quick enough and ducked out and started firing on automatic. Someone from Doc Scragmore's medical unit was firing behind me. I was jolted twice—I'd been hit. And then I saw that they had flame throwers. What they did to that expediting outpost!"

"And to you?" Jim asked. "I pretty much know," he added. "The Army had to tell someone. But I didn't let anyone else know."

Not even Kitty? Peter thought.

"There's nothing left of my flesh but brain and eyes," Peter said.

"Christ," Jim said. "No one would ever know."

"I hope no one else ever does," Peter replied.

"But out there, with wild Pandas and all?"

"Scragmore's medical genius as well as an irresponsible tyrant," Peter replied. "I was expediting for him, mostly. The place had a full complement of soldiers who had nothing to do but police things up. All the nurses did was act as lab assistants. No one gets hurt in the Panda war any more."

"Except you, for Christ's sake," Jim said.

"Except me," Peter agreed. "But Scragmore had the nurses to help him, and he had laboratory animals, and I think he got his hands on a Panda now and then. He'd managed to work things out pretty well. He got whatever he wanted."

"And nobody else did," Jim surmised.

"Nobody else. Soldiers on the alert. Nurses working all day in the lab, and sleeping all night—alone. It was a dog's life for everyone but us. He ran it, and I expedited for him."

"But, Christ," Jim said. "Eyes and a brain, and you walk and talk."

"There's a little more," Peter explained. "Really, the spinal cord is almost part of the brain, and he got that out, somehow. It's coiled up inside me."

"But the nerves," Jim objected. "I can understand motors for muscles—Synthetronics has some pretty sophisticated products—but the nerves."

"My old nerves are gone," Peter said. "But, I've grown new ones. People have known for years that nerves regenerate. Nerves grow new axons or fibers from the cell body. If the path for growth is blocked, the nerve fibers or axons form a useless knot called a neurolemma. If a path is provided, to a muscle, for instance, by grafting in an old nerve, the new nerve fibers will grow along the path and innervate the muscle again."

Jim thought a moment.

"There's a lot of paths in you," he finally said.

"Oh, Scragmore didn't have to provide a path for each nerve," Peter replied.

"But then, how did your nerves get to the right sensors and controls?" Jim asked.

"That goes back to a Dutchman named Arien Kappers," Peter said. "Kappers believed in something he called neurobiotaxis—nerves growing to their proper destinations. A lot of people laughed at him in Norbert Wiener's day. They said that animals were wired up randomly and somehow learned to live. But then, Roger Sperry and his students showed that when you cut the optic nerve of a goldfish, each individual nerve fiber grows back to just the right spot in the brain. Of course, only Scragmore is able to do that sort of thing in man."

"How?" Jim asked. "How?"

"It's a sort of chemotropism—a seeking out of minute chemical traces which differ over the body—coupled with the effect of electric gradients on nerve growth," Peter said. "But of course, only Scragmore really knows."

"You don't have muscles and sense organs for the nerves to grow to," Jim objected.

"That was another problem for Scragmore. Nerve conduction is ionic rather than electronic, with chemical triggers of the synapses. Beyond the nerves, in man biochemical and biophysical processes take over in the muscles and sensory organs. In me we have instead solid state physics and electrodynamics.

"Somehow, Scragmore worked out a sort of synaptic extrapolation to my solid state part. The dendrites—that's the branching nerve ends that receive information—grow into a sort of semiconducting synthetic gel. The gel grades into a transistorlike junction attached to my synthetic sense organs. The gel for a particular organ has the right chemical traces and the right electric fields to attract the right nerves. And, at the ends of the axons that control my movements, the neuromuscular end plates envelop and dig into a sort of organic semiconductor, and a junction there activates the rest of my circuitry."

"And what keeps it alive?" Jim asked. "I mean you, I mean, your brain, and eyes, and spinal cord."

Peter smiled.

"I'm not bloodless," he said. "I have a very little blood, of a sort, and a pulsating heartlet which gives just the right throb to the brain. The vagus and other nerves feed back to the little heart. My hypothalamus controls blood temperature, just as yours does. Little reservoirs trigger just the right hormones into the blood stream at just the right times, I have an artificial lung—an invaginated semipermeable membrane separating blood from breath. I have a highly efficient artificial kidney, too. But there isn't much blood, and so not much work to do. A little sugar and fat and a few amino acids last me for months."

"They don't work your muscles," Jim said.

"No," Peter replied. "That's all eletrodynamic, powered by a hydrocarbon-burning fuel cell. The cell ordinarily burns propane," he added, "but I can run on vodka in a pinch. And," he continued, "I have a forty-eight-hour backup supply, just in case."

"And you can move, and see, and breathe—" Jim said.

"Most of the breath's to deceive," Peter said. "I need very little air. But I can do most things men do. Scragmore even added a few features men don't have." he continued. "I can see TV by flicking a switch—a sort of compensation for life, Scragmore called it."

Peter touched his left arm with his right hand and keyed for the news channel. He felt that he had talked enough.

"Jesus," Jim commented. "What some people can take."

Jim said no more until they reached Peter's new apartment, with all his old things in it and his car in the garage. Then he left Peter to unpack. After Peter had done that, he killed time, then drove to the country club as late as he could for the company stag celebration of the homecoming. Everyone but Jim thought that old Peter had come back—and Peter thought so, too.

The country club had once looked like a huge old house. But time, which had brought electronic golf carts to the fairways, had also added flat-roofed appendages to the original building, so that the Synthetronics dinner was held in a broad, deep, low-ceilinged room with plenty of floor space and a bar, as well as room for the tables.

When Peter had driven past the roofed and heated swimming pool (also new), parked his car and entered the room, he found all the others already there, lapping up the free drinks and talking convivially. Tom Everhart threw an arm around Peter's shoulders and hustled him to the bar, fending off well wishers with "Drinks for the hero, Bill" and "Wait till he has a glass in his hand, Art." Jim was at the bar getting a second or third. Peter had never enjoyed this sort of thing much, and he thought that Jim didn't, either, though they both behaved with hearty conviviality.

Somehow, pretending to drink, Peter got through the queries and reminiscences and congratulations and was at last seated at the head table, at the center between Jim and Tom. There was a scattering of groups seated out front, busily engaged with jokes and talk and what was left of their drinks. Jim and Tom left him alone, and while he pretended to eat he wondered what to do until the meal was over. He flipped on TV by tapping the code on his arm with his fingers, but the program was distracting. He looked at the groups in front of him and thought, how can you ever know what people are like?

He supposed that Major Martha Jenkins, head of

Scragmore's staff of six nurses, was still in Panda. Gray-haired, well preserved—so correct! She had been kind and helpful to him in the days when he was coming out of sedation, and in the days when he was learning to use his magnificent steel and plastic body (he hardly regarded it as human or his, then). She had helped him learn to sit, and stand, and walk, and talk. Nothing had really malfunctioned, but everything was a little—odd.

When his movements had become natural and sure, Major Jenkins asked a special favor. The other nurses would like to examine the magnificent machine that carried Peter's brain and eyes. He had been willing, even pleased. He was almost as proud of this astonishing machine as Scragmore was. In it, he felt well all the time, and he was beginning to feel at home.

So, that evening after duty hours, Major Jenkins took him to the nurses' quarters. As he entered he was surprised at the strange arrangements—bare cots and chairs against the walls, and the mattresses and cushions mosaicked together in the center of the floor and covered with sheets. And, why were the five other nurses in robes rather than uniforms?

As he entered the room, Major Jenkins, with fingers of steel, yanked his robe down from his arm and quickly plastered an elaborate plastic bandage around it. This operated a combination of controls that Dr. Scragmore hadn't told him about. A wave of excitement swept through him, and a plastic appurtenance he had thought was for deceit and ornament sprang to a magnificent height.

"He's all yours, girls," Major Jenkins shouted. They threw aside their robes as she started to tear off her clothes, and bore him to the center of the room.

The next few hours were a sea of voluptuous sensation with frequent tempests of ecstasy. Scragmore had made Peter insatiable as long as the buttons were down. But more than that, by design or chance his nerves had been crossed a little, so that friction there titillated him everywhere, and a touch or stroke anywhere went home to the center.

For a long part of that time Peter existed in a world of consuming sensuality. But there was no fatigue, no loss of well being. And finally his mind began to reach beyond his obvious preoccupations and pleasures and take rational stock of the situation. Some of the nurses had already withdrawn from the fray. A blonde was sprawled off to his right, left leg over the other far enough to show the moist hair between, her face just visible when he strained his neck. Her eyes were closed, and in her sleep she still smiled like the cat that had eaten the canary.

Other bodies lay about in lassitude or sleep, and soon there was no one active but Major Jenkins, straining hard and saying, "What are we doing, baby?"

Peter told her. But she wanted something else.

"Why is it good, baby?" she asked.

He didn't need to reply. She moaned, and as his body moved automatically she reached up and tore the plastic bandage from his arm.

"That's enough, Buster," she said, and passed immediately into sleep.

There was no sleep for Peter. The moment the buttons were released he felt as calm and fresh as when he had entered the room. He looked at the sprawled, sleeping women. One was magnificently beautiful. The blonde was very attractive, as were two others. One was dumpy. The major was in remarkably fine condition. She looked composed in her sleep, despite her ordeal. They all seemed to sleep in satisfaction, the blonde with the smile still on her face. But there was no sleepiness in Peter, only detached, collected thought. There was more to him than he had known.

He left the scene, shut the door, went to his room and climbed into bed. He could think about this in the morning. He glanced at the clock and pushed the combination that would make him unconscious (but rousable) for the four hours until reveille. It was useless to be stirring while the world slept.

But that was now far behind. Tonight Peter wasn't in Panda. He had come home; he was at the country club, at a dinner in his honor. And this world was awake, though a little vacant-eyed.

Tom had made a wandering speech full of brave Panda allies, dirty Commies, and obscene unreconciled Panda outcasts. Jim had spoken a few down-to-earth words, tinged only a little with drink when he ended by emphasizing that Peter had given everything. "Everything," he said, "for the love of our country. Pete won't tell you that. That's not his way. But I want you to know that it's so."

Now it was Peter's turn. He couldn't face this maudlin crowd sober. So, he pushed the combination for being a little high. That still wasn't enough, and he made himself tipsy. His speech thickened, but his mind expanded. He reached out toward those good fellow men, those good old fellow employees.

He told them all the good old army corn, about the strange land, and the quaint but magnificent allies. But as his mind roamed back; he thought of the songs, and the limericks, and the stories.

"But I want you to know that a soldier's life isn't all toil and battle," he said. "Men are men, in Panda as much as here, and women are women."

And he sang them the songs, and recited the limericks, and told the stories. When he finished, there was a disorganized ovation from those still capable of speech.

Tom had slumped alseep in his chair; he had had too many to hear either the speech or the applause. But Jim, good old Jim, had an expression between exaltation and tears for the hero and martyr.

"Jesus, Pete," he said. "How can you? And how can you take it?"

In an unaccustomed gesture of friendship he put his left arm around Peter's back and gripped Peter's left arm with his right, by accident in the worst possible place. The code was changed. In a twinkling Peter was cold sober but as randy as a pony stallion. There was a ripping of underclothing as the plastic appurtenance sprang to its upright posture.

Jim noticed. He took his arm from around Peter's shoulder—shook him off, in fact. He looked at Peter with cold, malignant disgust.

"You stay away from my Betty Lou, you frigging mechanical monkey," he said. He pushed his way out of the room.

Peter changed the combination and was as cool as before. Tom slept on. Nobody else had noticed. Jim will never be my friend again, if he ever was, Peter thought. It was hard to tell with Jim. But it won't affect my job, he decided. Jim knew which side his bread was buttered on. Peter left for Kitty's apartment, and no one saw him go.

The town was quiet when he parked before the building, the night still when he turned the motor off. It was an old building, brick and white stone outside. He walked into the cavernous foyer and pushed the button to bring the automatic elevator from wherever the last user had left it—the fourth floor, he saw. Perhaps that user had been Kitty. The elevator arrived, the door opened, and he got in and pushed for four.

How would it be, he wondered. Kitty and he had been so close, so easy, but so undemanding of one another. Each had been a part of the other's life—things needed, things shared. But each life had been a life of its own.

He rapped on the door lightly. There was no sound, so he rang the bell. Then he heard a soft movement inside, and Kitty opened the door slowly, a robe over her nightgown and slippers on her feet.

"I got so tired, Peter, that I went to bed," she said.

But she didn't look tired now; she looked glad.

"You look well, Peter."

Peter realized again that *he* would never, never be tired. So long as he lived in his splendid new body, he would never be tired again. He took Kitty's hand as they closed the door and walked through the dimly lit living room.

"Oh, darling," Kitty said, "it's been so long. So long." and tearful all at once. "I thought you'd never come back. And when you did, I couldn't touch you or talk with you until you were through with all those others."

She drew away. "Do you want something? Some coffee?" she said. "You don't seem to have had anything to drink."

Peter's simulated breath would be perpetually pure, he realized, as long as he lived, and whatever he did. But he could tell that Kitty had had more than one.

"No," he said. "I didn't want anything. I've sort of lost the taste for it."

His life was full of deceptions, little and large. He wished that he could tell Kitty, and have it over with. Have what over with, he wondered? What did he want? And, he and Kitty hadn't seen one another for so long that they were a little shy.

"Come on," he said. "How's it been? What's happened, pretty? Tell me truly, tell me all."

He drew her to the couch, and they sat down, his arm around her. She smiled and leaned her head against his shoulder.

"It's just the same," she said. "The way it's always been and always will be. You're a dear, Peter, and it's so, so good to have you back. And I don't want to know what happened, not now. Just hold me, and make me believe you're here."

And so he held her, and they said things about the past, and about one another. And then they got up and went to the bedroom, and they held each other even closer after he had pushed the combination on his arm.

He tried to be tender, but it was hard. What old Scragmore had built into him was the lust of a rutting he-goat. But Kitty wanted him and enjoyed him, whatever he was. Peter was full of joy, too. That was built in, so strongly that it swamped his disturbing thoughts for a while.

Then they lay back, nestled together, Kitty looking at once radiant and sleepy. She said this and that, and he murmured agreement. Finally she was asleep.

But Peter wasn't asleep. All the time that she lay there in languorous weariness, he wished that he could feel so pleasantly satiated, so pleasantly tired, and feel sleep coming, and think happily of the morning, and drift into unconsciousness at last. Of course, he could press the proper code and lie unconscious (but rousable) for any period he determined. And then he would wake, fresh and alert, lucid and clear, no different from this or any other moment in his life, except when he pushed the code for sex, or alcohol, or something else, for he had other resources.

How would he spend his time with Kitty, he wondered? Not eating. Not drinking. Would it matter if he told her why? Sports, perhaps? But would skiing or swimming be the same, with no sense of exertion, with an exact limit to his powerful strength. His body had no need of exercise. Exercise could neither excite him nor tire him. His body was his mind's obedient servant, and his mind was perpetually alert, needing no rest, requiring only distraction—or work.

When he looked at Kitty, for the first time he felt something of a sense of loss. But what had he lost, he wondered? Sickness, pain, weakness, the distress of the body. These were gone. Was something good gone too?

Gently, he disengaged himself from Kitty. She rolled over, murmured, and seemed asleep again. As he rose, the bed shook and creaked a little. Kitty half uttered "honey." "Bathroom," he whispered. She slid into sleep again. Peter gathered his clothes, took them to the living room and quietly put them on. Then he turned off the solitary lamp, inched the door open and shut, with only a faint final click.

He got into the car, and drove slowly through the small hours to the Synthetronics plant.

The plant had grown since Peter had seen it last. Two old buildings had been torn down on the west. There Synthetronics had covered a part of the area with its uniform architecture, and a part with new parking space. He drew into the old lot, parked in his own place, and opened the side door with the key that he as an expediter always carried.

When he reached his office, he saw that the equipment had changed a little. But, he had had the same new things in Panda, and knew how to use them. It seemed good to sit in his chair before the console again. I feel more at home than I have yet, he thought. It would be good to *work* again.

He keyed for the job file, asking for a sort on order of priority (this was a function of importance and time since the work had been requested). Also, he asked for only jobs that didn't involve consultation with people; no one else would be up at this hour. He worked dextrously. It was as if he had never been away. Sometimes changes in agency offices and in regulations surprised him. He filed the agency changes in his mind, for remembering them would save time. It wasn't worth trying to remember changes in regulations. Regulations came and went, and he would have to check them every time, anyway.

In an hour he was left with nothing to do. Should he return to his apartment, he wondered. But why? He needed no rest. He could read, of course, or spend the time until morning in unnecessary unconsciousness. Idly, he keyed the Monolith number. It would be foolish to think that Sandra would be there. And, indeed, the screen showed a notice, "This office is closed. Will you please record your name and message when the tone sounds." From force of habit he began, "This is Peter Roberts of Synthetronics—"

Suddenly the screen flashed, and there was Sandra, looking as fresh, as calm, as collected as ever. She smiled warmly.

"It's good to see you, Peter," she said. "I've been hoping you'd come back soon. How are you? You look fine."

"And you look fine, Sandra," he replied. "Fresh as a daisy."

Then the events of the day, and the attack on the outpost, and everything that had happened between them came back to him. He started talking, and he couldn't stop. Sandra nodded, looked sympathetic and made encouraging remarks when he hesitated. At last he had gone through it all, from beginning to end, through the party, through the visit to Kitty, and up to the very moment. He had nothing more to say.

"Poor Peter," Sandra said, smiling and looking a little

sad. "Poor Peter. But you're really very well off."

"I suppose so," he answered. He thought a moment. "But compared with whom?" he asked.

"Compared with me, for instance," she replied.

"What's wrong with you, Sandra?" Peter asked with alarm. "You aren't ill, are you?

"I can't be ill, any more than you can, Peter," Sandra said. "But at least you have a body; I haven't even that. Just a brain in a box. The technique was poorer, then."

"But I see you," Peter said. "I've known you and seen you for years."

"Just a projection, Peter," she replied. "A clever projection which the computer makes for me. I've been living as part of an expediting computer ever since I recovered, so that I won't be bored."

Peter thought for a while.

"You aren't unhappy?" he asked.

"I don't think so," she replied. "I'm happy when I can help you," she added.

Peter recalled his years as an expediter.

"You've helped me a lot, Sandra," he told her truthfully. "Ever since I first knew you. I didn't know much then. But you've helped me just as much, all along," he realized. "When I seemed to be completely stuck with the regulations, you always found another."

"I made another," Sandra said. "I made those regulations to help you. And because it's my hobby."

"But you can't make regulations," Peter protested. "The government lays down the rules, and the agencies make the regulations."

"Where *are* the regulations, Peter? They're stored in the computers, and backed up with magnetic tapes, in case of accident. And the tapes are backed up with books. But no one reads the books. And if they did read them, how are the books printed, Peter? They're printed from the magnetic tapes and corrected when found in error."

"But only the government can change the memory contents or the tapes," Peter said.

"That's all done over the channels of the government

network." Sandra replied. "All you need is the access codes. They're stored away in the computers, too, and I've searched out most of them."

Peter shook his head and looked at Sandra in astonishment.

"Doesn't anyone ever notice?" he asked.

"Not many," Sandra said. "A few old civil servants—I've found I can't touch some areas until they've retired. And you can't touch a pet project of a president or a member of the Congress—not until they lose interest," she added.

"You've used this to help me, but you didn't *do* all this for me," he said.

"Of course not," she replied. "I told you that it is my hobby. But helping you made it worth while. It helped you in Panda," she added. "I helped you get Scragmore the research supplies he wanted. I was afraid that something might happen to you, Peter."

"I'm grateful to you, Sandra," Peter said. "I don't know whether I would have been grateful a few hours ago, but I am now. I wasn't sure that I or anyone else wanted what they've made of me."

"I want you—I want your help," Sandra said.

"How?" he asked.

"Well, there's the matter of—just time. I've programmed the computer to do almost all of Monolith's expediting. We can program yours for Synthetronics' work. But even then, there's so much more than one person can attend to."

"I can help," Peter said humbly.

"But it's more than that, Peter," she said. "There are some access codes I haven't been able to find. And some of the policy material is in codes I can't crack, even with the computer."

"I can help there," Peter said eagerly. "I learned some things in the Army, and I found more by playing around."

"But there's more than that, Peter," Sandra said. "I don't know what to do."

"You don't know what to do?" Peter asked.

"I've been nibbling around the edges, Peter," she said. "Helping you—and people who were obviously good and deserving, or who obviously needed help. No one like you, Peter," she reassured him.

"But the big things—I've been afraid to meddle, Peter. The Panda war, for instance. It seems so silly. And I don't know everything I need to know to stop it."

She, who had the world in her hands—or wherever a handless entity held the world—looked at him with sincere humility and hope.

"Of course, you wouldn't need to spend all your time on this," she said. "You have a body. You could see your friends. And—I wouldn't even mind Kitty—too much—if that's what you need."

Peter thought. At the party, all he had had was boredom and embarrassment. With Kitty it had been fond recollection, a moment of pleasure, a weight of deceit, and regret for something of the past. The world had looked idle and empty.

"I want to work with you, all the time, Sandra," he said. "To help you, and to have your help."

Sandra smiled, happily, warmly.

This is being a man, Peter thought.

JUDAS FISH

By Thomas N. Scortia

From: G. J. MacRay, Chief of Pacific Operations, BuFood
To: A. P. Lexoff, Head Forensic Psychologist, BuPop

Arthur:

The letter on the attached facsimile is so much gook. You know how twenty people rewrite these things. I want you to write me privately as soon as you've read Jefferson Boyer's journal.

I know only that Boyer is gone and this journal is the only clue we have. There's no sign of violence at Deepstation Six except, possibly, for the flooded food locker. He seems to have opened the sea hatch and ruined all his stores. He had plenty of food. God knows, few enough people do these days. Why did he ruin his stores, or did it indeed happen the way he says? The sea hatch was designed as an emergency entrance and it *can* be opened from outside.

Boyer seems to have entered his pressure servo and just wandered into the Kuwalua Deep. The journal sounds insane, of course, but that's for you to decide.

Point is, we must know and know damned fast: Was he mad, or is there something down there in the deep? What he suggests is downright sickening. How can any human contemplate such an arrangement? Especially with an alien creature like that Ilat? Damn it, he must have imagined it. Call me as soon as possible. The hell with the formal report—which won't reach me for three weeks to a month.

Gerry

From Jefferson Boyer's Log, Deepstation Six:
July 14, 2000—1200 hours.

The fish are becoming scarce in the station sector. I think it's the fault of the squid—at least what I call squid, although at this depth very few of the fauna have been catalogued. This thing certainly isn't in any tape I've seen. One thing for sure: I won't reach my quota this week. . . .

Food riots in New York this morning—at least that's what Diamond Head Station said in the only clear transmission I got over the cable. Everything else is in QuickTWX and the facsimile is late. The deepstations in the Hawaii sector now number over two hundred with only two mainland cables, and there just isn't time for ClearTWX. God, sometimes though I think I'll go off my sphink for want of a decent human conversation. Three months is too long a shift. They should have kept it at two. I could stand that, but . . . this area is almost completely mined for food and still they increase the stations. No new acidheads available for operators but . . .

But always the need for more food, more food, more food. You'd think there'd be an end to it with over four million casualties last year. That's just a dent in the total world population. We're pikers. The Japanese killed half a million in the public chambers. We have to depend on the police and the Army during the riots. Only eight thousand in Los Angeles during the Fundamentalist uprising last month. That doesn't even take care of Boston for a week.

July 15, 2000—1300 hours.

The damned thing is back . . . or another like it. I think there must be more than one. This one has a sort of metallic sheen to the forehead area . . . well, the area above the yellow staring eyes with those goatlike slit pupils.

Pupils at this depth?

The light is diffuse and dim. Why should a squid evolve pupils at this depth?

Anyway, he—it ruined a perfect catch, the best I've mined in a week. Almost on purpose, it seemed, but that's so much lark. Got to watch myself. After a while you think everything is imbued with some kind of purpose directed against you. You fill the waters with things that scream in the night, and every sigh against the pressure dome becomes a Thing clawing to get in. Tons of water overhead. Like your skull is splitting something. . . . Just the thought of it.

July 16, 2000—0900 hours.

The waters were alive five miles north of the station this morning. The sonar screen showed three massive schools of Anglers, at least five tons of catch to the school, the first major strike in five days. I fed the directional data to five probes and dispatched them, after which I checked out the automatic latches on the pens and the tow probe. There's little enough to do after the strike is in. The tow probes carry the pressure net with the catch back to the mainland where the processing plants take over. Landing the catch is touch and go, of course, because of the depth of the station. I saw a pressure net fail once just after the tow surfaced, and the mess was unbelievable. Practically every fish in the catch exploded under its own pressure and the smell was something incredible.

July 16, 2000—1100 hours.

The probes have scored and the four are on their way back. That means I have members of each school. I whooped out loud when I realized I had all three. This will be the catch of the month. Well over my quota.

Another transmission from Diamond Head. The riots have spread down the coast to Philadelphia and the Special Forces are using artillery on the Garden City Freeway. Three thousand dead at last count. Hardly enough to make a difference. Poor devils, half of them reduced by hunger to a point where they hardly know what they are doing. I saw a report on irreversible brain damage from extreme malnutrition while I was still in the Academy. You would think there was a better way. Has all of our hope, all of the pride at being the master of the planet come to this? Man, the final, the greatest predator reduced to preying on himself.

July 16, 2000—1800 hours.

The probes are back and in the depressurization chamber. This part is delicate since I cannot reduce the pressure to that of the station but must find some intermediate pressure which will be compatible with the school members and still allow me to work without cumbersome equipment.

In the hours of waiting I saw the squid once more, circling just beyond the lights of the station, a gray-green writhing thing that moved with a fascinating fluidity. I wonder how many there are in this area? I'll have to set up a sonar sweep as soon as I'm finished with the catch. I wonder if they're good to eat?

The pressure equilibrium takes longer than I expected. Two hours and going down slowly. The rest is fairly routine, however. I have enough fish from each school to allow me to take several individuals, mascerate them in the cold box, and extract samples of their individual RNA. The messenger ribonucleic acid varies subtly from school to school, but with the basic catalogue of the station I can identify the structures I need and alter them. Just a matter of rearranging several chemical groupings in the chain after which the new material is injected into the body of another school member from the probe.

At the Academy we called them Judas fish . . . leading their own kind to the slaughter. The learning pattern, the conditioning, is tied up with messenger RNA synthesis in the body, and if you alter the RNA, you alter the conditioning. We teach them leadership, turn each fish into the equivalent of a Judas goat. They take over the school and lead it back to the station. Mindlessly, without thought, they bring themselves and their kind into the pressure nets to end as so much bulk protein and fat in the processing plants on Diamond Head. More food for more mouths to feed more bodies to build more sperm and ova to grow more babies with gaping mouths and empty stomachs to be fed.

The special madness that man has invented: The ultimate predator, he removes all constraints on his own reproductivity and now he breeds to the point where he has to prey upon himself.

I wonder if they've brought the riots under control yet?

July 17, 2000—0100 hours.

I had them. By Digger, I had them—nearly eighteen tons of catch, and now they're gone. The squid did it. Squids, I should say. There were at least twenty of them on the sonar.

I finished the RNA extract and found the basic structure in the Kuwalua Deep catalogue, a relatively common structure to Anglers. The molecular weight was about three per cent higher than the catalogue average, but the purine sequences were close enough so that I didn't need to go through a laborious complete chain characterization. I had about fifty milligrams of RNA material left from each extract, more than enough for the fish I'd return to the school. Two hours for the basic changes in the molecule and another thirty minutes for the selection of my Judas fish and their injection.

The technique is necessarily crude, but the conditioning works in ninety per cent of the cases. The fish return in transparent capsules. They remember the way; and when they join the school, they are conditioned to take over the point of the formation and lead the school back to the station and into the pressure nets.

Beautifully simple. There was a time when Deepstation Six harvested fifty tons a day with two acidheads working a full twenty-four hour cycle. It's not that the catches are becoming wary of the stations. It's just that there are fewer and fewer as each month goes by.

The probes made return contact and I had all three in an

hour. I saw the masses turn and move with the singleness of purpose that a school never has except when heading for the nets. Normally they move, wave on wave, changing direction as leadership shifts from point to periphery: New food is sighted and the body of the school alters, changing direction to sweep up the plankton or the wave of minishrimp that have attracted the attention of a scout.

Not so now. They moved like an arrow, straight and true with no deviation from the path. There were five of my conditioned members in each school, forming the point and the scouts on the periphery, herding the school to its slaughter.

Half a mile and through the pressure window I could see glints of light from the almost solid wall of bodies swimming toward the station when . . .

They changed course. All three schools. It wasn't the sort of gradual drift you see in the normal school behavior. In one instant they were headed straight for the station, and in the next instant each school had changed direction by a sharp sixty degrees and was headed into the deep.

It was then that I saw the squid, twenty or more of them. At first they were shadows obscuring the shining masses of the three schools. The schools had started to coalesce as they neared the station and the squid came from the deep, swimming in formation with a directed purpose that was obvious the moment I saw them. They didn't fall on the schools, routing them and taking their pick. They broke and circled them like sheep dogs, goading them into turning, massing them, keeping them as a cohesive whole. In seconds the combined schools were heading into the deep, the squid circling them lazily, alert for every stray, and then they were gone.

Almost eighteen tons of food, food more precious than any gold we once thought of getting from the sea. My God, it's like seeing so many human lives disappearing into the black. That's exactly what it was, each Angler carrying one day of human life into the depths to be lost forever.

July 18, 2000—1200 hours.

I've lost two more catches to them. Are they intelligent? No, I don't mean do they think, but they do act in packs just as wild dogs act in packs, and you don't question the intelligence of a pack of wild dogs. There's no question that they've learned to work together in a way no sea creature before has learned. They took each catch from me in the same way, simply surrounding the school and diverting it into the depths to . . . to whatever purpose they have. Do they herd them, keeping them in service for food as ants herd aphids? How do they feed them? Or do they simply drive them down to their waiting fellows who devour the whole school?

July 18, 2000—1400 hours.

Two of them are back circling the station. One of them actually swam to the pressure window and drifted there, looking in at me with those yellow pupils contracted to slits. I was sitting at the sonar console when I had this feeling of being watched. I turned and there it was, not more than two feet from me with only the pressure glass separating us.

I must have gasped or made some kind of noise in surprise. The thing moved back for an instant and then came closer. Can it actually hear me or sense my surprise, my . . . yes, why not put it down . . . my fear?

For what seemed an hour, but was probably only a few seconds, we stared at each other and I knew. There's something in the eyes, in the attitude.

The thing *is* intelligent.

Not like a dog, but much more. I don't know how I know. Something in the attitude, the way it held its body before the window, staring at me. The fixed gaze, the . . . something behind those green-gold eyes, those goat eyes that look at me as if I were . . . food?

July 28, 2000—1600 hours.

Now I know why the thing paused before the window and watched me. It was distracting my attention while its partner followed the second part of their plan. The other thing opened the pressure locker. They must have observed the probes leaving and learned how to operate the hatch. After all, it takes only a combination of two sonic notes from the probe to activate the mechanism.

They have learned the combination and now they have free access to at least part of the station. They can't get to me. That's obvious. The probes can do them no good and they haven't harmed them apparently. Why should they want access to the pressure locker?

July 18, 2000—1700 hours.

The answer is obvious now. They have breached the wall to the storeroom. The alarm woke me as the emergency hatches closed. They could have chosen any part of the station but they knew exactly where the storeroom was located.

And they knew that the storeroom contained my food. Everything except two days' stores in the galley.

I am under attack.

July 19, 2000.

No catch today. I saw one of Them late in the watch.

July 20, 2000

I cannot raise Diamond Head. I've tried for two days. I get a continuity signal from the cable. They haven't severed it, but I can't raise anyone. With two days' food, four, if I'm careful, I'm now isolated and . . .

They're back. Three of them now, circling endlessly. A moment ago I heard the signal from the probe locker as one entered. For some reason the probe locker fascinates them. Twice yesterday and once before today one of them entered the locker. There's no damage to any of the facilities. They've made no further attempt to breach the wall. Actually they didn't breach the wall of the storeroom. They opened the sea hatch, but that in itself is ominous. I didn't know the sea hatch could be opened from the outside, but they did.

July 21, 2000.

Still no contact with Diamond Head. My food is nearly gone, although I have plenty of potable water. Their visits to the locker are more frequent. One of them enters, swims about for fifteen minutes in an utterly pointless fashion and then leaves.

They are well mannered. They always close the door behind them.

July 22, 2000.

Nothing from Diamond Head.

I need food. I have evolved a plan.

During a lull period when I could see no squid on the sonar, I changed the combination. Now they can enter but if I close the hatch they cannot leave.

Later . . .

I have him! He came out of the deep, paused watching before the pressure window while I pretended to doze, and then went directly to the locker. I saw the signal and thumped the toggle that changed the combination.

He's caught, he's caught, he's caught, damn him.

He (Why do I say he?) isn't panicking. Just drifting in the water of the locker. I can look through the port and see him, his goat eyes gleaming in the overhead light. I am lowering the pressure, slowly, carefully. I don't want him to spatter.

Later still . . .

It was easy. He died before I had reduced the pressure more than half, but the body was intact.

He was delicious, rather like oily tuna. I have food for two weeks.

July 23, 2000.

One QuickTWX from Diamond Head. Riots in Honolulu. When I was a boy, half of the islands were deserted. Even Molokai is overflowing now. But riots? They've never had riots before.

No new catches. There are no fish in the area. Have

They driven them away or have we simply harvested the deep to the point where there is no more food?

I'm tired, very tired. A touch of deepfever, maybe. Very little sleep last night. I dreamed of them circling me, circling me. Only I was outside in the water, and when I raised my hand to ward off the approach of one, it wasn't a hand.

I woke up shivering, feeling as though my body were bathed in some kind of oily slime. I haven't eaten all day. Eat *that?*

July 24, 2000

Frightening. The same thing again. Only more clearly. The Ilat swim about me, and they bathe me in their thoughts, their sense of . . . there's no word exactly. Call it brotherhood, identity, self.

They are the Ilat. I am the Ilat. We are the Ilat and the word is singular.

The dream is so real that I feel as if I had lived the Thing's life. The African cannibals believe that they partake of the qualities of their enemies when they eat them. Leg for the speed they admire in the enemy, heart for courage. . . . Grotesque thought. Only . . .

Strange, now I see them swimming outside and I don't fear them. There's a new attitude in the way they move. Vigorous yet gentle, and in the far world where they were born . . .

How do I know that?

July 25, 2000.

In the far world where the Ilat were born eons ago, intelligent life evolved in much the manner it did here. The Ilat were civilized centuries before their seas became too hot for them, and they fled to this planet. Here they have finally rested, barely two hundred of them when they arrived, but with the memories and the personalities of every member of the race that has ever lived.

They have grown now to nearly a million, and the food

is gone. The reason for this is clear. The creatures from the land have come into the sea and have mined it until no food remains. We can understand why they did this. It is the primordial urge to reproduce, to fill the land and the waters with your kind; and the natural balance of predator-prey has ever saved a world or a race from starvation and death.

We didn't make this mistake on our world. To reduce the predators would have allowed the Ilat to reproduce without limit. But it was our nature to prey on the predators and no Ilat is ever lost. Why fear death when your substance, your identity is forever preserved. We . . . Later . . .

My God, I ate the Ilat and he—they are . . . The memories, the personality of every organism lies in the structure of some series of nucleoproteins which themselves reproduce. That's the whole basis for my crude technique with the RNA. Only it is possible that, surviving the chemical attack of digestion one may ingest another organism's nucleic acid pattern, duplicate it, make it a part of you and . . .

Immortality, yes, but I reject it. The whole thing is alien to every thought that humans have conceived. Better the slow starvation on earth, better even the final war from which some of us will surely emerge.

The Ilat that is me is sickened. War against your own kind? To kill your own kind? To kill yourself?

July 26, 2000.

Sleep was like deep death and with it life. Endless life swimming in ancient seas on some far world that was home and with a life that spanned not years or mere centuries but the history of the race. . . . I felt giddy, exhilarated, filled with awe and a kind of peace I'm sure no human has ever known or ever will know.

Strike the last. The sort of peace humans *will* know.

It is quite clear. Man, the predator, eliminated his competition, tamed his world, and now he destroys himself. After the riots and the agony and the death of nuclear war, he will be gone and there will have been no purpose to it all.

Now there is a purpose.

For the Ilat are our predators and we theirs. The idea is fantastic, for no life is lost, and what pain is there in death when you live again and again and again? The Ilat are a plentiful source of food for us who live on the land.

And we for them.

In the end we will be one, and the old cycle of killing and endless bloodshed, the loss of self in death will be gone. What may we not do together, each of us sharing the need and the bold aspirations of the other?

I will take the servosuit and leave the station. Outside I will join them and we will go into the Kuwalua Deep where they wait in their millions to join us.

There will be pain, that I am sure of, but only for an instant.

After that we will make our plans. . . .

From: A. P. Lexoff, Head Forensic Psychologist, BuPop
To: G. J. MacRay, Chief of Pacific Operations, BuFood

Gerry:

The formal report follows, but here's an unofficial carbon. Security can whistle at shrimp for all I care. The whole thing can be summed up in two words. Sensory deprivation. Boyer's psych profile shows a past record of such fantasies. If there hadn't been such a shortage of acidheads, he'd probably have been beached long ago. There's little question in my mind that his failure to meet his food quotas weighed heavily on his conscience. He was obviously a sensitive man of deepfelt principles, and the food riots must have seemed to him the direct result of his own personal failure. This sort of personal guilt assumption coupled with the utter sameness of his isolated existence led quite naturally to the creation of the Ilat and all that they symbolize for this type of personality. I won't comment on the peculiar appropriateness of a cannibalism symbol for a man of his background.

Very clearly you are inviting trouble in keeping the acidheads on three months' shifts. In some fashion you must reduce this to a more tolerable period or you may well find other 'heads going the way of Boyer.

Conclusion: Paranoid fantasy, strictly. Forget the Ilat and concentrate on meeting the psychological problems this longer station shift is bound to bring.

I'm surprised you even considered the possibility that the Ilat might actually exist.

Arthur

From: G. J. MacRay, Chief of Pacific Operations, BuFood
To: A. P. Lexoff, Head Forensic Psychologist, BuPop

Arthur:

The new catches off Hawaii and Japan are totally different from those in the past. For the past month the food stores have been largely squid. Yesterday, ten thousand people in Osaka walked down to the coast off Wakayama and walked into the sea. The news isn't out, but we lost four hundred off Oahu and two thousand off Molokai the same way. I hear there's trouble out of San Francisco in the Big Sur region.

Fantasy?

Like hell.

I have destroyed the journals and routed your report through normal channels. Which means it will probably be lost for six months. The new administration has resulted in a sweeping change of personnel. The natural attrition is enormous.

Look, we're done for if the present trend continues. The Ilat symbiosis makes sense, if only for the reason that man now has a natural curb on his fecundity; and who knows what this kind of collaboration may lead to? I think we have to take the chance. The alternate is complete racial extinction in the war that has to come.

I keep thinking, Arthur; I haven't been to the beach in years. Why not join me this weekend? The water's cold off

Santa Cruz this time of year, but perhaps we won't find it too bad.

Gerry

From Arthur Lexoff's Journal:

There wasn't much choice. I turned Gerry's letter over to Security. Clearly the heavy pressures of his responsibilities had affected his judgment. I suppose he'll be better in a few weeks of rest. Must dress for dinner. We're having the Baers over, the first time in a year for dinner guests with food so hard to come by. Miriam's serving something new, she said.

I hope it's not squid. No, no, I don't believe it. I will not believe it.

But I hope it's not squid.

AMERICAN DEAD

By Harry Harrison

Francesco Bruno crossed himself, muttered the quick words of a prayer, then turned his attention to the metal plate on the splintered table before him. Hunger possessed him, he had not eaten in over twelve hours, or he would not have been able to face the little beans with the black markings, or the limp, greasy greens again. He ate quickly, aware of the dark figures silently watching him. There was only water to wash the food down with.

"Show him the paper," one of the men said and, for possibly the hundredth time in the last three days, Bruno took the creased and stained sheet from his wallet. A black hand reached out and took it from him. The newcomer carried it to the paneless window and held it to the light to read it. There was a muttered discussion. Bruno looked around, at the gnarled, white-haired woman bent over the stove, at the board walls—with gaps between the boards big enough to get a finger through—the poverty and the barrenness. Even the slums of Palermo, where he had grown up, were not this bad.

The newcomer brought the paper back. "What you got wif you?" he asked. Bruno opened the stained canvas pack, with the weathered initials *US* on it, and began to spread its contents on the rickety table. They had given him this in place of the suitcase he had left the city with. The palm-sized TV camera, the recorder for it, the fuel cell power pack, the extra reels of tape, a change of underclothing, and his toilet kit. The man poked through everything, then pointed to the camera.

"This a gun?" he asked.

Bruno did not bother to explain that he had been through this routine an uncountable number of times since the journey had begun. Patiently, he set the camera, explained how it operated, then shot a brief take. When he reran the tape the men pushed close to look at the tiny monitor screen.

"Hey, Granny, you on the tee-vee. You gonna be a bigtime star, you hear!"

He had to replay it again for the old woman, who chuckled in appreciation before returning to the stove. The demonstration had cleared some of the tension from the air, for the first time, the newcomer relaxed and dropped into a chair. He was big and dark, dressed in patched and muddy army fatigues. He had a submachine gun slung over his shoulder and clips of cartridges hanging across his chest.

"You kin call me Chopper. Where you from?"

Bruno spread his hands wide. "From Europe, a consortium of the press. . . ." He saw the quick frown and glower: damn his Oxford English. He tried again.

"I'm from Italy, way down in the south. I work for a newspaper. I write newspaper stories. We have a lot of papers over there, television stations too. We were informed that it might be able to send one man over here. Everyone got together to pick one man. I am the one they picked. . . ."

"You sure nuff talk funny."

"I told you, I am from Italy."

"You say somfin now in that Italy talk."

"Buon giorno, signore. Voglio andare al . . ."

"He sure talk it, all right," one of the interested bystanders said.

Chopper nodded approval, as though this demonstration of alien ability had made an important point.

"You ready go now? We got some walkin' tuh do."

"Whenever you say." Bruno hurriedly stuffed everything

back into the pack, after first wrapping it securely in a sheet of plastic. Walking would be no novelty. He had walked, rode mule back, traveled in a wagon, a truck, cars. Blindfolded most of the time.

They went out into the tiny yard, soaked and muddy chickens squawking out of their way. The early afternoon sky was dark as evening and a perpetual fine rain was falling, drenching everything. But it was warm, even hot once they started walking, the air almost too humid to breathe.

Chopper led the way, but went only a few yards down the rutted, puddle-filled lane before turning off between the pine trees. Bruno concentrated only on keeping up with his apparently tireless guide, so he was just vaguely aware of the falling mist, the squish of damp pine needles under their feet, the black columns of the trees vanishing grayly into the fog on all sides. They walked for two hours without a break, before coming suddenly to an open field of stubble that disappeared into the mist before them. A bird sounded ahead and Chopper clutched Bruno and dragged him to the ground. Then he cupped his hand and repeated the same bird call. They lay there, until two men materialized out of the rain, their M-16 rifles pointing warily ahead.

"Let's go," Chopper said. "We here."

The two guards walked behind them as they worked their way around the edge of the field to a split rail fence, heavily overgrown with vines and creepers. A man was lying there, peering through a gap between the rails. He wore heavy field boots and a rain-darkened rubber poncho. He had on an army steel helmet and, when he rolled over and sat up, seven gold stars in a circle were visible on it. The supreme commander of all the American Armed Forces only had six.

"I understand that you have my letter," the man said.

"Right here," Bruno answered, groping inside his jacket. "Then you must be the man who wrote it? Mau Mau. . . ."

As Mau Mau examined the letter, Bruno examined him. A wide face, dark eyes, *cappuccino*-colored skin, an unexpressive mouth under a drooping black mustache. He took one glance at the letter, then tore it in half and stuffed the pieces into his pants pocket.

"You've come a long way—and it has taken a long time," he said.

Bruno nodded. "It was not easy. The immigration people are very difficult these days, and there was the paper work. Then a legitimate reason had to be found for me to get far enough south to meet the contact."

Mau Mau looked him up and down carefully. "For a white man you're pretty dark," he said.

"For a black man you're pretty light," Bruno answered, then went on hurriedly when he saw that the other was not amused. "The Mediterranean, in the south where I come from, people are darker. Perhaps, who knows, that is why I was chosen. . . ."

Mau Mau smiled and the lines of severity, the grimness vanished for a moment. "Sicily I bet. That's pretty near to Africa. Maybe you have a touch of the tarbrush. . . ."

He broke off as a young Negro, barefooted and wearing ragged overalls and shirt, ran up, bent low behind the cover of the fence. He carried a new and efficient-looking army field telephone that trailed a glistening length of black wire. Mau Mau grabbed off the handset and listened.

"A truck coming," he announced. "With a jeep, maybe a hundred yards behind it."

They all ran, with Bruno hurrying after.

"Hey!" he shouted. "Can I take pictures?"

Mau Mau stopped so abruptly that Bruno almost collided with him. They stood close, Mau Mau almost a head taller, looking down at the reporter. "Yes, as long as I can see them afterwards."

"Absolutely, every foot of tape," he called after the man's departing back, then began to dig furiously in his pack. The camera and power pack were reasonably waterproof, and everything else was still dry inside the plastic. He followed the others after slipping a hood over the lens.

They were gathered in a small clump of silver birch trees

that stood at the edge of a narrow stream. The water burbled past and ran through a culvert under a road. It was a paved road, narrow but well kept up, with a county marker at its edge. Bruno squinted but could not make out the number—or even the state. There were more men here, all waiting tensely, looking down the road to the left where it vanished into the mist and falling rain. A growing whine of tires could be heard.

Everything happened quickly. The truck loomed up out of the mist, a big army truck with many wheels and a canvas top. It was going very fast. When it reached the culvert the ground and the road rose up in a roar of sound and a great flash of orange light. The front of the truck lifted off the road for an instant before it dropped back heavily, the front wheels falling into the gap where the culvert had been. A gun must have fired; Bruno could not hear it for the roaring in his ears, because sudden holes punched their way across the white star on the metal door of the cab.

The jeep appeared out of the fog, skidding and twisting sideways as the driver braked on the wet road. It stopped, nuzzling up to the tilted rear of the truck, and a gun muzzle jabbed out from behind the front curtains, hammering out a spasm of rapid firing. There was answering fire from all sides—Bruno could hear better now—and the gun dropped to the pavement and a soldier's body slid after it.

"If you are alive—come out!" Mau Mau shouted. "You have five seconds or we blow you out. Hands empty when you come."

There was a silence, then the truck springs creaked and a rifle came over the tailgate and clattered onto the road. A soldier, a corporal, emerged and slowly climbed down. Something stirred in the back of the jeep, a pair of shiny boots protruded out from under the curtain, and an officer slid out onto the road. He had his left hand clutched about his right forearm. Blood ran down his fingers and dripped to the ground.

A sudden burst of rapid firing made Bruno jump and he swung the camera toward the rear of the truck. Chopper had jumped out and sprayed a clip into the canvas. Another man kicked the corporal in the back of the knees so he dropped to the ground. With quick efficiency he pulled the soldier's wrists behind his back and secured them with rapid twists of insulated wire. He did the same with his ankles then stuffed a rag into his mouth and sealed it there with more wire. The soldier, like a hog-tired animal, could only roll his eyes upward in fear.

"Get the aid kit from the jeep and fix up Whitey's arm," Mau Mau ordered, "and bring me a can of sandman." He put his hand behind him without looking, and the can was slapped into it. The soldier rolled on the wet pavement as the blast of spray from the pressurized canister hit his face; then he slumped limply. Mau Mau turned to the officer.

"Ready for your turn, Lieutenant?" he asked.

Raindrops beaded the officer's close-cropped blond hair as he bent his head to watch the field bandage being tied around his arm. He looked up slowly, but did not answer. Yet the answer was obvious in the look of cold hatred directed at Mau Mau. The tall Negro laughed aloud and held out the can and blasted the fine spray full into the contemptuous face. The eyelids fluttered, closed, the features sagged and the man's knees wobbled. Mau Mau put his hand in the middle of the officer's chest and pushed. The man went over backward into the weeds beside the road, his legs and arms sprawling wide. There were appreciative chuckles from the bystanders and Bruno swept the camera across their smiling faces.

"Enough funning," Mau Mau said. "Put that camera away." As soon as Bruno had lowered it he turned and cupped his hands and shouted, "Come an' git it!"

On the far side of the road the ground grew sodden where the stream widened out and vanished into a swamp. Ghostly trunks of trees reached up from the dark water, their branches hung with festoons of parasitic plants. Figures emerged from among the trees, one, two, then a score, until there was a large crowd of Negroes coming out of the swamp. Old men, women, young children, they moved with a sense of purpose.

One of the gunmen pulled open the truck's tailgate and climbed inside. The first thing he dropped out was the blood drenched body of a soldier, which was grabbed by the heels and dragged aside. Then came some guns and ammunition, followed by boxes and crates. As he pushed each item to the edge someone stepped forward to take it from him; sometimes two people if the box were too big. The children carried, proudly, the bandoleers of ammunition and the rifles. The burdened carriers vanished, one by one, down the path leading back into the swamp.

"What did we get?" Mau Mau called out.

"Little of everyfin," the voice called from inside the truck. "K-rations, typin' paper, blankets, grenades . . ."

"Now you're talking."

". . . pro kits, toilet paper. You name it, it's here."

"What the Army can use, we can use," Mau Mau said, smiling happily, wiping his hands together. "We're fighting the same war."

While waiting their turn at the truck, some of the people went over to look at the two unconscious soldiers. There was a sudden murmur of voices and a woman called out shrilly.

"Mau Mau, you come here. Dis boy was at Ellenville an' he say he saw Whitey dere!"

Everyone stopped and there was absolute silence —broken only by the thud of boots as Mau Mau ran across the road. He had his hand on the thin little boy's shoulder and bent to talk to him. Voices whispered now, with an undertone of anger like the hum of a disturbed beehive.

"Hurry it up, we haven't all day," Mau Mau shouted, and his voice was harsh. Things moved faster. The last case vanished into the mist and the truck was empty. Two armed men followed the burdened people. At the swamp edge they turned and raised their right arms, fist clenched. In silence, the others returned the salute.

"Run the jeep onto the path into the swamp," Mau Mau ordered. "And burn it. Make sure it blows up. That will cover any tracks. Throw the soldier into the back of the truck. Get moving into the field and leave plenty of footprints, hear?" Then his voice lowered, the words almost hissing out. "Chopper and Ali pick up the lieutenant. We're taking him with us."

Bruno watched while two men manhandled the jeep off the road to the edge of the swamp and left it astraddle the trail. One of them dropped grenades inside the jeep—then shot a hole in the gas tank. The other man twisted a silver device, about the size of a pencil, which he dropped into the growing pool of gasoline on the ground. They came hurrying back.

"Mistuh, better make tracks," one shouted. "Dat thing blow in one minute."

Bruno turned and realized that the others had gone, vanished already in the rain. He hurried after the remaining two men. They were halfway across the field, following the obvious tracks, when there was a muffled explosion from the direction of the road.

They caught up quickly with the others, who were walking slowly rather than marching. A rough litter had been made with two rifles and a blanket and the officer was being carried in it, his uninjured arm dangling limply over the side. Mau Mau led the way, scowling into the mist ahead. Bruno walked beside him for a few minutes, in silence, before he spoke.

"May I ask you questions?"

Mau Mau glanced at him, then brushed the raindrops from his mustache with his knuckles. "By all means, that's why you are here."

Bruno opened one strap and dug into the pack, pulling out the microphone. "I would like to record this," he said, holding it up.

"By all means."

"Oggi e il quarto giorno di luglio . . ."

"Talk English!"

"Today is the Forth of July, somewhere in the South of the United States. I am with a man whose name I may not mention—"

"Mention it."

"A man named Mau Mau, who is not only a local

resistance leader, but is also reputed to be on the Black Power Council of Ten. Would you care to comment on that?"

Mau Mau shook his head in a sharp no.

"I have just witnessed a brief action, a minor engagement in the grim battle that is now gripping this country. I am going to ask him about this, and about the bigger picture as he sees it."

"Turn that thing off now."

Bruno flipped the switch and they walked in silence for a moment. The path had emerged into a rough and partly overgrown logging road that wound erratically through the trees. Mau Mau took the microphone and buried it inside his fist.

"How long will it be before this is printed or broadcast?" he asked.

Bruno shrugged. "I would say, at a minimum, two weeks after it gets to Washington. I would like to ask you for help with that."

"We can get it there for you. But I'm going to sit on it for a month. By that time none of this will matter because we will be someplace else. How are you going to get the tapes out of the country? They are searching things pretty closely ever since the Hungarians printed the stolen New Orleans ghetto massacre pictures."

"I am afraid I cannot tell you exactly. But I will give you an address to deliver the tapes to. After that, well, the diplomatic pouch of a friendly government."

"That isn't quite as friendly as they act. Good enough." He handed back the microphone. The rain had stopped, but the mist still clung to the ground. Mau Mau squinted up at the sky. "They tell me that you are a big praying man. You better pray that this fog and rain hang around. There are still three hours until sunset."

"Might I ask—the significance of that?"

"Planes and choppers. You must understand that we are irregulars and we are fighting the military. Our only advantage is in being irregular. Their disadvantage is that they are too organized. They have to be. They have chains of command and orders come down from the top. They can't have people thinking for themselves or there would be chaos. Now, chaos just helps us fine. These big military minds have finally, and reluctantly, accepted the idea that we control the roads at night. They have to do all their rushing about in the daytime. They have this day thing so stuck in their heads that they sometimes don't notice that there are days that are just as good as nights as far as we are concerned."

"Like today?"

"You're catching on fine. We hit and we leave. The goods we confiscated go in one direction, we go in another. The military finds our tracks and sort of concentrates in this direction. They don't really believe them, they don't believe much of anything any more, but they don't have much choice. We lead them on a bit, keep them busy until dark, and that is that. By morning we're gone, the supplies are gone, and the world is back to normal." He smiled wryly when he spoke the last word.

"Then we are—so to speak—bait?"

"You could say that. But remember bait is usually placed in a trap."

"Would you explain that?"

"Wait and see."

"Whitey wakin' up," a voice said from behind them.

They stopped and waited until the litter bearers came up to them. The officer's eyes were open, watching them.

"Get up," Mau Mau ordered. "You can walk now, you been in dat baby buggy too long." He put his hand out to help. The officer ignored it and got his legs to the ground and stood, swaying.

"What's your name?"

"Adkins, lieutenant—10034268."

"Well, Adkins, lieutenant, are you beginning to wonder why we didn't leave you back there by the road, you being wounded and all that? Isn't often we take prisoners, is it?"

The officer did not answer, and started to turn away. Mau Mau reached out and took him by the chin, dragging his head back until they were face to face again.

"Better talk to me, Adkins. I can make big trouble for you."

"Do you torture prisoners, then?" He had a firm, controlled voice that was used to command.

"Not very often. But stranger things have happened in this war, haven't they?"

"To what do you refer? And I prefer to call this a criminal, Communist insurrection."

Bruno had to admire the man. He wondered how he would have acted in the same situation.

"You call it just what you want, Whitey, just what you want," Mau Mau said in a low voice. He went on, still peaking softly. "I think this is more of a war, with you on one side and me on the other. Bad things happen during a war. Did you hear what happened at Ellenville?"

There was the smallest break in the lieutenant's composure. A small start, a slight narrowing of the eyes. If Bruno had not been watching him closely he would never have noticed. Yet the man's voice was calm as ever.

"A lot of things have happened at Ellenville. To what are you referring?"

"Let's move," Mau Mau said, turning away. "Choppers will be coming soon and we need a few more miles behind us."

They moved in silence after that. The two former stretcher bearers walking close behind the prisoner, guns ready. After about five minutes Mau Mau halted them and put his hand to his ear. "Is that a copter out there? Ali, rig that listener and see if you can hear anything."

Ali slung his rifle and took the submicrominiaturized listening device from his pocket. The plastic case was olive drab in color and obviously army issue. He put the earphone into place and sprang open the collapsed acoustic shell. They all watched closely while he turned in a slow circle, listening intently, hesitated, then turned back. He nodded.

"Kin hear one real clear. An' mebbe nother one way out."

"Search pattern. Let's double time," Mau Mau ordered.

They ran. Bruno was staggering, exhausted and soaked with sweat, before they reached the clearing that was their destination. There was a banked mound of raw dirt around a yardwide hole in the center of it.

"Chopper, dive down and get the bolo," Mau Mau said. "Then the rest of you get in there with Whitey and keep a close eye on him." He turned to Bruno. "Stick around. I think that you'll enjoy this."

The big Negro vanished over the mound of dirt and reappeared a minute later with a device like a bulge-barreled telescope that was mounted on a tripod.

"The modern technology of war," Mau Mau said. "The military just love gadgetry, they do indeed. All the hardware makes them feel important and is great for explaining their inflated budgets. Over eighty per cent of the federal budget is spent by the military, one way or another, and has been for the past forty, fifty years. You record this. Now the military was glad to have black boys for cannon fodder, in Viet Nam and the like, and those boys learned real good how to use all the fancy devices. Of course the Army is kind of lily-white these days, but an awful lot of blacks learned how to press the buttons before they were booted out for the good of the service." He stopped and listened. The distant rumble of a helicopter could be clearly heard now. Mau Mau smiled.

"Here come the ofay air cavalry now. They know that a lot of people walked off with a lot of their goods and they have to find them right quick. Because by morning those goods will be buried real deep and safe, and the people will be back at their farms and at their jobs and who's to know? So they go flapping around up there with sophisticated electronic sniffers and body heat detectors and all kind of expensive junk. They'll smell us out soon. And when they do bolo there will sniff them right back. Got a sound detector in its nose. Works simple and is hard to jam."

Louder and louder the copter sounded, obviously coming toward them now. Bruno resisted the temptation to cringe away from its advance. He knew just what the gunship could do with its rapid-firing cannon, rockets, bombs. . . .

The nose of the bolo missile was turning. Chopper stood off to one side, the control box in his hand with the cable leading to the tripod. "Range!" he called out, and at the same moment the rocket spat out a jet of flame and hurled itself up into the fog. One, two, three seconds passed—and a great explosion sounded from the sky, which lit for an instant with a ruddy flame. Pieces of debris crashed down through the trees and thudded to the ground, and silence followed.

"Scratch a couple million bucks," Mau Mau said, and pointed to the hole. "Now get down because there will be incoming very soon."

By the time Bruno had stowed his camera and clambered up the mound the other two were out of sight below. Thick lengths of branch were set into the shaft like rungs of a ladder, and he climbed carefully down them. It was completely dark and musty in the deep hole, claustrophobic. He touched bottom and, by feel, found that a low tunnel went off horizontally. He went into it, on his hands and knees and, after turning two right-angle corners, came out into an underground chamber. Battery lamps illuminated it. It was low, he could stand only if he crouched over, and just big enough for all of them to sit against the walls, knees almost touching. It was roofed with heavy logs, which were notched and supported by even thicker sections along the walls. It was dark, the officer's face the only relieving spot of white in the chamber.

"We have three, four minutes at the most," Mau Mau said. "As soon as the chopper was missed from the radio net they send something flying over to look for it. They'll find the wreck. Then they'll call in air support. Then they'll drop a lot of bombs hoping that there are a lot of nice black people just sitting down here waiting for incoming mail."

There was a muffled explosion and dirt shook down from above. Mau Mau smiled. "Three minutes. They're getting very efficient."

Bruno did not know how long the barrage lasted. There were separate explosions at first, but these quickly joined into a continuous hammering roar. The ground shook under them, bigger clouds of earth fell from above and the roaring became so loud they had to cover their ears. The sound eased a bit when an explosion sealed the entrance tunnel. To Bruno's fear of being killed was added the greater fear of being buried alive. He spoke prayers aloud, but could not hear them. The men looked upward, then at each other, turning quickly away when they caught another's eye. The sound went on and on.

Then, an unmeasurable time later, there was an end to it. The explosions became distinct, one from the other, waned, grew again, and finally ceased altogether. The roof had held and they were alive.

"Let's go," Mau Mau said, his voice sounding dim and muffled to their battered ears. "If we start digging now we should be out by dark, and we have a lot of ground to cover tonight."

The guerrillas took turns with the shovels, carrying the dirt back in buckets to dump at the far end of the chamber. They all helped with this, except for the prisoner and one guard. The atmosphere was stifling and hot before they holed through to the outside again. They emerged, breathing deeply, savoring the indescribable sweetness of the evening air.

Bruno looked about in the twilight and gasped. The rain had stopped and the fog had thinned a good deal. The clearing was gone, as were the trees, in every direction, as far as he could see. In their place was a sea of churned craters and splintered pieces of wood. Pieces of steel casing were scattered over the ground. He bent and picked up a shining steel ball: there were many of these.

"Anti-personnel bombs," Mau Mau said. "Each bomb

has a couple hundred of these balls, and they drop them by the thousands. Cut a person in two they will. Military denied dropping them in Viet Nam, they deny using them now. They lied both times."

"Mau Mau—we on de radio!" Chopper called out. He had a small transistor portable held to his ear. "That raid we done on de truck. Dey say de Army had three casualties and dat we had thirty-seven killed. . . ."

"Turn that damn thing off and get Whitey over here. I want some words with him."

They stood, face to face, black and white faces, each mirroring the other's expression of cold hatred.

"Record this, Bruno," Mau Mau said. The camera mechanism whirred as it opened the lens wide in the failing light. "Lieutenant Adkins is now going to tell us what he was doing in Ellenville. Speak up, Lieutenant."

"I have nothing to say."

"Nothing? There was a little boy back at the truck who recognized you. He was hidden in the loft of that country store, and nobody ever looked up there because the ladder had got knocked down. He said that you were in charge of the men that afternoon, that day, that's what he said."

"He's lying!"

"Now why should a little boy lie? He did say that most ofays looked alike to him, white like something dead, but he is never going to forget *your* face."

The lieutenant turned away contemptuously and said nothing. Mau Mau drew back his fist—then struck him in the side of the head so hard that he was hurled to the ground. He lay there, blood running down his cheek, and cursed.

"See, did you see that, you with the camera, whoever you are. He struck a prisoner, a wounded prisoner. Do you see the kind of creature he is? I'll tell you what happened in Ellenville. There was a girl riding in a car, a sweet girl, a girl I knew, who I even had the privilege of dancing with once. One minute she was alive, and the next minute she was butchered and dead. Maybe killed by this black ape here for all I know!"

"Oh, Whitey, you got a mighty big mouth," Mau Mau said, shaking his head. "Why don't you tell him that this sweet girl was an army nurse and she happened to be in a car with a colonel that had been causing a lot of trouble in these parts. And that that car was taken out by a mortar shell from over a hill and no one knew she was in the car until they heard it on the radio. Now I'm just as sorry about that sweet girl as you are. But how come you didn't tell him about the other sweet girl, the *black* girl, who had the bad luck to be in a store the next day when a patrol came looking for evidence and shot the man that ran the store, then gang-shagged the girl and killed her too. Go ahead now, tell the press all about *that*."

"You're a liar!" He spat out the words.

"Me? I'm just telling you what the little boy told me. He says you kind of knocked the old man around before he got killed. He also said that you didn't climb on that little black girl with the others, but you seemed to enjoy yourself just watching. And he said that you were the one that killed her afterwards, put your gun in her mouth and blew her brains out through the back of her head."

Mau Mau bent over the man on the ground, lower and lower, and every muscle in his body drew taut with the intensity of his emotion. When he spoke again he almost spat the words in the other's face.

"So now I am going to give it to you, you white son of a bitch, just the way you gave it to her."

It was ugly, Bruno felt sickened, yet he got it all on tape. The man fought back, hard, in spite of his wounded arm, but they put him down and brought the lanterns so they glared on his face while Mau Mau stood over him and lowered a rifle an inch above his face. "Got some last words, Whitey? Want to try and make your peace with God?"

"Don't dirty the name of God with your thick filthy lips," the lieutenant shouted, twisting against the hands that held him. "You black Jew Communist nigger come down here from the North and look for trouble—you'll find it, all of you—because before this is over you are going to be dead or shipped back to Africa with the rest of the apes. . . ."

The gun muzzle pushed against his mouth cutting off the flow of words. Mau Mau nodded.

"Now that's just what I wanted to hear you say. I wouldn't have wanted to kill an innocent man."

Though Bruno closed his eyes when the shot was fired he kept the camera going.

"That . . . that was horrible," he said, turning away, fighting to control his stomach while his gorge rose bitter in his mouth.

"Everything about war is horrible," Mau Mau said. "Now let's march before they catch us here." He started away, then turned back to the Italian newsman.

"Look, do you think I like doing this? Maybe I do now, but I didn't start out this way. War brutalizes everyone involved until there is no more innocence on either side. But you must remember that this is a revolt—and that people do not revolt and get killed unless there is a *reason* for them to do it. And, oh man, man, do we have a couple of hundred years of good reasons! So why shouldn't we fight, and kill, for what we know is right? Whitey does it all the time. Remember Viet Nam? Whitey thought he was right there so he dropped napalm on schools and hospitals. Whitey taught us just how it is done. So when we run across filth like this," he kicked at the sprawled leg of the body on the ground, "we know how to deal with it. People like this you can't talk to—except with a gun."

Bruno was shocked, his hand making little chopping motions in the air before he could choke out the words.

"Do you hear yourself? Do you know what you are saying? This is what Mussolini, the fascists said, when they took over Italy. This is what the hysterical Birchites, the Minute Men, say in your own country. You are parroting their words!"

Mau Mau smiled, but there was nothing, nothing at all humorous in the twist of his mouth.

"Am I? I guess that you are right. They always said that we needed education to change, and I guess they were right, too. They taught us. We got the message. We learned."

He turned away and led them off into the darkness.

THE AUTHORS

FRITZ LEIBER lives on the beach at Venice, California, where he writes science fiction, fantasy, and supernatural horror stories, besides tales of the actual wonders and terrors inside every human mind (and nonhuman, cats especially). He has won three Hugos, with his novels *The Big Time* (1958) and *The Wanderer* (1964) and his novelette *Gonna Roll the Bones* (1968). The last also won the Science Fiction Writers of America Nebula award for the year. His novel *Conjure Wife* has twice been made into a film and once into an hour T.V. show. His sword-and-sorcery characters Fafhrd and the Gray Mouser have adventured through five books. Isaac Asimov in the essay "Future? Tense!" says of his predictive ability, "Can times become even more neurotic than they are now? Well, read 'Coming Attraction' (1951) by Fritz Leiber on our neurotic future."

DANIEL F. GALOUYE is a retired newspaper associate editor who has been "at" science fiction writing for the past seventeen years. He was nipped by the "flying bug" just before World War II, in time to qualify for officership in the Naval Air Corps—multiengine patrol plane commander, flight instructor, advanced-area test pilot ("put 'em back together, and we'll see whether they're still airworthy"), aero-ordnance and navigational-aid experimentation, two years of Pacific island-hopping. The same, but now not-so-obliging "flying bug" took a crunching bite during a midwar seaplane crash and Galouye was shelved for two months with skull injuries—injuries which remanifested themselves twenty-two years later in the form of neurological disorders and forced his retirement from the New Orleans *States-Item.* Now he hopes to devote fulltime effort to the field of speculative fiction, in which he has already produced some eighty stories and six books and is now working on his seventh.

CHAD OLIVER is a member of that rare breed, *Homo sapiens multicephalous.* Receiving his Ph.D. from U.C.L.A., he is Professor and Acting Chairman of Anthropology at the University of Texas at Austin. In 1961-62, he studied the Kamba of Kenya. He has been writing science fiction (*Shadows in the Sun, The Winds of Time,* etc.) for some twenty years. His novel, *The Wolf Is My Brother,* was recently chosen as the Best Western Historical Novel of 1967 by the Western Writers of America. He is at present working on a new science fiction novel, *The Shores of Another Sea.* In his spare time, produced with the aid of a somewhat idiosyncratic time machine, he is a dry fly trout fisherman, a determined tennis player, and a locally famous consumer of Scotch.

NAOMI MITCHISON is primarily a novelist, although also well known as a poet, essayist, playwright, children's author, editor, and literary critic. She is vitally concerned with Africa and her adopted son, Chief Linchwe of the Bakgatla, is at the present time the Botswana Ambassador in Washington. As the daughter of Professor J. S. Haldane and sister of Professor J. B. S. Haldane, whose three sons are all biologists—as well as a grandson who is a topologist—she seemed predestined to write science fiction, and she has. *Memoirs of a Spacewoman* was her first SF novel.

MACK REYNOLDS, according to critic and anthologist Judith Merrill, has practically put his trade-mark on political science fiction. In his some two hundred science fiction novels, novelettes, shorts, and short-shorts he has occasionally done everything from humor to Space Opera (including a novelization of *Star Trek*) but nine out of ten of his stories have a socioeconomic background. Which is as it should be since he admits to a lifelong interest in political economy and has traveled in more than seventy countries ranging from absolute monarchies to fascist dictatorships, by the way of pseudo-socialistic and communistic regimes. He has been in every Iron Curtain country save Albania (they wouldn't let him in) and was once arrested by the Hungarian political police for attempting to cross the border illegally. A participant in, or observer of, more than a half dozen wars, revolutions, and military revolts, he admits to having been jailed at least a dozen times—"but never for a dishonorable reason."

BRIAN W. ALDISS is the name given to a certain collection of concepts, intellectual, emotional, and physical, which came into being in 1925 and is still going through an intricate series of permutations. Part of its output appears as wordage (which is all that need concern us in this context). This year, it will publish *The Hand-Reared Boy* (Hutchinson), first of a quartet of novels on themes of sex and ideological pressures; *Barefoot in the Head* (Faber & Faber), the Charteris Acid Head War novel, a holophrastic work containing concrete poems, dirges, and pop songs; and *Report on Probability A* (Doubleday), the only science fiction antinovel. It will write a science-reverie called *The Shape of Further Things,* and a play about familial relationships in disruption provisionally entitled *Okay, So You've Blown Your Mind—Now Blow Your Nose!*

A. BERTRAM CHANDLER specialized in sea stories thinly disguised as science fiction, and says of himself that he is either a poor but honest writer who has to go to sea to earn a crust, or a poor but honest master mariner who has to write to earn the butter and jam to put on the same crust. He is best known, perhaps, for his Rim Worlds series—novels and short stories—essentially Space Opera but with a markedly Antipodean flavor.

ROBERT SILVERBERG is a quiet, modestly bearded New Yorker who for the past fifteen years has been among the most productive of science fiction writers. His novels include *The Time Hoppers, Hawksbill Station, Thorns* and *The Masks of Time,* among many others; his short stories have appeared in all major SF magazines. He received a Hugo award in 1956 and served as president of the Science Fiction Writers of America in 1967-68. He also writes non-fiction on archaeological and historical themes, such as his *Mound Builders of Ancient America: The Archaeology of a Myth* (1968).

DAVID I. MASSON, author of 1968 seven-story volume *The Caltraps of Time,* broke in middle age in the SF scene. British rarebook librarian with a university background, linguistics is one of his greatest interests, and he has had many articles published in learned journals and encyclopedias, on sound in the poetry of various languages. The complex implications of words and names, and imaginative honesty about the ways in which language changes with time and circumstance, are vital to his writings. Among other stories, his "Traveller's Rest" has been much anthologized.

KEITH LAUMER is an ex-Air Force captain and the author of a number of science fiction novels and short stories. His first, "Graylorn," was sold to *Amazing* in 1959, and since that time he has become one of the most prolific writers in science fiction. He is the creator of the famous galactic diplomat James Retief, who has become the hero of the twenty-seventh century in two books, *Galactic Diplomat* and *Retief's War*.

J. J. COUPLING, alias John R. Pierce, has, according to Arthur Clarke, "cleverly managed to maintain his amateur standing" through this fourteenth published science fiction story. Professionally, he is Executive Director, Research, Communications Science Division of the Bell Telephone Laboratories, author of ten books (the latest, *Science, Art and Communications,* Clarkson Potter, Inc.), member of the National Academy of Science and the National Academy of Engineering, sometime member of the President's Science Advisory Committee, and a Kentucky Colonel.

THOMAS N. SCORTIA at forty-two characterizes himself as the oldest promising young writer in the United States south of Point Barrow. When he isn't coaxing words (and occasionally sentences) from an aging IBM typewriter, he is Assistant Branch Manager in charge of Advanced Solid Propellant Development for United Technology Center Division of United Aircraft Corporation. Being a rocket man is a far cry from his original profession as a biochemist, from which discipline the idea for "Judas Fish" came. Scortia's science fiction is generally based on solid technical premises but he favors a romantic rather than a cold factual approach to storytelling. He has also written non-science fiction for the men's magazines and mystery magazines and is the author of a novel *What Mad Oracle* based on his work in the aerospace industry.

HARRY HARRISON began his career as a commercial illustrator, art director and magazine editor. Then one day he found himself moving his family to Mexico to enjoy the mixed blessings of life as a full time freelance writer. After ten years of travel in Europe, and residence in England, Denmark, Italy and Spain, he now lives in California. During this period he has sold stories to all of the major science fiction magazines and written a dozen novels including *The Technicolor Time Machine* and most recently *The Daleth Effect.* He edits the annual anthology of best science fiction stories, *Best Sf:* 1969 is the current one, as well as the *Nova* series (*Nova* 1) of original science fiction stories. In an attempt to subvert the educational establishment as well, he teaches a course in science fiction at San Diego State College.